Damian worked the front door open silently and stepped out onto the concrete porch. Alexis's face peered at him from the driver's side window of a car across the street. Through the pain of her energy pouring into him, he stumbled over the yard and across the road. She got the passenger door open for him, and he fell inside.

"Go, go, go. I don't know how long we'll have before they notice we're both gone." He inched into a more normal position in the seat as she accelerated away. He slipped his shoes on, then buckled his seatbelt. "Give me your phone."

She handed it over. He rolled down the window and tossed it out.

"Hey."

"Sorry. I'll get you a new one as soon as I can. My brother tracked me once already through my phone. I'm not letting him do it again."

She nodded. "Where do I go?"

He leaned back in the seat and closed his eyes. "Work your way down the hill toward the lake. When we get closer, I'll tell you how to get to the marina."

"Are you ok?" she asked.

"Not really. But hopefully I will be soon. What about you?"

"I don't know. I've felt like I'm going to explode. But the pressure is lessening now."

His eyes snapped open. *Oh crap.* He studied her profile. *I think that was a close call. If I have no energy and she has it all…*

Exploding might not actually have been a metaphor.

Sundered

SIANA WINELAND

Published by Nine Tails Press.
ISBN: 978-0-9961331-1-1

Published in the United States of America

This book is dedicated to the Parsley King.

Acknowledgements

Thanks so much to my family, who as always have been a great support, especially my Mother in law Sedna whose unwavering support has made this so much easier. And I would like to thank the doctors and nurses at Swedish Cherry Hill who kept my husband with us so he could continue to nitpick my stories.

Chapter 1

HUMID DARKNESS SHROUDED DAMIAN. The lights and bustle of Capitol Hill in Seattle didn't reach him in the alley. He leaned back against the brick and stared up into the sliver of faint stars, barely visible through the narrow opening above. His black tank and dark jeans stuck to him in the August night. The need to hunt warred within him. He closed his eyes, breathing deeply, trying to control the urge. He'd just finished seducing the energy from a couple of humans. He'd gone further than he'd intended, their psyches pushed to the breaking point. He should have been satisfied with the amount of emotion he'd already consumed tonight. The fact that he wasn't left him unsettled.

Clenching his fist, he gave up the fight for control and reluctantly turned toward the door of Decadence. This club was a regular hunting ground for incubi and succubi—and one of his favorites. He had to have more emotion. Whether he *should* need it or not didn't matter. Psychic hunger pulsing, he prowled across the street, the denim of his jeans shifting across his skin with each movement. A soft breeze stirred the ends of his dark hair to brush against his neck. His mind ranged out to caress the line of people waiting to enter the building. Eyes turned to look at him, following him, heat rising in them from his mental touch as he paced to the front.

The burly gatekeeper rose, wariness entering his gaze. "Dae?"

A slow smile stretched across Damian's mouth as he crossed the last few feet to press into the man's personal space. He let his hand skim down the human's cheek, the stubble rough against his palm. His mind flickered out to brush against the other's psyche like a cat. The gatekeeper sucked in a breath.

The human suppressed a moan, then managed to get out, "Are you in control?"

"Never felt better," Dae whispered in his ear. "I just need to hunt."

Damian could see the guard didn't trust his condition. As the man reached for his phone, Dae let his power slip out and wrap the human's mind, fogging his concerns, the need to hunt overriding his judgment. "I don't need to be evaluated," he whispered. "I just need to hunt."

He left the guard fogged and passed the gate, stepping into the darker interior. The entrance hall opened up onto a wide industrial-style walkway and balcony that overlooked a large dance floor in the warehouse-like atmosphere of the club. Dae avoided the bar and tables to the left and took the set of nearest stairs directly down.

Loud music vibrated through Damian's body. The pulse of the beat spurred him through the crowded dance floor, the dim light brightened by the flash of color and strobes. Energy swirled through the air. A feast. He wanted to laugh; he just needed to turn the tide to the proper energy. His brother Isaac could fill up on all the happiness and joy that currently radiated from the crowd of humans, but Damian needed something edgier.

A body swayed into him, and he paused as the woman pressed deeper against his chest. The scent of flowers reached his nose from the heat of her hair. He inhaled and let his mind dart out and catch a strand of her emotions. Grasping the band he could use, he tuned it and felt a shiver race down her spine. She pulled away and leapt forward, plastering her mouth against what Dae assumed was her boyfriend. His gaze heated as he watched the two, and a sinful smile slowly pulled his lips. Then he circled around behind to brush his fingertips lightly across the back of the male's neck, using the contact to feed his hunger for lust as well. Hands came into play on their bodies, and Dae moved on.

Twining the thickening mental strand of desire in his grasp, he pulled, then fed it back into the crowd. Lust filtered into the air, and the movements on the dance floor subtly changed. Sorting and plucking the strands of energy that he could reach, he fanned the flames.

Standing in the middle of the dance floor, he closed his eyes and lifted his face to the ceiling, inhaling deeply, drunk from the emotion. Energy poured into him.

Yet still it wasn't enough. Frustrated, he opened his eyes and looked back among the pulsing crowd. His mind reached out and pressed harder. The energy grew. Along with the frantic movements of the mob. He pushed the crowd beyond what was acceptable. No longer dancing to the music, people wrapped about one another. Hands groping, mouths tasting. His breath labored, Dae drank in the frenzy, moans and gasps echoing in his ears, an undercurrent to the pounding music that still beat through Decadence's large, open room.

His mind drifting, Damian played the mob in a haze. The lust energy swelled.

A vise squeezed the back of his neck and a cold, wet blanket smothered his mind. With a gasp he jerked, his gaze clearing. The hot hand at the back of his neck propelled him forward and forced him quickly around the sprawling humans as his jumbled thoughts tried to catch up to his stumbling body. The hand released him after it shoved him onto the metal grill of the stairs leading up to the balcony.

A fast glance as he ascended showed Dae the thunderous face of the one enforcer he really wished he wasn't seeing. At the top landing the concerned face of Bob, the human who worked the bar, waited for him. But Damian didn't get a chance to speak. The enforcer grabbed him by the front of his shirt and yanked him to the balcony rail.

"What the hell are you doing, Damian?" Karry snapped.

All Dae could do was mutely shake his head. His wits still hadn't quite caught up. The other incubus shook him roughly, then pointed out over the floor. Dae turned his head slowly, as if moving through molasses. Enforcers worked the crowd, bringing the writhing humans down from the sexual high he had unwittingly taken them to, altering their memories of the event.

"You've closed this hunting ground for everyone, Dae. No one can hunt here for at least twenty-four hours. You're lucky I'm the one who heard the call come into headquarters. Breaking the law like this…"

He cleared his throat. "I'm sorry, Kar. I don't understand…"

The enforcer's gaze bored into his. Dae wanted to look away but couldn't. "Go home, Damian. Have Erik check you out. I'll get this cleaned up."

Karry released him and turned with his hands spread, gripping the rail of the balcony. His duster fell like dark wings down his back.

A hand landed softly on his shoulder and Dae turned. Bob's concerned gaze met his. "Come on, Dae."

He cast a last glance over his shoulder at the mess he'd caused down on the dance floor, then let Bob lead him to the hallway out. At the exit, they paused.

"You OK, Dae?"

A shiver ran down his spine, and he forced a smile to surface. "Yeah, sorry for getting carried away."

The human shook his head, and Dae could tell

that his reply hadn't reassured him. "Go home like the enforcer said."

"Sure. I'm full now anyway."

"Not surprising," Bob muttered as he turned back to tend his bar.

With a last glance at the enforcers, still systematically wiping the humans of their recent sexual experience, Dae walked out into the humid warmth of the night. The bright neon and bustle of humanity on Capitol Hill usually comforted him, but tonight he barely noticed. His attention turned inward.

Kar's right. What the hell? I haven't lost control in centuries. He walked the streets, making his way across the hill, heading toward Volunteer Park, near his home. His stomach growled, and Damian stumbled to a stop, his hand shooting to his belly. *I had dinner just before I left to hunt.*

Worry nibbling away at his mind, Damian continued his walk home.

Alexis Kingham flicked the hair off her cheek, again, and wished the air conditioning vent wasn't above her cubicle. Everyone else from the office had gotten to go home already. But Mathew had dumped Katie's folder on her desk half an hour before quitting time, so she was stuck. What the boss wanted the boss got. And if he wanted her to finish cleaning up Katie's designs before she left, it was either that or quit.

Good enough to touch up, but heaven forbid if I try and

design something myself. I have more talent in my nail parings than most of the graphic artists Mathew employs. Why did he even hire me?

She stabbed the save button, then started the image rendering. An impatient hand across her cheek shoved the cut ends of hair away again. The new hairstyle had not accomplished what she'd hoped for. The fresh and invigorated vision of herself had not come to pass. Instead she just had another irritation piled on a life that didn't seem to be going anywhere. Letting out a frustrated groan, she thrust her chair back but then stopped, forcing herself to take a deep breath, followed by lifting her arms in a stretch.

If I could just paint. She thought about the half-started, discarded canvases she had in her minuscule apartment. *Why did I move out here again?*

It was easy, now that she was trapped in this situation, to forget the unidentified impulse that had all but driven her to relocate from her small hometown to downtown Seattle. She had grown increasingly uncomfortable at home, to the point that she felt like she was going insane. Something had drawn her here, and when she set foot on Capitol Hill, where she found her apartment, she'd finally been able to relax. It had been months since she'd relaxed. Excited, she'd tried to start painting again. The restless need that had pushed her away from home had blocked her from painting as well, but she still couldn't make her visions come to life on the canvas. Almost a year had passed since she'd finished anything worthwhile.

She double checked all her equipment, then

grabbed her purse. Late sunlight streamed through the windows, and she glanced down to the busy street several stories below as she walked through the silent office door. Another summer evening gone. She sighed as she waited for the elevator. Her heels clicked on the marble when she boarded and pushed the lobby button on autopilot. Soundlessly the elevator dropped.

In the lobby, she flipped a wave at the lone desk operator as she passed, then stepped out into the wall of heat that the pavement and buildings in downtown Seattle had accumulated during the long summer day. A deep freeing breath stretched her chest. Even filled with exhaust, as opposed to the clean pine scent of home, it felt better than the stale refrigerated air of the skyscraper.

Thoughts of home settled into her mind. She still wasn't sure why she'd had to leave. She missed her family, and her job sucked. But she still couldn't bring herself to move back. She trudged up the hill in her heels, sweat dribbling between her breasts, when she heard her phone ring. She fished it out of her bag and looked at the screen—her sister Lydia. After plugging in her earphones, she answered.

"Hi, Dia."

"Hey, Lexi. Working late again? I can hear the traffic."

"There's always traffic in the city," she evaded.

"How can you stand it there? The noise must be overwhelming."

"It's not so bad," she lied. She missed the quiet of the country. *If I wasn't alone...*

The thought surprised her, and she tuned back into her sister. "...still doesn't understand. You've been there for six months now. Your lease should be up. Dad's really hoping you'll come home."

"Dia, I've told you all before, it's a great place to live. I like that it's full of people."

"All strangers."

Lexi sighed. Her sister was right. What was she doing here? She still wasn't happy and the constant searching for something was driving her nuts. But the thought of leaving tore her insides up. "They aren't all strangers. I've made some friends." *One.* She laughed to herself. "I'm fine, Lydia, really. Please tell everyone I love them and I'll see them when I come up at the end of the month." She waited for a light, then crossed at the signal. "I've got to go. I've reached home and it's not polite to be on the phone in the elevator. Bye."

She pushed end and dropped her phone back into her bag. Sadness followed in the wake. A form of homesickness engulfed her. The strange thing was that it wasn't for her family or home.

Up early, Damian quietly wiped the now clean dish dry, trying to get the evidence of his first, and private, breakfast tidied up before anyone came out to find it. Afraid that he knew what this growing hunger meant—along with his loss of control the other night at Decadence—he jumped when Maggie, the human descendant in charge of their house, entered the kitchen.

She smiled a motherly smile at him. "Up early again, Dae?"

He conjured a smile in return. "Thought I'd help you with breakfast."

She shook her head, the gray streaks at her temples shimmering in the overhead light, and told him to get the bacon out of the fridge. "This is normally the only time I have peace," she continued. "Kelusis may not need to sleep the same way the rest of us mortals do, but I can usually count on at least a few hours near dawn that you are all out from underfoot. Is everything OK?"

"Maggie, how many times do we have to tell you we aren't immortal?"

She rolled her eyes at him. "Whatever. From where I'm standing, close enough."

He slid bacon into the skillet and listened to it sizzle, mortality keen on his mind. *My hunger is growing too quickly, both the physical and psychic. I'm glad Erik harvested my energy the other night. If he saw my storeground now...*

That was one of the reasons why he was up. Unable to sleep, he had turned inward and took a good mental look at the psychic organ that the Kelusis used to store the emotional energy they harvested. Kelusis existed in both the physical and mental planes equally. One look at his ground and he'd wanted to cry.

Standing in Shadow, the world of dreams where his ground manifested, he had stared around the orchard that represented it, then sunk to his knees.

The trees were wilting as the loam turned to sand and could no longer support the lush growth. Which meant that his ability to store the emotional psychic energy he needed to survive was diminishing. He had entered what the Sundered called the fade.

I'm dying, he finally acknowledged to himself. Sorrow welled up that he quickly suppressed. He didn't need to draw Cassandra's attention. His sister was the sorrow link of the family and was specially tuned to that band of emotion. Just as he was the lust link.

Railing at fate would do no good either. It would have the same effect of attracting Callum's attention, the anger link. He turned the bacon and listened to Maggie stir batter in a bowl. *I just have to accept it. There's nothing I can do to change the fact that I was sundered. That we all were. No matter how much I want my succubus back, to be whole again, I can't change what happened. I knew that my life span was forfeit the moment I lost that half of my soul. The moment it was ripped from me. At least by bonding with the family we've all had these centuries. It's all I could have asked for.*

The catastrophe that had hit the Kelusis centuries ago still reverberated through their society. Fear, distrust, paranoia, all followed in the wake of the weeks that had broken so many of their people. The damaged, sundered Kelusis were pitied and treated as handicapped by the untouched Kelusis.

Pulling the bacon out to drain, he moved to the side so Maggie could finish getting the rest of breakfast done. He got plates out to set the table.

"I notice you didn't answer my question earlier,"

Maggie prodded when he walked by. "Are you OK?"

The stack of dishes rattled before he could steady his hand. "Nothing to worry about, Mags. I just have a lot on my mind with the conclave coming up. You know Erik has me doing a lot right now."

A relieved breath escaped her as she added more batter to the griddle. He finished setting the table as pounding footsteps thundered down the hall. Isaac slid around the corner, a goofy grin on his lean face, his short sandy hair tousled like usual. Though when Dae looked in his eyes, he could see his brother's weariness. Isaac was their joy link, and the constant high of the energy he harvested took a toll on him.

"Blueberry pancakes! You do love me, Mags."

She swatted his hand away with a laugh. "Go pour the orange juice, imp."

Trying not to draw attention to his hunger, Dae sat and dished up a serving so he could get extra in without it being obvious. Isaac sloshed juice for everyone, then plunked down in a chair, suppressing giggles. Cass joined them, rubbing sleepy eyes and shoving the long tangled curls of dark hair away from her face, but she threw a curious glance his way that he ignored. He wasn't sure if she was picking up remnants of his sorrow or if she'd noticed the quantity of food. He didn't have long to contemplate because Callum stomped in, a scowl on his rugged face.

"Shut up, Isaac." He yanked out his chair and sat.

Dae stuffed a bit of pancake in his mouth so he wouldn't laugh at the normal morning ritual between his brothers.

"Leave him alone, Cal." Erik sighed as he entered the room, still reading whatever papers he'd brought with him from his office. Tall, fair, and broad-shouldered, Erik's Viking heritage was stamped prominently on his physique.

Damian chewed and watched his eldest brother warily. None of them were related by blood. Selected to bond together after they were all sundered, they depended on each other to live. Four links were needed to harvest the separate bands of energy, and their center, the fifth member of the family, had been altered to draw the energy out of the links and combine it to feed them all. Erik could no longer touch any free energy, though he could still see and sense it. So now it took five to do what they each once could do alone when whole.

Focused on Erik, Dae watched, hoping that their center wouldn't notice anything amiss. His thoughts in turmoil over his newfound realization, Dae couldn't bring himself to break the news. *I'm dying. This has to be the fade. What else could it be? There's no other explanation for why I'm suddenly eating so much. My ground is deteriorating, and as it does, my body won't be able to process any nourishment. Either energy or solid food. I'll starve.*

He watched the others eat like this was any other normal day. Damian pulled a couple more pancakes onto his plate. *You know they're not going to let you go.*

Fear spiked his system and he took a calming breath. Even though he contained it quickly, both Cass and Callum still threw him inquiring glances from the emotion they had each picked up. Both of their bands were sensitive to what he was feeling. He shrugged and smiled, taking another bite, while inside he battled to hold himself together. *I'm going to kill them.* The sudden realization hit. *I can't tell them. As soon as Erik finds out, he'll open the bond conduit and bind us all open.*

That was the only option to give a fading Sundered a little more time. If the family's center opened the conduit that connected them all, then the whole family could support the fading link; the downside was that it drastically reduced the whole family's life span. *I can't steal their lives. I couldn't live with that. They will just have to bond with a new lust link.*

That would allow the family to continue for centuries more. *Maybe the Chirurgeons will finally have found a cure for us by then.* The Kelusis doctors had yet to figure out what had actually caused the sundering in the first place. They knew the mechanism, but not its origins. So far the best the Chirurgeons had been able to do was alter the Sundered psychically and bond them together so they wouldn't starve to death. They hadn't been able to stop the fade that eventually occurred, nor could they determine when an individual Sundered might become affected.

Dae sat quietly eating, watching his family interact around him. *The symptoms are coming on fast. I probably only have a couple more weeks left.*

"Damn it, Isaac, sit still," Callum growled.

Damian glanced at the joy link. Isaac's eyes held the truth of his feelings since his outward reactions were always manic and exuberant because of the energy he held. And right now Dae watched frustrated irritation skate across the brown. *Uh oh, he's spoiling for a fight.*

With an exasperated huff, Erik slapped his papers down, obviously recognizing Isaac gunning for Callum as well. "Isaac, here, now." He pointed at the floor in front of his chair.

The joy link bounced out of his chair with a loud whoop, and Dae saw relief sweep through his eyes. It was hard for Isaac to hold a coherent conversation once he had enough energy filling his ground. Unfortunately Erik couldn't hold the individual strands for very long, so he couldn't just siphon the joy link off all the time since the energy would just be wasted. But sometimes he made an exception.

Isaac crashed to his knees on the hardwood in front of their center. Erik placed the palm of his hand over Isaac's heart and the joy link groaned. Erik only relieved some of the pressure, so it was a fast exchange.

"There. That should help. Now leave Cal alone." Erik's lips twitched like he was trying not to let a smile out.

Isaac drew in a deep, relieved breath. "Thanks, Erik. I don't know why it's so bad right now."

He rose and walked much more sedately back to his seat at the table; there was only a tiny bit of bounce to his step.

Erik shrugged, but his attention was now on those around the table instead of his paperwork. Dae swallowed a big bite of food, not thrilled that their center was no longer distracted. Erik's gaze landed on him, and it took all of his willpower not to freeze under his brother's piercing stare.

"I need you to get the next set of papers out to Mr. Davies this morning, Dae. This should lock us into the house deal in Port Townsend for Jeremy's family. This house is perfect for his descendant's needs. And the family would really like a new location outside of Seattle."

"I'll put it on my list. Do you still want me to go out there?"

"Yes, but not until next week. When the final papers are ready. Today we just need to get caught up on stuff. Too much has gotten backed up with the conclave coming up. Speaking of, I have an extended council meeting tomorrow afternoon."

"Did it get on the calendar?"

"No." He sighed. "I just found out before breakfast."

"Right. Then I'll go through your schedule for tomorrow to make sure any conflicts are taken care of."

A warm smile lit Erik's face. "I don't know what I'd do without you, Dae."

Damian snorted as expected, but inside he felt gutted. *You'll find out soon, brother.*

The crowd bustled by in the late afternoon sunlight a couple of days later. Damian slid to the edge of the sidewalk and planted his back against the sun-warmed brick wall of a building, the edgy need burning through his skin.

Keeping his power leashed was becoming harder and harder. It went hand in hand with the insatiable physical hunger that grew. He raised a burrito to his face, inhaling the spicy scent along with the emotion the crowd of humans released on the street like wispy tendrils, waving in a psychic breeze. The little trickles of love and lust that pattered onto his storeground felt like water dropped onto a hot stove. The desert was spreading fast, destroying the healthy, energy-rich sections that remained.

The need to hunt pushed at him.

He took a bite of the burrito in his hand. The unwelcome ravenous hunger gnawed at his belly. He restrained himself from bolting it like a starving dog—barely.

Dark energy brushed up against his, and Cassandra settled her shoulder against the wall beside him. A flash of fear shot through him that he suppressed, and he strangled his power, holding it in, hiding from her the extent of his need. Her wild midnight hair stirred in the summer breeze.

"Keep eating like that, you're going to get fat."

He raised an eyebrow at her and cast a look out of the corner of his eye while he took another bite. *Then you don't want to know that it's my third.*

"I would have thought after the dinner you packed away at home that you'd be out hunting, not supporting Taco del Mar. I'm starting to agree with Erik. He sent me to check on you. You OK?"

Damian swallowed the last bite and balled up the foil. "I'm fine."

He cleared the gravel out of his voice and fashioned a smile to lead his sister away from the truth. Over the last few days, the hunger had gotten harder to control and harder to hide. He shook back the billowy cuff of his favorite white silk shirt and tossed the ball across the sidewalk, straight into a trash can. Cass snorted. He winked at her, then cast a roving eye across the hustle and bustle that was Capitol Hill on a summer evening, letting just enough of his power twine out to satisfy her. "I am hunting. There's plenty of lusty thoughts and feeling floating through a crowd like this. But you know I've got a weakness for a good Mondo Burrito. I couldn't help myself when I walked by. Tell Erik to back off."

She searched his face, then pushed away from the wall and shook out her multi-hued skirts. "Boy you've been grouchy lately. You left early again, so you didn't get notice that Erik wants to drain us all tomorrow. Make sure you come home at a decent hour. Where are you really hunting?"

A couple of young women clicked by, their heads tilted his way, their skirts inching up the backs of their thighs with each step. He ran his tongue across his lower lip and one smiled at him. The breeze stirred again, and the ends of his hair tickled the back of his neck. His power reared and he choked it back, letting the smallest tendril stir, reaching out lightly with his mind to brush the women as they passed. One of them ran her hand up her companion's arm to twine into her hair. He was rewarded with a burst of their heightened lust, and he pulled the wisp of energy in.

A smile cracked his lips and he let the couple move on as he returned his attention to Cass. "I'm going to head over to Decadence."

"Don't start another orgy."

He rolled his eyes. "Come on. Give me a break."

The corners of her lips tipped up.

"Where are your hunting grounds tonight?" he asked.

"I'm planning to ghost the halls of some of the hospitals on Pill Hill. Enough sorrow to fill an ocean. It won't take much for me to amplify it. I should fill up tonight." She fell silent.

"Now it's my turn to ask, are you OK?"

Her lips firmed. "I envy you, Dae. I'm tired of causing so much sadness. Will this ever end?"

He brushed a spiral of hair behind her ear, the loose sleeve of his pale shirt a stark contrast to the dark strands. Pushing away from the wall, he gave her a quick hug. "I don't know. My hope is gone, Cass. Only the family keeps me going any longer."

"I can't remember the centuries." She paused, then cleared her throat. "Tristan's family lost their sorrow link the other night."

"Damn, I hadn't heard. The Chirurgeons are working on it. You know that."

The cobalt of her eyes flashed. "Of course they are. And I'm sure they'll figure out a cure for us as soon as they quit hiding behind the court's laws and protocols. Even the king ignores his son. The rest of the Kelusis don't care what's happened to us. We're an embarrassment. Handicapped Kelusis that aren't worth acknowledging."

He shook his head. He didn't quite agree with her assessment of their people. He felt more like they treated the damaged Sundered as lepers. Leaning over, he kissed her forehead, which made her hiss in frustration.

"Knock it off. If I could still shift into my incubus, none of you would be so patronizing."

"It's not that and you know it, Cass. You *are* physically weaker than the rest of us, that's a fact, but more importantly you have the responsibility of taking in the hardest energy."

"No. Not the hardest. Sorrow is just the most depressing. All the links have challenges. Callum's anger, Isaac's insane happiness, your sexuality." She shook her hair over her shoulder. "Time to get to work. See you tomorrow."

He watched her saunter away, and the eyes of the crowd turned to follow the succubus as she passed.

With a sigh, he bent down to pick up the bag of burritos at his feet, glad that his sister hadn't noticed it and questioned him on the contents. He slipped into the flow of people. Twice as many eyes tracked him as had Cass. He reached into the bag as he wandered and pulled out more food while he let his mind loose to hunt. He just needed to keep control.

I can't believe Nathanial is gone. Tristan must be devastated. Lucky me, I get a preview of what my family will go through.

His stomach growled. It didn't stop growling anymore. He ate faster and looked at what was left in the bag. *I'm not going to be able to hide this much longer. I'm not far enough gone yet—Erik could still open the conduit.*

He continued to amble, his mind pulling at the threads of emotion accessible to him as he passed— but the trickles only hissed into the sand inside him, dissipating almost as fast as they landed. Only a fraction of the energy he took in remained in his storeground. Frustrated, he pushed harder.

When he neared Decadence, he skirted the entry line to avoid the gate and made his way quietly to a side door. Since he was Kelusis, he had free access to the private doors when he wished it. And right now he wished not to draw attention to himself. He could learn from his mistakes.

He passed out of the last of the sun and into the dim interior near the kitchens. Smells of cooking food assaulted his nose, and his stomach growled. Gripping his now empty sack tighter, he shoved it into the first available trash can he passed.

Music reverberated through the building. The kitchen hall let out near the bar, and he tried to slip over to the tables near the railing, but Bob kept a sharp eye on his domain.

"Damian, what are you doing here? I know you were told not to come back for a few weeks."

He froze midstep, then looked over his shoulder at the descendant. Bob swished a towel across the top surface, waiting. With dragging footsteps, Dae turned and walked over to the bar and took a seat on one of the stools. It was still early so the place wasn't too busy.

"Kar was pissed. He doesn't want another incident." The bald-headed bartender pulled a glass down and filled it with red wine, placing it in front of him. "Letting you stay...this could get me in trouble with the enforcers."

Dae rubbed the stem of the glass softly in his hand. "How would the enforcers find out? Are you going to call Karry?"

"The enforcers would most definitely pay attention if you break the law so spectacularly again, Dae. They aren't going to miss another orgy."

"That was an accident."

The descendant's fear of the Kelusis enforcers wasn't unfounded. As an individual, a human didn't stand a chance against any Kelusis, let alone an enforcer—not even a human descended from the Kelusis, like Bob, who had a greater chance of having heightened abilities. But as a species, the prolific and shorter-lived humans could pose a significant threat to their symbiotic nonhuman cospecies.

Bob's gaze darted around the room before he focused on Dae again. "Accident or not, you started an orgy. I'm not the only one here who witnessed it or who might call you in."

"Look, I won't go onto the floor. I'll stay up here. I promise."

"Up here?"

Damian looked away from the bartender's suddenly intent gaze, and his stomach took that moment to growl loudly over the background noise. The human's hand gently turned his head back.

"So that's why you lost control?" he said softly, his head tilted toward Dae's noisy middle.

Dae squeezed his eyes shut to stop the tears that threatened at the sudden understanding and sorrow in the descendant's gaze.

"How long do you have?" Bob asked.

He cleared his throat and pulled away. "I don't know. A couple of weeks...maybe? Don't tell Erik."

"You've managed to hide your fade that long? I won't tell them, but I doubt I'll have to. They can't miss it much longer."

The words shot an arrow through his heart. "I just need to harvest as much as I can to give them."

Bob shook his head, then moved to help a new customer who'd come up to the bar. Damian took his glass and found a table overlooking the dance floor below. He settled into the seat and started to tease out the threads of energy he could take in, the emotion dripping like acid rain onto the sunbaked sands of his storeground. Yet the need pushed him through the pain. Staying up here, the energy shouldn't slip his grasp enough to start another orgy. Not like if he was immersed in it down on the floor. Focused, he watched the humans below dance in and out of the bright flashes of colored light, their bodies gyrating to the thunderous bass that throbbed in Dae's bones.

A clatter on the table in front of him jarred him out of his focus. A plate piled high with steaming fish and chips now rested there. Silent, Bob met his eyes before turning back to his duties.

"Damn it," he muttered. Having a descendant

around—someone who understood what was happening to him—was annoying, but he picked up a hot piece of fish anyway, trying not to burn his mouth too badly. He wondered who had just lost their meal and went back to searching the crowd while he ate. A particularly enticing strand of energy wafted past his senses, and he grabbed it with his mind. His eyes followed the trail down to the base of the stairs on the left. In the shadows, a couple made out.

He swallowed the fish as he stroked the strand of energy and felt the response. He smiled and let his mind have more freedom. A careful crafting of images slid down the link. The man speared his hands into the woman's hair as he backed her against the wall. Her leg snaked around his knee as she kissed him back. His gaze locked on the two, Dae took an absent bite of fish and jacked up their responses. He couldn't hear their sounds over the music, but he could feel them through the energy— her moans and his groans as he slid his hands under her shirt.

The trickle of energy fleshed out into a rivulet. This held promise.

He sent them more inspiration. Soon the two writhed against the wall as they took their foreplay further than they had probably intended. The rivulet deepened into a stream. He sucked the power down into the sand of the once fertile loam of his storeground.

Completely focused on his work, he jumped when Bob touched his shoulder.

"Damian, you're taking them too far here." The bartender's eyes held pity. "Move to a new source or get them out."

"Don't tell Erik."

"Don't incite another orgy and I won't."

He nodded and Bob returned to his bar but kept an eye on him. His attention returned to the two below him. Her shirt was rucked up over her bra, and the flap of his jeans gaped enticingly. Stifling a groan of his own, Dae pulled back on the reins and watched the two rise to the surface of awareness for a breath. The man rested his head on the wall beside his partner while she quickly yanked her shirt down. Then he pushed away from the wall and buttoned his fly before grabbing her hand. They both made for the stairs. Dae twitched the reins. He pushed away from his table and moved to set his stage.

The stream of energy had lessened somewhat, but the current still ran swift. They were the best find in weeks. He savored the flavor as he used a light hand to direct them. He set a path to cross theirs. The two had eyes only for each other, so allowing them to run into him and ostensibly knock him over was easy. Hands reached out, grabbing his arms.

"I'm so sorry," the woman gasped.

"Sorry, bro. We weren't watching where we were going."

"Hey, no worries. Obviously I wasn't either." They hauled him up, and he pushed with a touch of the energy he'd collected so their pull yanked him into them seemingly on accident. He landed flush against the male, a hard ridge pressed into his thigh, and his eyes burned into the human's. Dae shifted his leg, caressing the length through the denim, and the man smothered a groan. "Nice," Dae whispered.

The woman giggled, and he peeled himself away sinuously, brushing his hand along the nape of the male human's neck as he put a paper-thin separation between their bodies. A zap accompanied the sinking of his psychic tracer line. He echoed the human's moan from the action and blinked, surprised. He normally had more control over his reactions, but then the woman squeezed his arm where she was still pressed to his side. He turned his attention to her. She leaned up and he let his lips settle over hers; his tongue snuck out to trace the seam of her mouth as his hand stole up to her nape. Another joint shock as his tracer sunk home. Instinct took control and his tongue plunged in.

"That is so hot," her partner whispered, his body closing the miniscule gap again. The warmth of the human male's hand settled on Dae's backside and squeezed. He moaned into her mouth.

"Damian."

He jerked back at the sharp reprimand. Bob's scowl penetrated the haze that had started to form.

"You know the law, Dae," Bob continued.

The human's hand continued to caress his backside and Dae shivered. *Law. Right. No sex with humans.* The woman nipped his collarbone, and he realized that she had pulled the laces of his shirt loose. He started to disentangle himself and ended up pressed tight against the hard chest behind him.

The man whispered in his ear, "We were on our way home. Care to join us?"

The wet tickle of her tongue inched lower through the vee of his shirt. He suppressed another moan. Then the male joined in the tasting, raking his teeth into the crook of Dae's neck. Energy ignited, and he couldn't stop the deep need that tumbled out of his mouth.

It took a moment before he could get a coherent word to form. "I wish I could. Unfortunately I'm expected elsewhere."

"Pity."

With a sigh the woman stepped back and scoured him with hungry eyes. "Maybe a different night?"

Tempted to break the law more than he'd ever wanted to since his succubus half had been ripped out of him, he nodded agreement. The man gave his rear one last squeeze, then took his partner's hand and started toward the exit, both casting hot glances over their shoulders.

The breath shuddered out of him, and he turned guilty eyes Bob's way. The descendant bartender swiped a towel across the wood and watched him. His steps heavy, Dae forced himself over.

"I need to bring in as much food for them as I can. Before..."

"You should tell them, Damian."

He shook his head violently. "No."

The descendant continued to wipe the bar, but Dae could feel his disagreement. He couldn't live with himself knowing he'd shortened his family's lives by allowing them to lengthen his. The lure of the trace pulled at him. He looked toward the exit the couple had taken.

"Thanks for the fish." He started away.

"Take care, Damian."

Dae looked over his shoulder and caught Bob's gaze, acknowledging the good-bye underneath the words. Then he turned to his trace and tracked the couple into the night.

The partying had only begun for the evening. Energy wisped around him as he walked through the crowded streets, but the potent lure of the two humans he'd already tasted drew him on. Their energy held a strength and purity he hadn't drunk in lately. The line led him through the night across Capitol Hill.

The crowds thinned as he followed the trace and moved into tree-lined residential neighborhoods. In and out of the pools of light the streetlamps threw, the trail turned to mount stone steps. He eyed the old brick apartment building across the street and watched a light snap on in a third-floor apartment, then the woman's figure paced by the glass. With a sigh of relief, Dae lowered himself to the grass at the curb and leaned against the rough bark of a big chestnut tree. Siphoning off a portion of the energy he was pulling in, he used it to bend the light around him, effectively rendering himself invisible, and set to work.

His eyes fixed on the square of light across the way. Regret unexpectedly hit as he watched the two return to their heated embrace through the glass. He could still feel their hands on his body. He shifted on the ground, the seam of his jeans pressed uncomfortably against his erection. He'd sprung to life at their first touch and had yet to subside.

The stream of lust he was tapped into swelled, and he pulled himself out of his thoughts and turned back to work. They had moved away from the window, but he didn't need to see them physically. He could see them quite clearly in his mind as he started the first of the fantasies he needed to push them to the edge. The place where he would get the purest energy. The most filling food for his family.

The energy grew, tumbling and rushing like a river rising to flood stage. The sounds and sights echoed in his mind. The reality of their physical acts overlaid the waking visions he sent them in his mind. He pulled the reins this way and that as he rode their psyches alongside the riverbank of their energy. But then the reins slipped briefly in his grasp.

Slammed by the images they sent, he became immersed in fantasies of their own, involving him, even though their encounter had been brief. The sights, sounds, and touches in their psyches were so real that he couldn't stop his body from responding. He groaned and pressed the heel of his hand into his groin. The fever in his blood intensified, and he ruthlessly yanked back control.

Ignoring the warning in his head, he pushed harder, driving them into a moaning, screaming frenzy. He could feel the first seed of doubt, the trickle of fear that wormed its way into their minds when they couldn't halt their own momentum, when they couldn't stop the lust that coursed through them and their bodies' responses to it. Beyond caring, he drank in the torrent. The sand inside him sucked it up and greedily demanded more.

The humans' passionate wails could now be heard on the street. He throbbed under the heel of his hand and sent the desire consuming him down the link.

On a piercing crescendo, he finally allowed them to climax, and sweat-soaked and trembling, they tumbled into unconsciousness in each other's arms.

Dae blinked and focused on the darkened street. His breathing was harsh in his ears, the searing hardness under his palm unexpected and unwelcome. The desert inside him demanded more as the flood of lust energy waned once the couple passed out.

He tried to turn his mind and appetite to hunting new prey, but the stream that still trickled into him from them was too tempting. Approaching death took the threat of breaking the law out of consideration. For the first time in thousands of years, he plunged into Shadow, into the world of dreams, with the intent to feed.

In Shadow, he wove the scene, then pulled the two humans into his world. They came with a gratifying eagerness. His lips descended to hers, their lush softness open and roving of their own accord. A large hand returned to his rear, and he pushed back into it, moaning into her mouth. Wet heat trailed up the back of his neck. With a shudder, he surrendered to the power. His appetite insatiable, he pushed them further than they ever could have gone alone—riding them into exhaustion, demanding response after response. Their fear mingled with their pleasure. And the power poured into Damian.

After an indeterminate length of time, his toys' responses faded, like the batteries run out in a Christmas gift. And he took a good look around for the first time, realizing what he'd done. What he'd allowed to happen.

Thank the stars I stopped in time.

The two humans lay sprawled, exhausted. Mind, body, and soul. If he had kept going, he would have killed them. The temptation to continue, to drain their energy dry, to the point that they would die, seethed under his tenuous control. Only when young did a Kelusis have to worry about draining the energy of another's psyche to the point of death.

Backing away from what he'd done, Dae fled the shadowscape and disengaged from the dream with a jerk, slamming back into his physical body. It still clamored for relief. Disgusted with himself, he pushed to his feet and took a quick mental look at the two humans in their apartment. They would feel the effects of his carelessness long after tonight. Physically, emotionally, mentally drained, they would be sore and tired inside and out. He had pushed them hard just through the trace, but continuing in Shadow scraped the pulp out of the shell. It would take them weeks to rebuild their reserves.

I can't go home tonight. Erik will be able to tell. Bob's right. I won't be able to hide this any longer.

Shoving his hands into his pockets, he kicked a rock with enough force to chip the glass of the car window it hit across the street, and he spun on his heel to stalk into the night.

⚜

"Another pointless attempt," Alexis mumbled and viciously plunged her brush into the jar. "Why do I keep trying? Why am I still here?"

She sat back and stared at the mess on the canvas. No life, no spirit.

It looked like a person, the picture that was slowly appearing before her. But that was all. "I might as well draw stick figures."

She absently grabbed a rag from the stand next to her chair and scrubbed at her finger without looking at it. *Maybe if I add some more blue to the dress?* She ducked her head to wipe the sweat from her temple onto the strap of her tank top. The August heat baked her little upper-story apartment during the day. But even at ten o'clock at night, it still hadn't dissipated.

She sighed and continued to stare at the blobs of paint. Slowly in her mind they merged and swirled as she daydreamed a new pattern. It consumed her thoughts as she closed her eyes and relaxed. Instead of the Victorian lady next to a pond that she'd been working on, hillsides of gilded rows of trellised vines took shape, so real she felt she could reach out and touch what she saw. Her hard chair no longer beneath her, she could feel the sun vie with the crisp air that was the cause of the leaves changing. Damp earth and leaf mold filled her nose. Cropped grass carpeted the spaces between.

Heart pounding, she looked around. Her gaze pulled down one of the aisles, she craned her neck. In the distance an immense stone building watched over the grapes. The feeling of remembrance swamped her. She knew that building.

The memory of a sharp pain pierced her chest as movement caught her eye down the row. A broad back, encased in pale linen. Dark waves of hair caught in a cue at the nape of the neck. She stood frozen, anticipating, longing for him to turn.

Sound carried to her on the breeze. Leaves rustling, birds, the rumble of a familiar voice that echoed in her head.

Breath seizing, she watched as he started to turn.

The wail of multiple sirens on the city street jerked her in her seat. The pale washed-out hues of blue on the dress blended with the pond background on the canvas before her. No sunshine. No breeze. No vineyard.

She blinked. Haphazard canvases tilted here and there in the mess of her apartment. Just where she'd left them when she decided they wouldn't suit. Clothes, supplies, and other belongings drifted out of boxes scattered between. She hadn't bothered to do much in the way of unpacking when she'd moved in.

She shook her head, trying to clear the fog. *I guess I fell asleep.* Though the vivid images felt more real than any dream she could remember.

Stiff, she rose from her chair and stretched. Edgy energy infused her, the picture still vibrant in her mind. A sense of longing engulfed her, and she clenched her fist to keep from sweeping the unsuitable painting from her easel. Slipping around it, she stalked through the pathway of her possessions to the open sliding glass door.

A breath of cooler air swirled around her when she leaned against the rail, and the colorful lights of downtown Seattle twinkled in the summer night. Their cheery energy seemed at odds with her introspective mood, her unexplained longing—and underlying it, an unfounded yet undeniable anticipation.

Chapter 2

A FEW DAYS LATER Damian once again settled against the warm brick of a building. A block off of the busy street of Broadway he leaned against the backside of a grocery store and faced the residential neighborhood. There was still a crowd coming and going here though it was thinner. His phone rang off and on as his family tried to reach him. His absence had been noted. He couldn't stomach condemning them to a wasting death though, so he maintained his silence. Normally one of them could disappear for a few days and not cause a stir, but Dae could feel the panic starting to rise from his family based on the number of calls. *They must have picked up more clues than I thought since they aren't giving me any leeway.*

He pulled a pastry out of the bag he held, biting into it with a moan. He needed food almost constantly now. After scarfing two, he slowed down a bit and worked on bringing some control to his energy harvest. He couldn't spend time in a crowd like

Decadence anymore. He'd cause another orgy from his lack of control, and it wasn't just his family he needed to avoid now. Any Kelusis would recognize the signs, and that would bring the enforcers—followed by the Chirurgeons—down on him.

The energy from the pedestrians on the streets posed plenty of difficulty for his control as it was. He worked to hold himself in check. It was hard not to mentally push too much in an effort to heighten the level, because what little emotion he could passively draw in from the pedestrians sizzled on his ground.

He pulled the next éclair out then froze before he could take a bite—the most tantalizing energy he'd ever felt wafted across his senses, and it wasn't something he'd pulled into being. Starvation forgotten, his head snapped up and he scanned the area. Plenty of people walked the neighborhood, but only one drew his senses. A woman meandered her way along the sidewalk across the street, grocery bag slung over her shoulder. Luscious curves filled out her denim shorts and simple T-shirt. The light breeze played with the feathery ends of her short hair, giving mouthwatering glimpses of her ivory neck.

She reminded him of a little bird, the way she would pause and tip her head to study a flower or something in a garden before moving on. His feet moved of their own accord, but he decided he agreed with them. Her energy was like a leash straight to his groin.

And strangely it didn't feel like steam exploding against his sand. It felt like a gentle rain, a healing balm on scorched skin.

He followed in her wake, but it wasn't good enough. When he passed near a shady shrub, he used some of the energy flowing into his ground and bent the light around himself, becoming invisible. Now he picked up his pace until he fell into silent step right behind her. Her energy was almost intoxicating, and her scent filled his nose.

She whipped a look over her shoulder that nearly made him jump, but the warm chocolate of her eyes stared through him exactly as they should. Still, her pace increased. He scanned ahead and a plan formed. Stepping off the sidewalk he gave her some room and jogged before her to round the corner. He let the light slip away from his grasp and moved into position. He pretended to turn his gaze to the ground and started back around the corner just as she turned.

They collided.

Her soft body molded to his in the briefest of contacts before she bounced back in a flailing stumble. The cloth bottom of her shopping sack split and her groceries tumbled to the pavement as her arms pin-wheeled. A squeak passed her lips as he snagged her before she completed her fall and joined her items on the ground. Her eyes rounded in surprise.

His own brand of shock coursed through him and he gulped in a breath. The physical contact turned the sufficiently intriguing stream of energy he pulled in from her into a wild torrent. Body surfing along, he had no intention of looking for shore any time soon.

෪෧ඁ෯

Alexis stared into the gold and green sparkles of the most beautiful eyes she'd ever seen. Hazel, her mind finally supplied the right word. The warmth of his hands on her bare arms made a potent reminder of the split second she had pressed flush against his hard body. The contact would remain indelibly imprinted on her, she was sure. His fingers pulled away, reluctantly it seemed, when she steadied on her feet.

"Here, let me help you."

The soft huskiness of his voice held a hint of elsewhere. An accent she couldn't place. Then what he said penetrated. "My groceries!" she yelped and started to lunge after the apples that had rolled into the street, but a hand yanked her back to the safety of the sidewalk.

"Not worth it. They'll be bruised anyway." He slid a crushed green pepper to the verge of the sidewalk with his foot. "And it doesn't look like any of the rest is salvageable either."

She stared at the splatter of fresh tomatoes and the torn open bag of pasta, the shattered jar of sauce. Egg seeped out of the side of the cardboard carton where it lay on its side.

She pressed her face into her hands. This just hadn't been her day.

"I'm really sorry, Miss...?"

Lexi dropped her hands and looked back into his beautiful eyes. She swallowed. "Alexis."

He smiled and held his hand out to her. Slowly

she clasped his, warm strength enfolding her fingers, and she felt them tremble as butterflies launched in her stomach.

"I'm Dae. I'm sorry about your groceries. Please let me make up for costing you your dinner? Charlie's Grill is just around the corner."

She slipped her hand behind her back after she pulled away and bit her lip. He was right. Her meal now lay crushed all over the sidewalk. So not only would her dinner be late, but she was out the cost of the groceries and would need to buy them all over again. She sighed at the dent to her bank account. She had splurged to have a nice meal. *I guess I'll just go with more normal replacements.*

"Come on. Charlie's is great."

She rubbed her palms against the denim of her shorts. Sparkles of friendly challenge radiated in his eyes and sent a weakness down her limbs that surprised her. "I do love Charlie's…"

His smile turned into a grin, and he brushed his palm down the skin of her arm to clasp her hand, then gave her a light tug. A shiver of awareness followed his touch and settled into a low ball of heat.

She let him lead her back up to Broadway. More people filled the sidewalks on the busier street and she relaxed a little. She tried to think past the physical impact he had made on her and remember that he was a complete stranger, whether he felt like one or not. She cleared her throat. "So I'm assuming you live nearby?"

The repetitive soft brush of his thumb across the inside of her wrist sent shivers over her skin.

A smile lit his hazel eyes. "Yes, over by Volunteer Park. You? Have you lived in the region long?"

Waves of sable hair brushed the collar of his rumpled white poet shirt. She already knew the hard muscles hidden by the flowing fabric. She blew her bangs out of her eyes. *Careful, Lexi, he's awfully smooth. Probably way out of your league.*

She pulled out of her thoughts and answered, "Almost six months. I came here for a job. Love the neighborhood, hate the job."

"I'm sorry to hear that. What do you do?"

"Graphic design. What about you?"

"My family and I have a house near the park. Erik is the executive of the family, but we all spend time in the family business."

"Which is?" She glanced at his left hand. No ring or obvious indent where one was taken off. *A successful, cute hunk. Which means that he probably likes to play.* She sighed.

He didn't get a chance to answer because they arrived at the door to the restaurant. He held it open and let her pass. The weight of his hand came to rest in the small of her back as they walked up to the podium. A waiter took them straight to a table that looked out onto the circus of Broadway as it came to life for the evening. She settled into the wingback chair and looked across the table at her companion.

With his clothes, her whimsical mind had no difficulties picturing him sitting in a chair like that a couple of centuries ago. She smiled at the image then picked up the menu to hide it. It only took her a moment to decide on the Monte Cristo sandwich, since it was her favorite here.

In an effort to divert her attention from her unexpected companion and hopefully get her nerves and body to settle down, she studied the large stained-glass starburst that dominated the ceiling of the dining room. Soft light illuminated the colored glass where it shone through.

"I'd like to say I'm sorry I ran into you again, but then I'd be lying." He laughed. "This is much better for my evening than I had planned."

She smiled back into his twinkling eyes. "A lonely dinner is what I had planned. I think I have to agree."

"So graphic design, huh?" His phone rang and he glanced at it, but then silenced it and set it on the table.

"Yeah, not my most favored position, but at least I sort of get to use my artistic talents."

"Sort of?" He toyed with his water glass before he took a sip, his eyes never leaving hers.

She took her own drink. "Mostly I get to touch up the other designers' projects instead of doing any of the creating on my own. I shouldn't let it bother me. It's decent pay and really I prefer to paint anyway."

"Is that what you hope to do? Paint?"

She sighed and looked at the table top, tracing circles in the drips from her glass. "I don't know actually. I feel like I've been searching or waiting for something, but I have no idea what. I love to paint, but making a living at it is pretty difficult. It's just a dream."

"Dreams are as existent as real life, you know."

She glanced up and got caught by his stare again, heat flushing through her. She took a hurried drink of her water. "So what do you do?"

He cocked his head and it felt like his eyes could see right through her. And the funny thing was that she didn't mind. Her thoughts had drifted enough that she missed the first words of his answer.

"...dabble in this and that. Investments, you name it. Erik runs most of it. The rest of us do what he tells us to." He chuckled.

"So you live with family?" Feeling self-conscious for fishing, she wasn't surprised by the corners of his lips twitching up and she felt her face heat.

"Yes. I have three brothers and a sister. We all mostly get along, so none of us have moved away. The business does well for us all and keeps us busy."

"Sounds nice. My family is still working through their distress that I left the hometown." She laughed. "I loved living in a small town, but I was missing something. They keep trying to get me to come home."

"Do you plan to?"

"No. I don't think so."

The waiter set a large appetizer down, and Dae started dishing plates up for both of them. Her breath escaped when his fingers brushed hers as he handed her the plate. Shocked at how much she was responding to his nearness, she fumbled the plate to the table top. When she looked up, his gaze caught hers knowingly.

She quickly took a mouthful, then from under her

lashes she watched him bite his lip to unsuccessfully suppress his grin. He settled deeper into his seat and ate steadily through the large appetizer he'd ordered for them.

"You moved away from home?" he prompted.

"Yes. This last winter."

"Winter? That's when we returned too. We tend to travel and hadn't been in Seattle for some time. It's nice to be back."

"Where do you go? I've always wanted to travel."

His fingers brushed her hand on the table top, then he grasped it, lightly rubbing his thumb across again. "We were in France."

Strangely, she didn't feel the urge to pull her hand away. "I bet that's beautiful."

"It is, but there's beauty everywhere."

Her insides quivered when she realized that he hadn't taken his gaze off of her. "My family have always been homebodies. I have two sisters and a brother plus both of my parents there. My grandparents died when I was a kid, along with our family history."

Their dinners arrived and they settled in to eat. His phone buzzed a couple more times, but his attention stayed on her. The conversation bounced around and she realized how much she enjoyed his company. For the first time since she'd moved away from home so restlessly, she felt free.

She passed up dessert, but he managed to consume a huge brownie with ice cream. She couldn't imagine where he was packing all the food away to. He must have an incredible metabolism.

And considering his beautiful body...she sighed.

He settled up with the waiter then held out his hand to her. After helping her to her feet, he kept her hand in his and walked with her out onto the neon-lit sidewalk of busy Broadway. He ignored the chatter and press of bodies and steered them in a leisurely walk.

It felt nice to stroll along with a companion for a change. The breath of warm night wind that circled through the streets caught her hair and she ducked her cheek to her shoulder to brush the short strands off her face. He tucked her hand into the crook of his arm and pulled her closer to his side. The silk of his shirt slid along the skin of her arm with each step.

Eventually they passed a clock on the side of a building. "Ten, already?"

He squeezed her arm to his side briefly then said, "Time to go home?"

"I'm afraid so. I have to get up early for work."

"May I walk you to your apartment?"

She was silent for a moment as they continued down the sidewalk. Eventually she made up her mind and said softly, "All right."

He squeezed her hand again then relaxed, allowing her to take the lead in their direction. She took the next street to the left and started them west. The lights of downtown Seattle occasionally peeped through between buildings as she led him toward her apartment.

"I'm sorry you lost all of your groceries," he said after a few minutes. "But I'm not sorry we ran into each other. This has been the best evening of my life."

She laughed nervously. "Oh come on. Of your life? I find that difficult to believe."

"No, really. I haven't enjoyed another's company like this in longer than I can remember." His hand settled over hers in the crook of his arm, the soft brush of his thumb over her skin a definite distraction. "I don't suppose you could call in sick tomorrow and spend the day with me?"

Tempted, she thought about it for a moment but then shook her head. "I can't. As much as I'd rather work somewhere else, I still need this job."

"What about after work?"

She nodded and said slowly, "OK. I could meet you then."

She caught the flash of his grin. They exchanged phone numbers, then he said, "Tell you what, give me the address of your work and I'll pick you up there. I'll get to see you sooner that way."

"I need to change out of my office clothes."

"You could bring some with you."

If she did that, she wouldn't have the half-hour walk up the hill home. "I can do that."

They had arrived at her building. She led the way up the steps and fished her keys out of her pocket. He didn't seem inclined to let go of her arm, so she let him escort her to her floor, then turned to face him at her door.

"Thank you. I had an enjoyable evening too," she said softly.

He tucked her hair over her ear, his fingers brushing the back of her neck, and she jumped at the zap, her stomach flip-flopping. He jerked his hand away and rubbed his fingertips. "Sorry, static," he mumbled.

Their gazes met and he smiled. "I look forward to seeing you tomorrow."

"Me too." She turned and fumbled her key into the lock, barely cracking the door open to slip inside so he wouldn't see the mess of her apartment. When she looked out the peephole, she met his hazel eyes and gasped because she could swear he knew she was looking at him. He smiled, then turned and walked down the hall.

She spun and planted her back against her door. A grin slowly emerged. Giddy, with an exciting fire burning in her veins, she kicked off her shoes. She knew exactly what she needed to do. She shoved piles of belongings over in her small corner of living room, unearthing a canvas, then dug through totes until she found her brushes and paints. For the first time in months, she *had* to paint.

Dae let the outer door of Alexis's apartment building close behind him, then he turned to look up at the windows. The reaction he'd had when he'd touched the back of her neck to set the trace shocked him. The whole evening shocked him. The things her energy did to his body.

It was like nothing he'd consumed in centuries.

Setting a trace should have been an impersonal action. It should not have left him feeling needy and turned on. A trace allowed a Kelusis direct access to an individual human's energy, granting them greater distance to harvest, but it also allowed them to mentally find the other end of the line when they went into Shadow.

Is this another side effect of the fade? I haven't heard of it as a symptom. Then again, setting a trace is against the law.

He couldn't see her, but he knew which set of windows were hers. He could feel her presence as if she pulled him. He crossed the street and started the walk to his car, which was only a few blocks away. Her energy still flowed into him, strong and pure. He let his mind wander over all they'd talked about and what they'd done.

It had been nothing but the truth when he'd told her it was the best evening. She had no understanding what that meant to him. Since the start of the sundering, the Kelusis had been forbidden the sort of contact he had made with her tonight. They were allowed to hunt the descendants with more depth, but a full human was against the law. To direct a human's waking energy was acceptable, as long as they didn't take it too far. Like the orgy he'd caused. The Sundered had to remain in the background. Never anything truly intimate.

He wanted her. He hadn't wanted like this in centuries. But having her was also against the law, and unfortunately the craving to stay near her was stronger than he could deny. So he'd set up a forbidden meeting with her anyway. He shook his head and stopped next to his car.

It won't be dangerous. I can hide her for a day or two

and get as much energy as I can for the family. I can wipe her mind. Then I'll be dead and no one will be able to find her.

His ground had sucked up her emotion greedily, but even with the distance the trace gave him, the stream faded and the hunger pains—both physical and psychic—descended upon him.

He got in his car and started it. Lowering the windows to let in the warm night air, he wove through the streets down to the marina where the family's boat, the *King's Ransom*, was docked on Lake Union.

The bright lights of a late-night pizza takeout near his destination caught his eye, and he pulled in. A few minutes later he tossed four large boxes into the trunk and finished his drive to the boat. After parking, he got out, juggled his keys and the pizza boxes, then navigated his way down the gangplanks and docks to the slip his family's boat was tied up at.

I doubt they'll think to look for me here, and it's not like I have a bunch of options. I need more sleep than I'll get in the cramped quarters of my car or on another park bench, as much as I'd like to stay closer to Lexi. I can't rent a hotel room. Erik's going to be looking for my charges by now.

He hopped onto the boat and then got the door open to descend the steps into the cabin. A slice of pizza in one hand, he walked around turning on lights and adjusting the thermostat. He didn't bother with the generator. The batteries would be plenty for the night.

He plowed through one pizza while he sat in the

galley with the gentle rocking of the boat. Even full he still felt hungry, but he slid out from behind the table. His body just couldn't pull the nutrients out of the food anymore. He washed up, then turned most of the lights off and went to his bunk. They all kept a few items on the boat, so he'd be able to change his clothes in the morning after a shower.

For now he just stripped and fell into bed and pulled the covers up. After several nights of not sleeping in a bed, the narrow bunk felt heavenly. The Kelusis needed sleep, just like humans. And just as humans needed to dream, so did the Kelusis, but for them it was different. They had to walk in Shadow or they grew sick.

The Shadow world was just as real as the world of the light. Though the laws of nature were different. Humans visited Shadow every time they dreamed, but most held very little control over the nature of the world and remembered even less when they woke. Unlike the Kelusis. For them, time spent in either world was necessary and each was experienced and remembered.

Dae's body relaxed immediately, and he found himself in a featureless gray mist. He took a deep breath and let it out in relief. Tempted beyond measure to use the trace and hunt down Alexis, he resisted. He was too unsure of his control. He didn't want to harm her, and that would be easier to do in dreams.

The law against hunting humans in Shadow followed after the sundering, like so many others. A law he hadn't been tempted to break in the thousands of years since it was made...until now.

Turning away from the pull to find Alexis, he focused his thoughts and visualized the vineyard at the family's seat in France. He always found peace and solace there.

He let the energy unfurl and the gray mist swirled around him, but instead of finding himself on the road up to the manor house, he stood on the dense-packed dirt in front of the Alamede Posting House. Carriages rattled by and he hurriedly stepped to the edge of the dusty road on the brittle brown grass, taking in the dark timber beams of the inn, the stark whitewashed walls, and brilliant flowers in bloom in pots all over the flagged courtyard. He stared at the Kelusis gathering location in bemusement.

This is not where I was going.

Incubi and succubi thronged the place. Laughing, talking, gaming. The Kelusis had many gathering places in Shadow, places anchored by an individual or group, where the public could come and meet. For business or pleasure. The anchor kept the mist of Shadow formed and prevented too much disruption by the other minds who visited. Not that small shifts didn't occur, of course. That was the nature of the dream realm. It was not linear like its reflection in the light.

He didn't have the energy to fight the currents and try to get to the Shadow equivalent of their home in France, so Dae walked up the flagged path and ducked inside the posting house. At least here he could sit, have a tankard of ale, and let the world of the Kelusis drift by. He would only have a few more days to reminisce. A few more days before he was gone.

He found a stool at an empty table near the roaring fireplace. An antique transistor radio blared behind the long wooden bar, giving a play by play of a current athletic event. A bunch of Kelusis dressed in the colors of two different teams shouted good-naturedly at each other, while a small group garbed in Elizabethan finery tried to ignore them as they ate an authentic multicourse meal at a table on the other side of the room. His ale arrived and he smiled at the succubus who brought it. The sound of steel clashed from outside, and Dae saw several laughing incubi through a window start a bout in the courtyard. He took a drink, then stiffened as familiar energy wrapped him.

The stool beside him scraped and his center settled onto it.

"Where the hell have you been?"

"Go away, Erik. You threw a line out and pulled me here, didn't you?"

"What did you expect? You haven't come home. And we knew you'd have to walk soon. You feel like shit; you haven't been sleeping or we would have found you sooner."

"Leave me be, Erik."

"You're kidding, right? What the hell's going on, Dae? We need you to come home. Now. Cass told you the other day that we were set to harvest so I could combine all the links' energy and feed everyone."

"We've gone longer."

"So? It's not like we have to. What is up with you?"

"I'll come home when I'm ready, Erik."

Erik's hand settled on his shoulder and squeezed lightly. This let Dae feel the energy his center gathered just before he went to unleash it.

"No!" he shouted and ducked out from under his eldest brother's hand, spinning off the stool. He saw the worry flash across Erik's blue eyes as he yanked the Shadow around himself and dissolved his location. Fear followed the worry as Erik's face faded from Dae's vision and he found himself back where he started, in the nebulous gray mist.

Only a moment later he felt the tug, a tug that grew as another line, then another, and another added to it. The rest of his siblings were throwing in their weight with Erik, working to draw him back.

If he let them succeed, combined they would be strong enough to contain him, then they'd be able to trace his physical location. He cut the ties with Shadow and dropped back into his own body, working to anchor his psyche to his physical form. He couldn't chance dreamwalking anymore tonight. Not with the family out hunting for him. And he needed to sleep. He only had a few more days to harvest. Then the fade would be advanced enough that they couldn't stop it and he could turn over one more full feeding to them before he died.

He snuggled into the pillow and let his body relax again, willing it to sleep. The last thought he had was of Alexis.

꩜

Dae wandered through the misty shadowscape. With each step he became more aware of his surroundings. The terrain flickered. One moment the mist concealed a wooded glade, the next possibly a sandy beach, or a mountainous vista, or a perfectly normal house. The more Shadow shifted, the more aware he became of his lack of control. Surprise surfaced next. Being an incubus, dreams were his forte. The fact that he was in Shadow again, after he thought he'd ensured he wouldn't walk again tonight…

Eventually the terrain settled into a beach. He strolled out of the mist onto warm sand. Sun caressed his skin. He looked down and found giant hibiscus flowers covering his swim trunks. He laughed.

So not my style.

The salty breeze ruffled through his hair and he kicked his feet in the sand while he walked, the shifting grains tickling his legs. He felt good and that surprised him. Carefree. Recent memory surfaced and he remembered that he was dying, but it couldn't hold sway. He paused to stare out over the ocean. The waves pounded into the beach.

The sensation of eyes traveling over him broke through the trance.

He tipped his head to look over his shoulder. Alexis stepped out from the shadow of the trees. She paced across the sand in an unhurried saunter, a hungry gaze roving over him.

I like how my mind thinks.

She reached him and soft hands spread across his back, then traced over his shoulders and down his front. The tips of his nipples hardened under her palms as they slid by. Lips, hotter than the surrounding air, branded his shoulder blade and he groaned. A husky laugh sounded over the surf. He trapped her hands on his chest and turned in her arms to face her.

Velvety sable eyes laughed up at him. Her hands started to dance up and down his spine, tracing every vertebrae. His gaze traveled over her full curves, and his mouth watered. It had been so long since he'd allowed himself the memory of touch. The orgy he incited the other night in Decadence had started a craving. He sent his hands skimming over her silky skin. Then he bent his head and nibbled a path from her shoulder up her neck to her ear. He soaked in the sound of her soft moan and sent his hand to cup the back of her head, then gently wrapped a fist in her hair and pulled her head to the side to gain better access. A shiver slid across her skin and he pulled her closer.

His skin rubbed against a tantalizing combination of damp spandex and flesh. His other hand slid down to squeeze her rear and she pushed her hips into him, her hands still busy touching everywhere she could reach.

His thoughts swam up out of the haze. *I haven't had a dream like this in...*

Then he noticed the shifting of power. The movement of emotional current that he controlled when he hunted flowed between them. Shocked, he pulled away.

Power definitely soaked into his storeground. *This isn't possible. I can't feed in my own dreams.*

Alexis took advantage of his preoccupation and started to nibble on his chest. Her tongue flicked out across a nipple and he gasped, his body responding beyond his control. Groaning, he pushed her back to arm's length. *She's here?*

Her energy most definitely flowed into his ground. The exquisite sensation shuddered through him. *She's really here? Or is this a product of my need? I know my body is on the boat.*

He wrestled for control—of himself, of the dream.

"Wait. Alexis, slow down."

She frowned and backed up out of his reach. "Doesn't it just figure?" she muttered and turned away, stomping across the sand, every luscious curve hugged and displayed by the spandex of her suit.

He caught up to her in a couple of strides. "Doesn't what figure?"

She blew the feathery ends of her hair out of her eyes and glared at him. "Even in my dreams someone as hot as you doesn't want me. I suppose my subconscious is just giving me the truth."

He grabbed her wrist and yanked her to a stop. Then he took her hand and pressed it hard against the steel that rested uncomfortably between his legs. "Does this seem like someone who doesn't want you?"

She gasped and tried to yank back, but he pressed

into her hand more firmly, his other hand capturing the back of her head as he swooped in on her mouth. His tongue swiped across her lips, then dove inside. He kept her off balance, dueling with her tongue, nipping her lips, all the while rocking in her hand. His breath shuddering, he pulled back, then lightened his hold so her hand rested lightly on his erection. "Don't insult me by jumping to conclusions. I just wanted to talk. It was moving too fast."

A dazed look on her face, she nodded. Her fingers twitched on his groin, then tentatively traced its length before she pulled away. He let her hand go on a suppressed groan.

She whipped her hands behind her back once she regained possession of them but couldn't stop her gaze from remaining riveted to where she'd been holding. He pressed his lips together to stop the smile; he doubted she knew how the movement presented her breasts to his eyes, a feast waiting to be unwrapped.

He shaped his thoughts, and using some of the power swirling around them, formed what he needed out of the Shadow. With a soft smile, he waved his hand and directed her to the blanket he'd created in the shade a few feet away. She cocked her head and stared at it for a second in confusion but then shrugged and allowed him to lead her to the blanket.

They sank down. He studied her face. Confusion and uncertainty chased across it. He understood how she felt. This was not how he had expected to spend his resting hours. Not after pulling away from his brother at the posting house. He thought he'd locked down his psyche so he wouldn't walk and take the chance of his family finding him again. Apparently his desire to follow the trace and find her was stronger than he'd realized.

But then the currents moved around him and he had another shock. This wasn't *his* dream. He tested the mists and found that, yes, she was the anchor. Human. Yet she'd drawn him here like a seasoned succubus. And after he'd locked himself down.

He stretched out on his side and laced his fingers with hers, his thumb rubbing across the back of her hand.

"How did you get here?" he asked softly.

She shook her head and stared out over the ocean, her chin resting on her knees.

He slipped his thoughts out, assessing the situation. Testing the levels of control. The dream world was as solid and real to him as the physical, and he had centuries of experience. He slid control out of her grasp. That wasn't difficult—he didn't think she was actually aware of where she was or what she was doing. In effect she was sleepwalking, or dreamwalking, as the case may be. The big question on his mind was *how*.

How is she doing this? She managed to pull me into the dream. And smoothly enough that I didn't realize it wasn't mine.

She sighed, then answered the question he'd asked. "I've always wanted to come to a place like this. I've seen pictures, but I've never been."

He continued to caress her hand. "Why did you bring me here?"

Her head jerked around to face him. "Bring you here? What are you talking about? You were just here…"

He met her eyes.

No, sweet, I definitely didn't set this stage. "Well I did want to be here." He raised her hand and moved his lips across her knuckles. She exhaled.

"You are so cute. What harm is there in having a dream?" she whispered.

"None." *Now that I know this isn't only a dream. It'll be much safer for both of us now.*

His tongue traced the peaks and hollows of her hand, then started to nibble past her wrist. He felt a shiver and her attention turned away from the horizon and back to him. Her energy pulsed like the surf into his ground.

"I thought you wanted to talk? That I was moving too fast?" she breathed.

"I've talked enough." He drew her down onto her back and stretched his weight across her chest. He met her eyes. "It was the hardest thing to leave you after our date."

He lowered his face and his lips pressed against hers again. The soft surface shifted, the tip of her tongue sneaking out to wet his. He tipped his head and dove into the kiss. As her hands snaked into his hair, he groaned, and the pulse turned into a flood on his ground, making him dizzy. He moved from her mouth and sucked wet kisses down the column of her throat. Soft sounds punctuated his path and her hands branded his sides as they traveled south. The hard peaks of her nipples pressed into his chest through her swimsuit.

Strengthened, his energy reared up and grabbed the threads of lust, slamming into her mind. His thoughts and images surged as her body bucked under his, with a drawn-out groan snapping him back to reality.

I'll hurt her. That's why I didn't want to hunt her in Shadow.

He pulled his mouth away from her hot skin, but that didn't stop hers. He shivered. She threatened to pull his tenuous control out of his grasp again. He tried to back out of her mind, but she held him firmly, her anchor in Shadow solid once more.

Sleep, he coaxed, realizing that was his only choice to regain control. He let his mind coil around hers and lured her to sleep. Her movements slowed, then her lashes sank down to make dark crescents against her skin, and her body relaxed into sleep.

Wishing he didn't have to leave, he kissed her forehead, then willed himself home. His eyes opened to the dimness of the boat cabin, his body hot and unfulfilled. Even more unhappy—if that were possible—about his coming death, he squeezed his eyes shut to stop the tears he felt threatening and tried to go to sleep again.

Erik ran his hand through his hair. His footsteps echoed loudly in the hall as he crossed the threshold, flanked by heavy oak doors. The council chamber occupied a huge open room in the old downtown building. The Kelusis had had the building built when the city was in its infancy. It housed a majority of the region's government, royal suite, audience chambers, historical archives, headquarters for the enforcers, as well as ballrooms and housing for members of the royal court. Erik walked down the aisle through the spectator gallery filled with dozens of empty chairs.

Well, mostly empty.

Erik's spine crawled from the enforcer's gaze. He pretended to ignore Kar's scrutiny as he joined the rest of the council milling around the large slab table that occupied the end of the room.

Erik wasn't pleased to see Kar sitting in the gallery. Or to have such undivided attention. He'd managed to avoid the other incubus for over a decade now—mostly thanks to his childhood friend's understanding. A reminder of what he'd lost when he was sundered.

But now he'd seen Karry twice in a month. The echo of the enforcer's words the night Damian had started the orgy at Decadence bounced through Erik's head, taking on new meaning with Dae's fleeing.

He could feel Kar's gaze follow him up to his seat at the council table. As second chair, he pulled his place out next to Dante's, the council head. Exhaustion pressed and his hand clenched the chair back. Losing Dae in Shadow last night had taken an emotional toll on the whole family.

Damn you, Damian. Don't think I don't know what you're doing. How stupid do you think we are? Obviously too stupid, since he'd run. He thought back over the last few weeks and connected the dots. *We're stupid enough, since we didn't see it sooner.* The growing physical hunger, the secretiveness. *The orgy, for stars' sake.*

Preoccupied with his worries, he missed the start of the sentence Dante directed at him about the meeting's schedule.

"Sorry, what was that again?" Erik asked.

The council head narrowed his eyes and said, "When's the last time you and your family fed? You are not on top of your game here, Erik."

The question brought Damian's flight front and center again, and his storeground protested its empty state, but Erik forced a smile, ignoring the piqued interest from Kar and the now worried looks the only other two Sundered on the council threw him.

"When did *you* hunt last, Dante?" he returned, drawing attention to how rude the comment was. *If it's acceptable to ask a Sundered that in public, then you'd better bet I'll turn it back on you. None of the other families are strong enough to stand up to the rest of the Kelusis. I wasn't raised to back down to anybody.*

Dante tipped his head. "My apologies. I was just concerned. You seem preoccupied, and your energy feels scattered."

Erik shot a glance out of the corner of his eye at Kar. *He didn't talk to the council, did he?* "Just a lot happening with the conclave coming up and getting ready for the decade court." *And the missing member of my family. Kar's already pushing me to get Dae to the Chirurgeons.* That conversation hadn't gone as well as he could have hoped. The enforcer had almost taken Erik's lust link in on his own. Damian's total loss of control — to the point where he'd started an orgy — made it well within the enforcer's right to do so. Only his loyalty to Erik had delayed that action. But Kar had insisted that Erik see to it as soon as possible. *And there's no way in whatever hell you believe in that I'll let one of those butchers near my links.*

Unfortunately Erik was one of the only Kelusis, Sundered or not, who believed that. The Chirurgeons held a powerful place in their society. Psychic doctors to the long-lived Kelusis, they took care of the normal health and well-being of them all. But when the sundering had started, the doctors had quickly developed a special class. On one hand, they all had the Chirurgeons to thank for quickly figuring out how to alter their bodies to save as many individuals as they could. The death toll had been high in those first weeks. On the other hand, over the centuries Erik had come to question the true necessity of some of the yearly procedures the Sundered were subjected to. He questioned enough that he'd managed to secretly avoid having his family go through the cauterization procedure for about five years now. He didn't need the Chirurgeons examining Dae too closely and figuring that out.

He still held enough influence and loyalty among his society to accomplish that much at least. To protect his family. He pushed regret away and sank down into his chair, starting to lay out his paperwork. Who was he kidding? He retained more power and influence than he truly wanted. He should be grateful that the royal court allowed him as much peace as they did. He actually held a place on the council. The other Sundered with him were little more than a concession to give the illusion that the Sundered had a voice.

Dante settled into the seat beside him, but Erik ignored the assessing glance. The council had a lot of work to do. Not only did they have the day-to-day tasks of their geographical region to attend to, but the yearly conclave was about to start—and just to add fuel to the fire, it was this district's turn to host the decade court. Every ten years the Kelusis gathered in one of the world's regions for the king to oversee issues that could not be settled by the councils for the various districts. The court traveled throughout the world continuously, but it was only during high court that certain grievances would be heard. The three months of high court were also when laws and other needs of government would be looked at and altered, and the gathering also served as an excuse for the high courtiers to hold all kinds of events.

For the Sundered it was a particularly dreaded time. Forced attendance and much higher scrutiny caused the families pain.

We aren't like them anymore. Erik reshuffled a stack of his papers needlessly. The Sundered had had to adapt to survive. They no longer thought or felt quite the same way as before they were torn in half. *The Kelusis have no idea the heartache they cause us, forcing us to be around full Kelusis again. Or the shame they inflict by treating us the way they do.*

Emotion swirled around him and Erik gritted his jaw. His storeground clenched at the reminder of how hungry he was, but he suffered the curse of having been altered to be a center. He could sense all the currents but had been completely cut off from them. He stood behind a glass pane and watched the world pass by in emotional strands of power that he could do nothing about.

His control wavered and the power fluxed around him again, reluctantly drawing his gaze up. Kar met his eyes.

His old friend lifted his brow. Erik cursed his astuteness. It was obvious to him that Kar was well aware of the puzzle pieces he was putting together. Hiding what he'd done with his family would be more difficult now. He had to track Damian down and get him home.

Before the enforcers figured out he was on the loose.

Chapter 3

DAMIAN STRUCK HIS FIST against his steering wheel rhythmically as he waited in the slow traffic and wished he was an anger link. He'd have a plethora of food from the trapped humans surrounding him then. Lust energy was much scarcer in this situation.

He rubbed his chest and tried to ignore both grinding hungers. With Erik tracking him in Shadow last night, he'd had to lay low today.

I'm sure they have all of my normal hunting grounds watched. Question is how and by whom? Erik's not going to want to bring Karry into it.

He'd had to settle for trying to bring in the trickles he could manage to elicit from the docks.

It hadn't seemed to make much difference in the relentless hunger.

But now he was almost to Alexis's work. Giddiness quickly replaced the frustration. And the strength of his reaction sobered him as he realized she was much more than just food. He *wanted* to be with *her*. It wasn't just that her energy was the best he'd found in more time than he could remember, she fed more than just his storeground. He hadn't felt this whole in...

Damn it. Why couldn't I have found her a century ago? I could have hidden her away and kept her safe. I would have had her whole lifetime with her. Now I'll have a few days before I have to wipe her memory—to keep her safe once I'm gone.

The traffic opened up and he was able to turn onto the downtown street her directions gave him. He eased to the side of the road to wait and glanced at his watch. She should be out any minute.

It was her energy that let him know she was near before he saw her. Muscles that he hadn't realized were tensed from pain relaxed as her energy started to pour into his ground.

He pulled forward to where she stood on tiptoe, craning her neck to look. He reached across and popped the passenger door. "Come on, get in."

She hesitated out on the sidewalk, then her hand steadied herself as she slid onto the leather of the seat. He put the car in gear and eased out into traffic. He felt her gaze settle on his face.

"Nice car. Did you restore it?"

"Thanks. No. I'm not that great with mechanics." *And there's no way you'd believe that I've had this beast since it rolled off the line.* He chuckled to himself.

She petted the buttery soft leather, a smile peeking out. The traffic continued to flow slowly but steadily. He shifted lanes and wove through the cars, making better time. The energy in the cabin grew and he glanced out of the corner of his eye at his companion. Her chest rose and fell, drawing his gaze, and she turned to look out her window, but not quickly enough to hide the flush on her face.

He smiled and plucked at the strand, remembering the time he'd spent in Shadow with her last night. How her body felt against his. The taste of her lips and skin. The sound of her breathless voice. Damian squirmed in his seat and let the energy flow into his ground, but it ramped up too fast. She was so responsive to his mental touch. He cleared his throat. "So, how was your day?"

Not only did the emotional energy come across loud and clear, but images flowed along as well. So his memories of their Shadow walk had a strange Doppler effect, his own overlaid by her unconscious remembrance of the experience.

Her voice husky, she answered his question, and Dae was able to moderate the energy build by keeping her occupied with conversation.

Curiosity wound through the lust energy, and he smiled at her but kept his lips shut on their destination. He wanted it to be a surprise. He knew from her choices of anchor places in Shadow that she'd love the picnic he had planned.

Her voice filled the cabin of the car, and he let it flow through him like her energy did. Then his phone rang with Erik's ringtone. He didn't need to look at it on the dash. Her voice paused but then continued when he ignored the summoning. It still damped down the energy in the car. All of his siblings continued to try contacting him in rotation. Sadness snaked through him. He missed them. And he knew how uncomfortable they must be, needing a full feeding from Erik. He needed one too, but not at the cost. *I can't...they'll die. I don't want to die, but I can't live with them...*

He shook off the dark thoughts and threw himself into Lexi's company. He turned the car down the twisting road that led to the parking areas for Golden Gardens Park. Luck was with him. He found a space near the beaches and pulled the car into it, turning off the engine.

"Hope you like picnics?"

Her laughter lightened his heart as they got out. He handed her a blanket from the trunk and pulled out the heavy picnic basket he'd put together that afternoon.

The blazing summer sun shone down on them as they wove across the thronging sand until they found an empty patch. She spread the blanket out, then settled to the ground, her gaze roaming out over the sparkling waves before coming back to him.

Her attention roved over him while he unpacked the basket, and he couldn't help reveling in it as well as playing with the flow of energy that she continually emitted. He hadn't felt this good since he realized he was in the fade. Even with how hungry he was, both physically and psychically.

He handed her a plate and joined her on the blanket with his own. She cocked an eyebrow at the quantity and he coughed and pursed his lips, trying to suppress the smile that wanted to come out at her teasing.

She seemed to like the choices he made. Though

the nervousness he could taste in her energy also showed in her movements, in the way she nibbled and fidgeted. It was twined with the sexual tension that he continued to heighten.

So responsive. He shifted on the blanket, his own body responding as well. Almost as if she played on his energy to match. He still couldn't get the time he spent with her in Shadow out of his mind. All day he'd replayed what had happened until it had blended with their dinner at Charlie's, the only time he'd spent with her in the waking world until now.

Close to obsession. He pushed that thought away. *She's human. I just need the energy. So what if I get a bonus of wonderful company. Beautiful company.*

He couldn't look away when she met his eyes. The energy flared. The rest of the beach forgotten, they talked and laughed, ate all the food, and watched the sun sink behind the Olympic Mountains across the water. Memories of their dream never drifted far from his thoughts.

He got lost in her energy again and it wasn't until his phone rang that he snapped out of it.

Erik.

A sudden surge of uncertainty flooded the energy she released. Alexis stared at the phone.

He clenched his fist around the vibrating object and decided to silence it. He hadn't had the heart to cut that tie. That let him know they still cared and he was important.

"Sorry," he mumbled.

"You can answer it. It sounds important, if it keeps ringing."

He snorted. "Depends on your point of view. It's just my family."

"Now that's one you can't run from for very long."

"You don't know the half of it. But I'm not really interested in talking to them just now." He turned away, cutting off the topic, and pulled out some strawberries and grapes and a container of Nutella for dessert. "Besides, this is much better than talking about my family. Almost as good as making out on the sand, even if it's not as warm as tropical sand." He swirled a strawberry in the chocolate.

He lifted the berry and saw that her face had gone pale as snow. Or the sand that they had lain on in Shadow.

She can't *remember!* He stared into her eyes, memories flickering in their sable depths. *She's human. She can't remember Shadow like we do. It would have faded like mist in the sun.*

Images too detailed not to be memories flooded the trace, and Dae had to stifle a moan at the overwhelming surge of lust that hit him. He mentally grabbed back the control, trying to ignore it. His hand continued on its path and he pressed the berry to her soft lips.

With her gaze still locked onto his, she took a bite, her tongue flicking out to catch a drip of chocolate as it dropped from the fruit.

He managed a smile. "It's Friday. Tell me you don't have to work tomorrow? Will you come to the zoo with me? For the day?"

Her lips glistened. He focused on them, wanting

to taste the last of the chocolate still clinging there.

"No. I mean, yes," she fumbled with a breathless answer. "What I mean is, no I don't have to work tomorrow. And yes, I would love to spend the day at the zoo."

He hadn't realized he'd held his breath, so he let it out in a whoosh and she snorted.

Laughing, they packed up the last of their picnic. Hand in hand they strolled along the sand as the waves lapped at the beach. Lights twinkled off the water. In a roundabout manner, they worked their way back to his car.

Quiet conversation punctuated the drive as he slowly crossed the city to her apartment. He pulled into the drop-off zone and put the car in park. His fingers tangled with hers, stopping her from getting out.

"I'm really looking forward to seeing you tomorrow," he said.

"Me too," she said softly.

Dim light from the street pole down the block illuminated her face as he leaned in closer. Still holding onto her with one hand, he raised his other and brushed her cheek before sliding his fingers into her hair. His lips settled over hers lightly. The reality of her taste proved how tangible the Shadow world was.

He licked across the seam of her lips and she opened, inviting him in. Their tongues brushed and twined. When her hand burrowed under his shirt, he couldn't stop the groan. The kiss grew hotter.

He let go of her fingers so his other hand could

help hold her head steady. She pressed closer, a moan deep in her throat, and his hand clenched in her hair. Lust flooded his ground. But the shock of his own emotion getting amplified by hers slammed him with cold water. He pulled away, leaving her dazed.

She blinked at him. His hand trembled as he ran his fingers through the short strands of her hair. The air in the car felt charged around them, like when lightning was building up in a thunderstorm.

"The morning can't come soon enough," he said roughly.

She touched her lips, then fumbled the car door open. It took all his willpower to let her walk up the steps to her apartment building's front door alone. His body hadn't needed like this in centuries. It would be so easy to throw all caution to the wind and just join her. The night would be glorious.

But reality intruded. *I wouldn't be able to control the hunger. I'd drain too much and she'd die. I just need to harvest the energy that I have been and be content with that.*

Once inside the locked door, she turned and met his gaze through the panes of glass. After a moment he touched his fingertips to his window, wishing it were her warm skin, before putting his car in gear to drive into the night.

Alexis watched the taillights to Dae's car disappear before she turned away from the lobby window. Her fingers rose to touch her lips again as she absently pushed the elevator button. Floating in a haze, she walked to her apartment—his touch still imprinted on her body. His hands in her hair. His lips hot against hers.

She unlocked her door. Inside, the smell of paint mixed with his scent still fresh on her skin. For a first kiss, it had been incredible. *But it wasn't the first kiss,* whispered through her thoughts.

She stopped.

That was just a dream.

She stared at the painting she'd done last night. Another dream. Sort of. The vineyard she'd envisioned stretched before her, a stone mansion in the background, with rows of grapes turning for the season. And Damian.

Arms resting on top of one of the posts, his smile seemed to reach out to her, taunting, teasing, turning her on.

She'd captured him perfectly for only having met him that night. The pressure of his lips slid across her neck and she shivered as she stared at his image in the painting. Wishing she'd had the courage to drag him back to her apartment for the night, she dropped her bag by the door and drew closer to her painting.

Memories of his weight pressing her to the sand in her dream blocked out her apartment and she shook her head to clear her vision. His voice echoed in her ears. *Almost as good as making out on the sand, even if it's not as warm as tropical sand.*

A flash of fear, like lightning, twined with the

lust, enhancing it, and she gasped at the clench it caused between her legs. But her rational mind immediately supplied the answer.

Who wouldn't think thoughts of tropical beaches when out on a date on a beach? Sheesh, Lex, get a grip.

She went into her bedroom and stripped out of her nice clothes, grabbing something that could get covered in paint. The picnic had been wonderful. The best date she could remember being on. The food, the location, the conversation…

Doubt wormed its way through the contentment when she remembered the ignored phone calls. A nebulous thought formed. Was he hiding something? Or running from something? But the dream images of Dae, exploring each other's bodies on that tropical beach, continued to overwhelm her thoughts, placing their mark on her body and scattering any other concerns. She left her room.

She took the canvas from last night off her easel and got set up to start a new one.

The feel of his hands across her body.

She wiped her forehead with her arm and gathered paint tubes.

His breath across the back of her neck.

She groaned and dropped into her chair, blinking to bring the blank canvas into focus. The comment he'd made during the picnic still tickled the back of her thoughts. *Good thing it really* was *just a dream. Or I'd never be able to face him at the zoo tomorrow.* She worked to push the erotic dream aside and picked up a brush.

Chapter 4

I HAD TO LEAVE her. It's too strong. I'll hurt her. Dae pounded on the steering wheel as he felt the torrent of Alexis's energy dwindle the farther he drove away from her. As the power waned, the debilitating hunger ripped into his stomach with razor talons. He turned away from his intended destination, the *King's Ransom,* and went in search of more food.

He couldn't chance staying in their neighborhood or visiting any of his usual haunts. After dreamwalking with Erik last night, the family were sure to be out in force looking for him. He turned the car north and headed for the University District. *The Ave is always busy late. College students never sleep. So there will be enough people around for cover.*

The tune to "Born to Be Wild" sang out from his phone and he sighed. Reluctantly he picked it up from the console to see what Erik's text had to say.

"Damian. Answer your damn phone! I know you're looking at this."

Then Erik's ringtone started and his picture

flashed on the screen. Dae stared at it for a moment. Too many memories to name flashed through his mind. The love and care Erik took with all of them. But he hardened his heart and ignored the call like he had all the others.

He cruised up and down the Ave, looking for a parking place. He'd been right, the street was packed and it took a while before he could tuck his car up to the curb.

A multitude of scents filled the air. So many different restaurants to choose from. He decided he'd just eat his way up one side of the street and down the other.

A couple of hours later, he walked out of what he decided would be the last restaurant of the night and rubbed his taut stomach. His hunger had become insatiable. He physically couldn't fit any more in his body, but he still felt like he was starving. *I don't think I'll be able to stay on the boat any longer. I'll need to camp outside Lexi's apartment. Her energy seems to diminish the hunger—it doesn't hold it at bay completely, but at least I can function if I'm near her.*

At some point during his restaurant tour, his family quit trying to call him. He hadn't wanted to turn off his phone again and cut that last little bit of contact with his siblings. While it hurt to ignore them, it still was comforting knowing they were there. He felt less alone.

The crowds remained thick given the lateness of the hour, and he wove between people on his way to his car. His phone vibrated in his pocket, but instead of a ringtone a strange pinging beep shrilled out of it.

His steps froze and he yanked the phone out of his pocket to stare at the screen. Not a call or text this time. They'd activated the find phone app. A message flashed on the lock screen.

"Damn it, Dae, you've seriously pissed me off."

"Shit." He tossed the phone like a hot potato into the bush he stood next to and took off at a run. He dodged in and out of the pedestrians and turned off the Ave at the first cross street. *Can I get to my car? I have to get out of range. If Erik gets too close to me, he'll be able to find me through the bond conduit.*

He pelted down the quieter street, then dodged into a darkened alley. One that would allow him to work back toward his car. He paused to catch his breath.

Cold rooted him to the spot.

He sucked in his breath and stared wide-eyed down the empty alley as the familiar energy washed over him. His thoughts spun and he told his legs to run, but they didn't cooperate.

A warm hand wrapped itself around his throat and slammed him into the brick wall. Erik shimmered into view as he let the light go.

"You little shit. You made us fucking search the whole city. I know what you're doing. How dare you hide this from us? I wouldn't let you commit suicide when you were Sundered, what makes you think I would allow it now? If I didn't love you so much..." Erik's gaze bored into his, rage not quite covering the deep fear in his center's eyes, and Erik placed his free hand on Dae's chest while he held him pinned.

"No…" Dae wheezed.

His usual gentleness absent, Erik ripped the power out of him. Dae struggled because he knew his brother didn't plan to stop there. His vision tunneled black, and his movements grew feeble as the hemorrhaging continued; the only point of light left was his focus on the blue of Erik's eyes, which widened in shock as his center assessed the purity of the energy.

"Don't…Erik…" he tried to whisper.

Erik's fingers flexed, then as the last drops of power were wrung out of the sand of his storeground, Dae felt him turn his will and focus a scalpel of energy. His center plunged into him, slicing away at the psychic structure the Chirurgeons had created so long ago to keep him alive.

At least for a time.

When the Chirurgeons had altered the sundered Kelusis, they knew it was only a temporary solution. A solution to span hundreds of years, but still, eventually every Sundered would begin to fade, just as Dae had done. When that happened to a link, their family had two choices: either watch their link, whom they had been bonded to for centuries, starve to death, or have the center tie the whole family even closer together.

With the first choice, the family had to find a new link or they would die within a few weeks. But with the second choice, they all supported the fading link, which kept them all together; unfortunately it drastically reduced the life expectancy for all members of the family.

And that was a choice that Dae had gone to a lot of work to take out of his family's hands.

In a form of field dressing, Erik hacked a crude and temporary pathway into the shunt, the structure that allowed Dae to take in the mixture that Erik created when he harvested all of their energies. He modified it so that Dae would receive a continuous stream of energy braided from all of them.

In effect, they put him on life support.

His legs gave out.

Erik let him collapse to his knees while he pulled his phone out of a pocket. "Cass, pinging the phone worked to flush him out of the crowd. I've got him. He's not going anywhere now, I've made sure of that. Call the others home. I'm bringing him in, and we'll need to finish this."

The effort to remain upright became too hard, and Dae slumped forward. Hands that now held a degree of gentleness caught him, and Erik lifted him into his arms.

"Damn you, Dae."

"Next time I'll throw my phone away sooner," he mumbled into Erik's chest.

"There won't be a next time. You can be sure of that. You're grounded."

Erik's steps jostled him as his older brother repositioned to get the car door open. He felt the leather of Erik's backseat embrace him, cool against his cheek. He tried to pull his knees to his chest. The door slammed, then Erik took the driver's seat.

"You should have respected my wishes and let me go."

"Get a clue, Dae. We are a family. We all go down together." He paused, then continued quietly, "Did you kill anyone? Your power was awfully pure."

"No. It was close. But no, I didn't kill anyone."

The engine roared to life and almost succeeded in covering Erik's sigh of relief. Traffic was sparse after they got a block away from the Ave, so the drive home only took a few minutes. Sooner than he wanted, he felt the car bump into their driveway and come to a stop. He tried to crawl out, but he was too weak. Erik hauled him up again. His head lolled onto an unforgiving shoulder, and through his impacted vision he saw Cassandra come running out the front door.

"How bad?" She brushed his bangs back with a soft hand.

"He's much closer than I like." Erik's voice rumbled in his ear where it was pressed to his chest. "But I think we're in time."

"He hid it so well, Erik. I thought he was fine on Wednesday."

"Don't, Cass. None of us saw it."

"Aye, lass." Callum's voice joined in and the sound of the door to the carriage-house-turned-garage scraped shut. "Don't beat yourself up. All of us should have seen."

The scream of a high-performance motorcycle zeroed in and skidded to a stop.

Great. Now the gang's all here, he thought.

"You were right, Cassandra." Isaac's voice, muffled by his helmet, reached Dae. "Bob over at Decadence did know. It took some threatening to get it out of him, however. He said Dae only had a week or so left. Are we in time, Erik?"

"I think so. Let's get him inside and finish this."

The fabric under his cheek grew wet. "Please, don't."

Erik's arms hugged him tighter and didn't let go. "Shut up, Dae."

They reached the steps, and Dae could finally see their descendants waiting on the porch. Maggie's ancestors had run this residence since the founding of Seattle. They had other family lines that tended their other residences around the world and acted as the human face for the property in question.

"Maggie," Erik addressed the matriarch of the family. "Please get Dae's bed ready. Then we'll probably want dinner. I don't think anyone wants to go out tonight."

"Yes, Erik." She cast Dae a worried look before hustling up the stairs.

Dae was carried up silently, and he railed against his inability to stop this. The soft cotton of his sheets welcomed him when Erik laid him down, the rest of the family surrounding him. He stared up at the ceiling and refused to participate. A tug at the laces of his boots and Cass got them off his feet while Erik stripped his shirt. Thankfully they left his jeans.

"OK, Callum, come here," Erik said.

Dae tried to ignore the feel as Erik placed a hand over his heart and his other over Callum's. He gasped as Erik tied the strand in. *Two more to go,* he thought and held back a sob.

"This is the way it should be, Damian," Callum whispered in his ear.

Next Isaac was tied in. "If you think we'd let you go, little brother…"

Dae turned his face to the wall. Wet splashed onto his skin near his ear and Cassandra placed her cheek against his, more tears joining the first.

"Don't leave me," she whispered.

Her energy twined painfully with the rest.

"I'll monitor the connection tonight," Erik said, "but from the looks of it, we made it in time. Why don't you all go get dinner dished up?"

Feet shuffled and a few gentle caresses brushed across him, then he was left alone with Erik. It took effort, but he managed to get his body turned to the side in a blatant "leave me alone" message to his brother.

He could feel the elder incubus's eyes staring at him. After a few minutes, Erik broke the silence. "I'm sorry you're upset, but so are we. What you did was not kind or fair to us."

"And you think me killing all of you is?"

"And how are you doing that? It was just a matter of time. One of us had to be the first to fade, and the rest would follow. Sure, tying us all to you will speed it up a bit, but so? It's inevitable unless a cure is found. Our lifespans were forfeit as soon as we lost our other halves."

"You could have had centuries. Now what? Decades?"

"We've had centuries. And great, now we have decades. That's better than the mere weeks you were consigning us to by refusing us. Did you really think we would bond with a new link? We all would starve in a couple of months after you were gone. The Chirurgeons haven't found anything yet. And you know as well as I that they aren't trying very hard. We would rather all go together than one at a time. You're outvoted. So deal with it."

"Deal with it? Right." He suppressed a hysterical sob that tried to force its way up from his chest.

"Well you have plenty of time to come to terms with it now." He paused, and Dae felt Erik's hand come to rest on his shoulder. "You know this will keep you alive. But it will take days before all of the effects fade and you're back to normal. The hunger will still be there for some time. I'll have Cass come up and help you eat. Your body should regain enough strength to be able to get up by tomorrow."

Erik squeezed his shoulder then left him alone, his thoughts in turmoil.

A few hours later he still hadn't resolved his feelings. Cass brought up a tray of food and the needs of his body proved stronger than his anger. She lifted him to a sitting position and hand-fed him. Ravenous, he wolfed down everything she offered. Tears sheened her eyes as she helped him.

"Why?" she eventually choked out.

He stared at her hands fiddling with the tray on her lap. "Now I know you're doomed with me. The only hope I had was that you would all live on. You could have found another lust link. Saved another from the waste. Maybe made it long enough to reach the cure."

"I would think after close to three thousand years you would know us all better than that."

"So, by the same argument, why are you all surprised by my choice?"

"Oooooh, you make me want to hit you."

"Go ahead. It's not like I can stop you at the moment."

She grabbed his face with both hands, her eyes staring into his, a flash of frustrated anger lighting their depths. "Will that help with the guilt, Dae? You hurt me. You hurt the others, but what hurts the most is knowing how much pain you must have been in, yet you didn't ask for help. Knowing you were suffering, and that I could have helped…" She had to stop to swallow. "But that I didn't notice…"

"I'm sorry, Cass," he whispered. He managed to get his arm up to rest shakily on her wrist.

After staring at him a while longer she sniffed, then said, "You will be."

She helped him lie back down, then left him to his thoughts again. Life was going to be fun for a while. He sighed. Frustrated that he couldn't get out of the bed, he cursed Erik for putting him there. His center hadn't needed to drain him so thoroughly. But Erik had obviously wanted to cut out Dae's ability to fight back. Normally this level of empty would have left Dae on the weaker side but not incapacitated. The severity was due to the fade, he realized.

His stomach still argued with his backbone, but the pain had become normal—normal enough that it receded into the background. Which left him free to dwell on the yawning emptiness of his storeground.

Erik did a thorough job. I don't think I've ever been this depleted. As if the physical hunger pain wasn't enough, now I have to contend with the need to hunt. His memory surged. The brief time he'd spent with Alexis whetted his appetite. Thoughts of her became centermost. His body stirred, but he could do nothing about it, too weak to even give himself relief. Exhaustion soon pressed and he faded into sleep.

Chapter 5

SUNLIGHT STREAMED IN THE open windows and finally penetrated the fog of Alexis's sleep. Wisps of the new dreams she'd had of Dae dissipated, and she groaned in frustration. Her body ached from more than sleeping in an unusual position in front of her easel. Sexual tension thrummed though her, the act of sitting up sending shock waves through her body. And the sight that greeted her didn't help. Propped to dry on her easel, the painting taunted her. Dae's image stared back at her. Like a photograph, every detail crisp, he reclined on a white sandy beach. She could almost hear the sound of the surf, taste the sweet fruitiness on his tongue. She shook her head as more images from her dreams overlaid her consciousness. The throbbing between her legs turned insistent.

She shifted in her seat. He smiled at her from the canvas. A glance at the clock showed her it was at least still morning, but barely. *Where's my phone?* she thought in a panic.

That got her out of the chair. She tossed around some clothes and a few other items until she found her phone underneath her sweater from yesterday. She blew her bangs out of her eyes and pressed the button to light up the screen.

No missed calls or texts. Disappointed, she slid the phone into her back pocket and headed to the kitchen to find something to eat. Her attention stayed riveted to her phone the entire time.

After cleaning up the kitchen, she puttered around, killing time.

He said he'd call me. She shoved her insecurity down. Something must have come up. *He seemed genuinely interested, so I don't believe that he's blowing me off.* The memory of the ignored phone calls insinuated itself into her thoughts. Patience wasn't her strong suit. Her fingers twitched to text him, but she held back, not sure if he just finally couldn't avoid his family anymore, or if it was her.

She spent the rest of the afternoon cleaning until the pull to her art was too much and she grabbed a canvas she'd prepped the night before. Quickly she became lost in the world in her head as paint spread across the fabric. Since the first night she'd met Damian one picture had lodged in her head—a visual that she had pushed to the back to avoid. The visceral pain that came with it left her breathless, but it would no longer be denied and started to take shape.

She shrieked when her phone vibrated in her back pocket. Dropping her brush with a splat, she fished the buzzing thing out. With a swipe she brought up the text from Damian.

"I'm so sorry. This day has not gone how I planned. I would much rather have spent it with you. This is the first chance I've had alone to contact you."

She started typing. "Are you OK? What happened? I was getting worried."

"I couldn't avoid my family any longer."

She paused, her fingers trembling. Then she typed, "Is that a problem?"

He sent a text frown, then, "Yes, no. It's too complicated to type out. If you would like to meet for just a few minutes, I've convinced them to take me up to Cal Anderson Park for a bit. I'll only manage a few minutes alone though. I've missed you all day."

"Sure, I can come up to the park."

"I'll be there in half an hour."

Alexis slipped her phone into her pocket, then stared at the roughed-out painting blindly. The tone of his texts sounded off. Worry gnawed at her. The phantom pain came and went again, and she picked up her brush to correct a line on the bed taking shape on the canvas. She could see the picture in her mind like it had happened to her.

She dropped her brush into the jar and got up to change. She didn't need her clothes to be covered in paint, she had enough on her skin, most likely. She grabbed a pair of shorts and a tank top, then fished her jogging shoes out from under the bed.

After switching her phone to her new clothes, she headed out, locking the apartment behind her. The jog up to the park only took a few minutes. She turned off of the concrete sidewalk and onto the crunch of the gravel path. She made her way past the reflecting pool and the rapids that coursed down from the huge cone-shaped fountain. Her eyes scanned the crowded park. Something in her chest relaxed when she spotted him through the lounging crowd, reclined on the grass in the sun at the base of the picnicking hill, his face turned up to the warmth.

She shifted from her jog to a walk, and his head swiveled like a lodestone in her direction, his hazel eyes opening to stare at her approach. A strained smile spread across his lips, and she watched him try to hide the struggle it took to sit upright.

She sank to the grass at his side and reached out tentatively, but pulled back before she touched the bare skin of his arm. "What happened? Are you all right?"

He smiled ruefully. "Didn't hide it, huh?"

"With the trouble you just had sitting up? What'd you think? Your texts had me worried enough. What did your family do to you? Are you in danger? You said you would only have a minute alone. Do you need help?"

"There's nothing you can do."

"Don't be so sure of that. Did they hurt you?"

He huffed out a cynical laugh and looked up into the sky briefly. "My family? Yes, but not in the way you think. I've been sick. That's why I was avoiding them. I knew they wouldn't agree with some decisions I made, and boy was I right."

On reflex she gripped his arm; she would have pulled back, but he trapped her hand with his. The warmth of his skin sank into her. "Sick? Are you all right? Why didn't you tell me?" And suddenly all of the ignored calls made a whole lot more sense. On an emotional rollercoaster, she bounced from anger to worry to concern and back again.

He sighed and she swore she could see her emotions reflected in his hazel eyes. "It was nice to be with someone who didn't feel bad for me, who I could just be me with. I'm sorry. I know it wasn't right...but I liked you so much. You made me feel better."

He watched her so intently that she found it hard to pretend that the building obsession she felt toward him wasn't reciprocated. The breeze, she was sure it was the breeze, whispered across the back of her neck and circled the spot that still felt sensitive from the static days ago. Images from the dreams she'd been having every night rushed to the surface and her stomach did a flip-flop. Obviously her body had no problems feeling attracted to him even if her mind found some things odd.

Dae licked his lips, then continued, "There was a procedure I knew they would want for me that I didn't. After they caught up to me last night, the four of them made sure I got it. So now I'm weak as a kitten." He growled that last.

"You can hardly blame them for wanting to help you."

He let go and rubbed his eyes with his fingers. "I know. I would have done the same for any of them. But my wishes should have been taken into account. What they've done affects the whole family so much.

I wanted to avoid the pain and hardship they've now shouldered to care for me."

"But if they love you, how could they not?"

He smiled halfheartedly at her. "Zing."

"Will you tell me what was wrong?" She plucked at the grass and avoided his gaze. "Will you be OK now?"

"Yeah." He sounded sad. "I'll be fine. It was a genetic problem, and my family will have to supply what I need for the rest of my life now."

Alexis heard his words and wondered why she felt a lie beneath the truth of them. A faint echo of a voice sounded in her head, the words not making any sense. *He'll be fine for my lifetime at least? Huh?* She shook her head and said, "So why are you even here in the park? It seems strange to me with how weak you appear, that they would let you out of the hospital."

He slowly wrapped his arms around his raised knees. "I'm weak, but other than that I'm fine. Being out in the sun among people is the best medicine really. But they aren't going to let me be here long. They're barely letting me out of their sights after hiding from them. Isaac only left me here alone for a couple of minutes because he knows I'm too pathetic to go anywhere," he said in disgust.

"You are not pathetic. And I'm happy to sit here with you until your brother gets back."

"No," he snapped, taking her aback. "You are my secret. Something that is only mine. I don't want them to know where I spent my time or with whom. I'm not ready to share you with them. Or have you deal with their inquisition. There've been too many fortune hunters in our background. My family is so close, and they feel like they have the right to be involved in anything. I want you to myself."

His gaze bored into hers. She thought about how nosy her siblings were and could sympathize. She licked her lips and asked, "Then what?"

"Will you meet me here again tomorrow? I'm sure I can arrange another outing."

"I have to work tomorrow so I can't get here until at least six. Is that OK?"

"I'll make it work. And I can text when they aren't looking over my shoulder."

"I would like that."

He captured her hand, letting his thumb rub gentle circles on her palm. "I want the weekend back where I could do whatever I wanted." He raised her hand to his lips for a brief brush. "You'd better go. Isaac will be here any moment."

She rubbed her thumb across the spot his lips touched and rose to her feet. "I'll see you tomorrow."

Unable to quit staring at him over her shoulder, she moved into a jog and started on her way home.

Dae watched her leave, his body clamoring at him, his mind raging at him to make her stay. He fell back to the grass and closed his eyes. He didn't have the strength to let himself down with any degree of control. In fact, he was just as surprised as she was that Erik had let him out of the house. Though with how thoroughly his center had drained his storeground, Dae figured Erik must be feeling bad—or at least taking pity on him enough to let him try and regain some strength by harvesting the ambient energy of the humans at the park.

Not that he was retaining any of it. At least until Alexis arrived. The moment she got close enough, her energy started to flow into him. The desert inside sucked it up like a sponge. It took everything she was willing to give.

The warmth of the sun disappeared as a shadow fell across him. He opened his eyes and met Isaac's currently sane half smile.

"I thought you'd be about done in. And I brought you this." Isaac held out his hand.

Dae struggled to a sitting position and accepted the foot-long sub from the joy link. Now that Alexis had retreated far enough away, her energy had dwindled and his hunger returned with a vengeance. He tore into the paper.

Isaac clucked and sat down beside him, saying, "I saw you working, so I waited until she left."

His mouth full, all Dae could do was grunt and glare at his brother. *How much did he hear? He couldn't have heard me arrange to meet Lexi again or he'd be all over me.*

Isaac sighed at his sullen silence. "You're going to be mad at us for a while, I take it?"

Dae swallowed. "What do you think? Erik took my choice away. You all agreed with it and helped."

"Your choice? That's the most selfish, self-centered

thing I've ever heard you say. I'm going to chalk it up to pain and the side effects of the fade. It was never just your choice. We are all dependent on one another to survive. The Chirurgeons made sure of that when they altered us. Without you we will all starve to death."

"You could have taken another lust link."

"Right." He snorted. "Now, tell me that you would have accepted another joy link if I were gone."

Dae buried his nose in the sandwich.

Isaac chuckled. "I thought as much."

Dae felt a hand riffle through his hair, then Isaac continued, "We won't let you go. But you know that from how hard you tried to hide from us."

They sat silent for a few minutes, the sounds of the park around them. He finished the sandwich and balled up the wrapper. Running his tongue across his teeth, he looked at Isaac from under his bangs. "You seem unusually sane today."

"Erik drained all of us more than normal last night. My storeground is begging, but I'm going to put up with the hunger pains for a few days of freedom. It's nice not to feel manic and high for a change. Besides, we only have two weeks left until the conclave. If I stay a sober joy link, I'll have enough mind to help Erik, with you no longer available to work. He has meetings scheduled up the wazoo. Not to mention you and he were in the middle of that deal for Jeremy to secure the house in Port Townsend for his descendant family. And even if you were up to doing paperwork, which you aren't, you're going to have your hands full trying to get back to normal before court."

Dae groaned. The royal court of the Kelusis had been a thorn in their side for centuries. This year would be worse than normal. The regional conclave happened every year, where the local legislative business for the Kelusis was conducted. They were such a long-lived species that they didn't need it more often. But once every ten years the full court convened. This decade court rotated through the different regions of the world. Kelusis representatives from all the regional districts were expected to attend the king during that time. But for the Sundered, every family and every individual were required. The Chirurgeons did a full census of their injured brethren in conjunction with a symposium, ostensibly to work on the problem of the Sundered.

If they didn't show up, the enforcers would be sent for them. But with Erik as their center, they wouldn't escape notice regardless.

The full court was set to take place here, at Yuletide. "The Chirurgeons will know how close I came. They might question the cauterization."

"There's no help for that. Maybe knowing Erik won't have forever will get the king off his butt."

"I'll believe that when I see it. They've had thousands of years and haven't done squat."

Isaac shook his head, then stood. "Come on, little brother. Let's get you home and back to bed."

With his help, Dae rose shakily to his feet. Then, depending heavily on Isaac's support, he let the older incubus lead him to a car at the edge of the park.

The next afternoon Dae hobbled down the stairs, leaning heavily on the banister. He sank to a seat on the bottom step and caught his breath. His stomach growled and gnawed—and his ground remained excessively low. He'd been drawn into Alexis's dreams again last night. He hadn't gotten to stay long, thanks to Erik pulling him out of Shadow. The tiny trickle of energy she'd passed him was long gone, and he missed her company even if it was only in dreams.

Rubbing his palms over his bare knees, he hauled himself to his feet. He managed to fish his loafers out of the closet and went in search of Callum. He found his older Celtic brother in the kitchen. Maggie had just pulled muffins out of the oven. The way to Cal's heart was always through his stomach.

Maggie smiled when she saw him shuffle into the room and took another plate out of the cupboard, which she piled high, then handed to him. He carried it to the breakfast table and joined the anger link.

Callum pushed the butter his way. "How're you doing?"

Dae shrugged and slathered on butter. The piping hot muffin melted in his mouth. "Ohhh."

Callum grinned, the expression briefly eclipsing the rage that usually sat in his eyes. "Yeah, I'll agree with you there."

Dae swallowed. "I need to feed, Cal."

The anger link stared at him while he ate his muffin, then said, "Not surprising. Erik drained you dry. Didn't you get some yesterday?"

"Yes, but it wasn't for long. Isaac took me over to the park. I was hoping you could take me today. Erik won't let me out alone yet."

Cal snorted. "Of course not. Are you surprised?"

Dae picked apart one of his muffins sulkily. "It's not like I can run again."

"That's not the issue and you know it. You're too weak to defend yourself if any humans decide to hassle you, but sure, I'll take you."

Damian glanced at the clock on the wall: five thirty. Time enough to finish his muffins and get Callum to the car. The thought of meeting Alexis at six buoyed his mood. He stilled inside. *It's just the energy. I just need her energy. It's so good.*

Maggie came over and cleared their plates when they'd finished. When they both rose, Callum's eyes watched him like a hawk. It was obvious the anger link saw how weak he still was. The large Celt hovered like a nursemaid and Dae began to plot how he was going to get out of Cal's earshot to spend time with Lexi.

I'll have to walk. If I can convince him to sit on the hill, he could see almost the whole of the park. I'd only be out of his sight at the far side when we passed the old reservoir building. That could work.

It taxed his strength when he dragged himself up into Callum's SUV, but thankfully the anger link missed it. One less piece of ammunition Cal would have. Once at the park it took longer to find a parking space than to drive the few blocks over. But luck was on his side. A space opened up on the north side of the park, the side nearest the observation hill. He slid out and Callum joined him on the sidewalk. He started to slowly make his way along the gravel path toward the cone-shaped fountain. When they drew near the hill, he glanced at his watch and stopped. A few minutes to six.

"Cal, I'm not going to be able to hunt with you dogging my heels."

"Tough."

He bit his tongue to keep from lashing out. "Anger. Lust. That's not the sort of explosive mix I'd like to encourage in public. I need to find a donor, not just sit on the hill and pull in ambient energy floating around. I need a more direct line tonight, Cal."

"Nice try. I'm not letting you out of my sight, kiddo. So you're not following anyone home."

"I wasn't proposing that," he said in exasperation. "I don't need to push anyone into sex. I just thought some focused time could give me more than sitting on my ass and pulling in stray energy. I was just going to walk the paths and find someone to have a bit of one-on-one time with. I could use the easy exercise anyway. And if you hang out on top of the hill, you could see me through most of the park. I won't drop down to the ball fields. OK?"

Callum crossed his arms, a frown in his eyes. But then he looked up at the hill and out across the park. "OK," he finally sighed.

"All right then." Dae smiled and started slowly off down the gravel path. He looked over his shoulder and saw Callum watching him—and tried to walk a little more smoothly. Scanning the numerous park goers looking for Lexi, he finally spotted her sitting on a bench near the west entrance. She looked so uncertain. He smiled. Her physical personality placed a strong restraining hand on who she was inside. The Lexi he'd met in the dream world held no uncertainty. He'd just have to coax her out.

Today, instead of workout clothes, she wore a summer blouse and light capris with sandals. Perfect, no jogging; he wouldn't look pathetic trying to keep up with her with his body so weak. They could just stroll and not draw unwanted attention.

Her face lit up when she saw him, and he felt her energy bathe his desolated storeground.

"I'm glad you didn't have to work late." He stopped in front of her.

"Me too."

"Let's walk for a bit?"

She leapt to her feet. "Are you up to it? You still don't seem too steady."

They started walking back the way he'd come. Joggers and bicyclists passed them as they slowly strolled the gravel path. "The exercise should be good."

He felt Callum's gaze and glanced up the hill. The older incubus lay back, reclined on his elbows at the summit of the little manmade hill. Clusters of picnickers dotted the slopes around him. Dae stumbled, then cursed himself. Lexi grabbed his elbow.

"Then again..." He chuckled.

She tried to join his laugh, but her face looked worried. He trapped her hand on his arm when she started to pull away. The physical contact enhanced the energy. He savored the flow as they continued to pace the gravel circuit.

She cleared her throat. "How'd you manage to get away? I would have thought they wouldn't let you out of their sights still. It's only been a day."

He squeezed her hand on his arm. "Well, I didn't quite. My brother is watching from the top of the hill." He felt her tense, but she resisted the urge to turn to look.

"So...your family's pretty mad at you?"

He snorted. "Yeah, you could say that."

She looked at him out of the corner of her eye. "What about you?"

"What about me?"

"How's your anger?"

He glanced away, surprised at her insight. Underneath it he could feel caring, and he realized that his need had become more than just energy. More than just a food source. He couldn't deny it anymore. If he looked back at his time with her, it was always more than hunting, even if he'd tried to pretend that he hunted her only because of the strength of her power.

Amused sympathy circled him, her energy changing flavor with it. "Am I that obvious?" he asked.

She rubbed her hand briskly on his arm. "Obvious? I don't know."

Callum's regard remained, hitting a bull's-eye on his back, reinforcing the realization of the tightrope he was walking. He had to maintain the outward appearance that she meant nothing. That he was just using her to feed. Or the consequences would be unthinkable.

He kicked a pebble. "I don't know that 'angry' is the right word. I was, and a part of me still is, but mostly I feel smothered."

"They were scared for you. So what happened to them not knowing about me?"

"Well they don't...exactly. I convinced him to let me wander by myself since he could still see me. And since he hasn't charged down here, he probably thinks I'm trying to use my wiles to pick up a girl." He cast a glance out of the corner of his eye and caught her gaze. "Is it working?"

She snorted and shook her head. "So how long is this weakness going to last?"

They paused to rest on a bench in the sun, the sound of children at the playground nearby creating a pleasing backdrop. His fingers toyed with hers. "I don't know. It was worse than I imagined. And I imagined a lot, which is one reason why I ran." He sighed. "Getting out like this, especially to see you, is the best medicine."

"So how did they find you? And I still don't understand why you wouldn't let them help."

"Don't get me started on the medical jargon," he evaded. "I don't get it. The simplest explanation is that I was physically fading away and by getting a rare type of transfusion from each of my siblings there was a chance they could stop it. But the medical procedure would likely hurt them, and I didn't want to be responsible for causing them pain. I hid from my family how sick I had become. Then I met you and I just wanted to enjoy my time. Unfortunately they didn't agree with my decision. So as soon as I quit returning their calls or coming home, they knew. As for how they found me—the stupid 'find phone' app. They hunted me down, and four to one meant that I didn't come out the winner in that confrontation. So now I'm weak and slowly recovering."

He rose and she followed. They continued along the path.

"I'm betting you weren't thinking very clearly. Choosing life is better. And your family obviously agrees. It sounds like they didn't want to lose you."

"You have no idea," he mumbled. They rounded the playground and continued past.

"Well I'm glad to know you'll still be around."

He watched the blush color her cheeks, and he pulled her to a stop as soon as they crossed into the shade of the old reservoir building. Out of Callum's sight. He backed her up to the stone of the wall, then let his fingertips brush the soft skin across her cheekbone before gently cupping her face with both hands. He gazed into her eyes.

"I've never felt so close to someone before. I want the weekend back. I want to be free to spend my time with you and only you."

"I'm a little scared at how much I want that too."

His thumb caressed her cheek. "They won't believe us. How close we feel. That it's real. I can't let the family know about you yet. It would bring endless hardship for you as they put you on the spot, searching your background, grilling you…"

"Why?"

"There've been problems in the past. Relationships that have had drastic repercussions for our whole family. So they are all overly protective, I guess you could say." *Damn it. Why can't I stay away? This is becoming dangerous for her.* Unable to resist, he lowered his head, slowly giving her the opportunity to pull away.

Their lips brushed. Her eyelids fell and he pressed harder. Her arms slid around his waist, and he opened his mouth just enough to let his tongue snake out and brush against her lips. She pressed closer, her lips parting, so he took advantage and licked inside. He touched the sweetness of her tongue, rubbing and coiling against it, encouraging her to come and explore his mouth. After a few minutes he drew back.

Both of them were breathing heavily. Her eyes were unfocused. He shook his head to clear it and remembered Callum. He'd be on the way if they didn't get a move on. He did not need his bond brother catching him kissing a human.

He brushed her hair back once more and smiled into her eyes. Placing her hand on his arm again, he started walking. When they rounded the building, he looked down the length of the park and saw Callum on his feet. The anger link made an abrupt gesture as soon as he spotted him, telling Dae he was through. With a sigh, he stopped with Lexi at the bench he'd met her at.

"I have to go. My brother is waving at me up on the hill. I'm surprised he let me have this long."

"That's understandable."

The thought of leaving her twisted his gut, so he blurted out, "Will you meet me tomorrow night?"

"If you don't want them to know about me, how can we keep meeting?"

He desperately wanted to pull her into another hug, so he stuffed his hands into his pockets to keep them to himself. He couldn't let Callum see anything inappropriate. The dread of walking away began to build—then the starvation would descend and the sand would consume him. "What allows me to meet with you is that I have four siblings and I've set up our meetings to look like chance encounters. If you join me at Decadence, I should be able to keep Isaac busy elsewhere while we hang out up at the bar."

"If you're sure…"

He smiled. "Trust me, I'm sure I want to see you. I'll be at Decadence by eight. Please say you'll come by?"

"All right." She smiled, though he thought it looked more nervous than excited. He chuckled.

"Don't worry. It's a fun place. It's only a few blocks south." The desire to bend down and kiss her overwhelmed him, so he took a step back. Callum stomped down the hill in his direction. "I'll look forward to seeing you tomorrow. Bye, Alexis."

"Bye." He heard her reply softly after he'd turned to go meet Callum.

The anger link stalked over to him. "What the hell, Dae? You were supposed to be hunting. Not making friends."

Uh oh. "What are you talking about? I told you I needed more than ambient energy. And since none of you will let me out to hunt normally, I had to form a quick link with one individual. Still wasn't enough to even make an impact, but it took the edge off."

His stomach took that moment to growl loudly.

Callum huffed. "You can't hunt normally yet, not until you recover some more, so knock it off. Come on. Maggie should have dinner ready for you."

He walked with Callum toward his car, but he couldn't resist a look over his shoulder. Alexis was already gone.

Chapter 6

"YOU'RE DRAWING ON THE wrong layer."

Lexi squeaked, her heart jumping. But her eyes flashed a look at the toolbar and saw the layer highlighted. "God damn it." Growling, she jabbed at her keyboard.

"Fix it after lunch," Mathew ordered.

Her shoulders slumped and she took her tablet off her lap, setting everything to hibernate. Then she grabbed her bag and left the office for the break room down the hall. A few others were there, including her friend Amber, the secretary for her office.

Amber pulled a chair out next to her, and Lexi wove through the round tables to sink into it. She pulled her lunch sack out of her bag and opened it in defeat.

Not saying anything, Amber chewed thoughtfully and watched her. Lexi tried to ignore her, but she could feel the clock counting down to the inquisition.

"Mathew's noticed you aren't operating at your normal level of expertise."

"Great," she muttered around a mouthful of sandwich. "How bad?"

"A bit of grumbling. But that's it so far. You've done more than your share for months, so he really doesn't have anything to complain about."

Amber continued talking, but Lexi's mind drifted again. Like it had all day. The real memories she had made with Damian blurred with the vivid dreams she kept having every night. Worry had started to gnaw at her over her inability to tell the difference between reality and fantasy. She took another slow bite of her sandwich.

Fingers snapped in front of her face.

"Earth to Lexi. Come in, Lexi."

"Sorry, Amber."

"See, that's my point. Your concentration is focused elsewhere. So who is he?"

"What?" She choked on her lunch, but Amber smiled.

"This level of distracted daydreaming can only come from one source. A guy."

She dropped her sandwich. "No."

"Yes," Amber mimicked. "I've seen this plenty of times. You've been getting more and more distracted for days. So who is it? Anyone I know?"

Alexis sighed and started to pick pieces out of her food, crumbling the bread. "No one you know. I ran into him on the street. Literally. We came around the same corner and—*bam*. He took me to dinner since my grocery sack broke and all my food was ruined."

"Gallant." She smiled and leaned back in her seat. "Go on. What else? What's he look like?"

Lexi snorted, but her thoughts turned inward, her mind always too ready to supply his image for her to paint. "Amazing. Think Greek god. But with the heart of a poet. Dark wavy hair, longer than normal. The most expressive hazel eyes. Not an ounce of fat on him." She smiled ruefully and turned her gaze back to her friend. "He took me on a picnic to the beach. I've seen him a couple of times at the park just to walk and talk for a couple of hours. Tonight he's asked me to join him at some place on Capitol Hill. I'm trying to decide if I'm going to go."

"Why? You seem plenty smitten with him."

"Spending time with him is great. But I'm really out of his social strata. And, I have no idea what to wear, or what to do." She felt her face heat and turned back to picking her food apart. *And I should seriously think about trying to get him out of my system.*

"Well, first, where are you going?"

"Some place called Decadence."

"Oh, great dance club. You'll love it there. And it isn't too far from your apartment."

"Dance club. Ugh, I can't dance." *Guess that's how he's going to distract his brother.*

Amber laughed at her. "Don't worry. There's more than just dancing. Now what you should wear is…"

Dae wandered through the house. The walk yesterday had done him some good, but his body still continued to recover from the stripping Erik had done to his storeground. His energy, both physical and psychic, was at minimal, bare-survival levels. Tired of the walls of the house, he shuffled through rooms—already sick of the tether he could feel keeping him alive.

He glanced at a clock. *Only five.* He still had three hours to wait. Oh, and arrange to even get there first. *They won't let me get far without an escort.* He sighed. *It'll have to be Isaac. Cal would remember her from yesterday. Cass hates going to the club, so she'd do it but wouldn't leave my side the whole time. And that will hardly do. And Erik is too observant.* He glanced in the door of Erik's office but backed off. He was meeting with Adam, the court liaison for the conclave.

The news of his state would be out soon, but the longer they kept it quiet, the better. Well at least easier, especially for Erik. *His father is going to flip.*

He continued down the hall and into the formal living room. He sank onto the leather couch and stared out into the gardens. Beyond the flowers and manicured trees, the sky opened up to show a view of water off in the distance and the bare peaks of the Olympics. But the expensive view didn't hold his attention. Remembering his dreams did.

Alexis somehow was managing to call him to her. The unheard of experience was thrilling. More than that, the time they spent together was managing to keep him stable.

Her laugh. Their conversation. Her body pressed against his. They hadn't managed much more than making out for lack of time, thanks to Erik yanking his psyche home every night. But the drive for more with her continued to grow.

Isaac sauntered into the room, and Dae pulled his gaze away from the window. He blinked and looked at his watch. He'd sat for two hours? *I don't have much time.*

"Hey, little brother. What're you doing?" Isaac plopped down on the chair opposite him.

"Starving, that's what."

"Like that's a surprise. You let the fade take you; you could have avoided the worst of it, but you made your choice."

He glared at the joy link but continued, "Not my stomach, my ground. Erik still won't let me out. Will you take me over to Decadence?"

"I don't know. Have you cleared it with him?"

"Come on, Isaac. I need to feed. The park hasn't been enough. The club will have a ton of energy, and once my level gets high enough I'll be able to start orchestrating and harvesting properly again."

"You aren't strong enough, Dae."

"Of course not. Not for normal hunting. But I can sit at a balcony table and harvest from there. And if you were down on the dance floor..."

Isaac pursed his lips.

"You're too sane," Dae said. "You haven't fed at all since...well since, you know. Have you? Your ground must be getting to you; you can't wait much longer. And you would get the crowd really producing. We've always worked well together."

Isaac stared at him, eventually conceding. "You're right. You weren't the only one Erik drained so deeply. The others have already gone out to hunt, I just wanted to keep my wits a bit longer. I'm willing to take you, but I'm clearing it with Erik first. Wait here."

Damian sat up, resting his elbows on his knees and looking at the floor. A few minutes later, footsteps returned down the hall.

"Get ready. He says not to be out for long."

"Yes." He pulled himself to his feet but had to catch himself when his leg muscles didn't support his weight at first. He brushed Isaac's worried frown aside and reassured him with a laugh. "I'm ready, let's go."

Isaac's frown turned into a rueful grin, and he held out his hand. "Give me your keys. We sure as hell aren't taking my bike, and I'm not letting you drive."

Dae rolled his eyes but fished in his pocket and pulled out the key and fob. They slowly made their way out of the house, and Isaac walked ahead and got the carriage house doors open. Dae ran his hand over the roof of his car as he walked along the side, then got in the passenger seat. The supple leather embraced him, and he closed his eyes while Isaac backed them out and started wending through the neighborhood.

He would have plenty of time to get into the building and get settled—and figure out how to get Alexis in if there was a wait.

Decadence, since it was descendant run, had a private parking area that they could use under the building. Isaac punched in the code and pulled into the garage. He managed to get a space near the elevator and turned off the car, but he gripped Dae's arm before he could get out.

"Physically you aren't strong enough, Dae. So stay off the floor. I don't care what thread of energy you find. Next, Erik doesn't want you out all night, and he's right." The joy link paused and looked out the window before returning his gaze. "You know what I'll be like afterward, so don't be stupid. OK?"

That's what I'm counting on, brother. "Me? Stupid?"

Isaac shook the arm he gripped in warning. "I can turn right around now, so don't push me."

"Sorry. I'll stay up on the balcony. I promise."

Isaac let him go and they took themselves through the basement entrance into the club. The power of the music throbbed through Damian's body, even this early in the evening. He got an escort all the way up to the bar where Isaac turned him over to Bob.

The bartender chewed on his cheek, and Dae was sure it was to keep from outright laughing over the leash being handed over to him. Dae glared at both in the dim light. Isaac patted him on the cheek with a smile and bounced toward the stairs to the dance floor, the energy already having an impact on the other incubus.

Dae turned back to Bob. The bartender pursed his lips, but his eyes twinkled brighter than the ceiling lights.

"So...I guess you weren't able to keep your secret."

"Fuck you, Bob."

"Temper, temper. You're starting to sound like Cal. Well, come on over here. There's a table overlooking the floor still."

He followed slowly in the descendant's wake and tried to ignore the sympathetic knowing in the human's eyes. Bob pulled out a chair and Dae dropped into it.

"Isaac's one scary mofo when he wants to be and isn't amped up on his power. I told you I wouldn't tell, so I'm sorry about that, Dae. But I'm not sorry they found out and saved you. Does the court know yet?"

He shook his head. "No. The family is trying to keep it quiet for as long as possible. It's going to be hard on Erik. But it'll be out as soon as one of the Chirurgeons gets a hold of me."

"OK, I'll stay quiet then, to give Erik more time. I'll get you some food and let you get to work."

Dae reached a hand out to stop the human. "Wait."

Bob turned back to him.

"Could you do me a favor?"

"That depends. I don't want Isaac gunning for me again."

Dae glanced over the railing into the mob under the flashing lights, then back to Bob. "Could you take a message to the door for me? I have a friend who might join me, and since Isaac said that Erik wants us home early, I want to make sure she can get in quickly."

Bob looked at him funny. "...OK. That's a little odd. I'm assuming she's human or this wouldn't be an issue?"

"Yes."

"Dae?"

"Please, Bob. No one needs to know. I'm not going to get you into any trouble."

"I shouldn't. I should tell Isaac."

"You do and I'll start an orgy down there that'll make the last one look like a church picnic."

"Don't threaten me, Dae. Erik will take you apart if you do that, and you know it." He crossed his arms and stared at Dae for a minute. "I'll do it. I don't know why, but I will."

Relief washed through him. "Thank you, Bob. Really. There's nothing in the laws about making friends," he added.

"Maybe not, but I'm sure there would still be raised eyebrows."

He let himself shrink down in his seat. "It's nice to be with someone who doesn't know. Who doesn't send pity my way."

Bob closed his eyes for a moment, then nodded. Dae passed on Alexis's name and description, and the descendant promised to get the info to the door. After that, he sat back and watched the dance floor. As drained as he was, plucking a likely thread proved difficult. So he watched his brother work. The happy, exuberant energy started to spread in a wave as he watched Isaac become the center of a growing group of jubilant dancers. Then he noticed Asher saunter out—the joy link for another family.

Uh oh. Two hunters on the same ground. Hope they keep it under control. But, good timing for me. They'll keep each other busy.

A glass of wine appeared, followed by food a short while later, and still he had trouble accessing the free-floating energy. He kept glancing at his watch. Eight twenty-five. He sighed. *Maybe she isn't coming.*

But then a whisper of energy drifted across his storeground. He looked up, and she stood uncertainly on the bridge near the entrance that overlooked the dance floor. He half rose and lifted a hand. She swiveled in his direction like a lodestone. A look of relief swept across her face that he could see even with the distance. He had the perfect opportunity to admire her as she crossed toward him. Her jeans hugged her luscious curves, while the bright flower overshirt framed her chest. And like a bee, he zeroed in on the goods bouncing softly in his direction.

"I'm glad you made it."

"Sorry I'm late."

They both spoke at the same time, and he chuckled, pulling a chair out for her. "Did you have trouble getting in?"

"No." She sat and fiddled with her shirt tails. "There was a bit of a line, but I wasn't in it long. Someone came and asked my name and who I was meeting, then they escorted me past the line."

"I'm friends with the bouncer and bartender. They were willing to do me a favor. I'm still on limited time and didn't want to waste it with you in line."

"Still have a keeper, huh? You kind of thought you would."

"Yeah," he groused, then added, "At least we have a few hours…"

"So, Damian, what will your friend have?"

Dae turned and gave the curious descendant a look. "Alexis, this is Bob. Bob, Alexis."

"Nice to meet you, Alexis. Dae hasn't brought friends here before. So this is interesting. What'll you have?"

"Shut up, Bob."

"I find that hard to believe," she said at the same time. They smiled at each other, then she turned back to the descendant. "I'll just have what he has, thank you."

"Right. Be up in a minute."

"I don't believe that for a second. That you don't bring girls here," she repeated as Bob walked back to the bar.

"Well, believe it. I don't have many friends I socialize with. It's mostly work and spending time with the family."

"Speaking of, you've managed to dodge the question of what you do each time I've asked."

"That's easy enough. Erik's the head of the family and CEO. He runs most everything. We do what we're told."

"Really? Another thing I find hard to believe."

She jumped when Bob snorted behind her, and Dae glared at him.

"Do what you're told? Right, Damian. I'll believe that when I see it." He laughed and set Lexi's drink down, along with another plate of food. "What he's not telling you is he's a playboy, sweetheart."

"Keep this up, Bob, and you won't have to worry about Isaac."

"And to reiterate, I'll tell Erik."

Dae growled and Bob laughed as he walked away again.

"Interesting people you know, Damian."

"I like it when you call me Dae better. And to set the record straight, I do lots of useful things. I'm usually helping Erik with the business, but they've restricted me right now because of the recovery. And, well, Erik's still pissed at me."

"For you not telling them?"

"Yeah."

"Well, I'm sure that's just a matter of time. I'd be mad at my family too if one of them did something similar. But it wouldn't last forever."

He sighed and rubbed the spot over his heart; he could still feel Erik branding him there with his hand. "I hope you're right."

"If they love you, then I am."

"I'll work on remembering that. Thanks for coming tonight. It means a lot. You must be busy. Work, friends?"

She fidgeted with the stem of her glass and shrugged. "Too much of one, none of the other. My family wants me to come home. But, I never fit in there, and they won't ever believe that. I always felt like something inside kept pushing me away from there. It wasn't until I came here that it settled. I like it here. Even if I'm not completely happy with my job. I feel like this is where I'm supposed to be. Kind of silly, huh?"

"Not really. There's a lot to be said about feelings and emotions. They have more power than most give them credit for."

"Thanks." She took a drink. "I need this after today."

He stole a bite of food off of her full plate. "Bad day?"

"Have you ever drawn on the same layer? Repeatedly? It's a nightmare."

"Layer?"

"Of art? On the computer."

"Whatever happened to brushes, paint, and canvases?"

She snorted and tried a bite of what he was stealing. "Actually I prefer those, but they don't pay the rent. Unless you're Thomas Kinkade."

"So, what happened?"

"I haven't been sleeping well lately, and I couldn't keep my mind focused. Too much wandering, and so I screwed up. They aren't too happy with me I expect."

"You haven't been sleeping well?" His stomach dropped.

"It's nothing."

"It can't be nothing if you're getting in trouble for it at work. Why aren't you sleeping well?" he pressed.

Her gaze rose, holding his, and he knew. "I've been having a lot of vivid dreams, that's all."

She blushed and looked away. *Damn. She actually remembers our time in Shadow? That shouldn't be possible. I could see dream fragments disturbing her sleep…*

He put his hand over her clenched fist on the table and squeezed. "I've had my share of vivid dreams as well."

A strange look crossed her face, but they were interrupted by Bob clearing his throat. He topped off their drinks, then left with a pointed look. Dae removed his hand quickly.

"So which one is your brother?"

He turned to look over the balcony with her and spent some time directing her through the crowd from their height.

"It almost looks like he's having a contest with that other guy."

He chuckled. "You could say that. That's Asher. A close friend. We grew up together with his family."

The two joy links were really pushing the envelope. The infectious mood had swelled with the two of them feeding it. Dae could feel the energy they were causing from the gathering. But with Alexis's energy blanketing him, he didn't feel the normal pain of separation from not getting to access the bands he'd been cut off from. He basked in the novelty of not missing it while the two of them sat quietly watching Isaac and Asher turn the crowd into a seething mass. Bob came over to check on them and noticed the level down below.

"Dae, you need to get Isaac home. If they take it any further, we'll have injuries that will result in police, and the enforcers won't be pleased to have to come and control the results. They had enough trouble containing what you did. I'll call Martin to come collect Asher."

"Damn it. I wasn't ready yet," he muttered. He turned to the inquiring look from his companion. "Sorry, looks like it's about time for me to go.

Sounds like Isaac's had too much."

"Not a very good watcher for you if he goes and gets drunk with his friend."

He laughed. "Yes and no. I sort of tricked him into it so I could have time with you. Any of the others would have been a nuisance. I knew Isaac would leave me be. Though he did sic Bob on me." He took her hand and looked into her eyes. "Will you come to dinner with me tomorrow?"

He felt a flutter go through her hand, but she smirked. "What sort of dinner would it be with a chaperone?"

He exhaled and bit his cheek to keep from laughing. "I think I can manage to get out by myself tomorrow. But if I can't, I'll call or text you."

"I would love to have dinner with you, but are you sure you'll be up to it? Even if they let you out of their sights?"

He lifted her hand to his lips and pressed a kiss to the knuckles, then his tongue flicked out to taste her skin and he was rewarded with a sigh. "Being with you is worth it."

Her fingers trembled in his grasp, and she looked at the tabletop. He could see in the dim light that a blush stole across her face. He smiled. "Come on. I'll walk you over to the door to see you out before I gather up my plastered brother."

He stood slowly to hide any weakness from sitting for so long, then took her hand again to walk over to the bridge near the exit. There, after a quick glance over the rail for Isaac, he framed her face with his hands and kissed her good-bye.

The lure of her lips sucked him in and instead of a quick kiss it turned into an inferno. Lost, he didn't notice the people who came and went around them. Her energy washed through his sand, saturating it. And he could feel the haze of lust that usually swirled around him click into place, blazing into the atmosphere.

She kissed him back, with more heat than any of their prior encounters in either the waking world or Shadow. He backed her against the wall, his body pressing lightly all along hers. Her tongue swept across his, her hands clutching at his shoulders.

"Damian." The shout broke across the distance.

He stiffened. After a last nip to her lips, he pulled his head back and looked down into her eyes. "Dinner. Tomorrow."

"OK." Her tongue flicked out to swipe across her bottom lip. He barely concealed his groan.

His fingers swept across her eyebrow and down her cheek. Then he turned her and startled her with a swat to the ass. She jumped forward into the doorway, then turned a halfhearted glare over her shoulder. He smirked at her, and she shook her head as she left the club.

Only then did he turn and catch hell from Bob's stare. He also realized that Isaac, while still moving on the dance floor, had his attention turned on him. He groaned. Dragging his feet, he returned to the bar.

"You don't kiss a *friend* like that, Damian. I'm sure that was not within the bounds of the law." He swiped at the bar aggressively.

Nothing he could really say to Bob. The descendant was right. What the hell was he doing anyway? All he knew was that he couldn't stop. He rubbed his eyes and felt her energy fade away the farther she got from him. He wasn't quite so energy hungry—yet. But since his storeground had dried up and turned to sand from the fertile soil it once was, it no longer held the energy for long. None of the others yet realized his ground was permanently destroyed and that was why he wasn't recovering as fast as they thought he should. Opening the conduit should have prevented the complete deterioration. Truthfully he should be dead already with a ground like his.

"I can't go down to the floor to get Isaac, Bob. If you want him out before the two of them become a problem, you'll need to send someone down."

"Already have. He should be up in a minute."

He turned away from the disapproving descendant and waited for his brother. One of the bouncers herded him up the stairs. Isaac laughed maniacally while the guard did his best to withstand his influence—though it was a losing battle.

"All right, Isaac," Bob drawled, "you and Asher have had your fun. Now go home."

"But, Bob, Asher's still here. It's not fair."

"Not for long. I've already called Martin. Take Damian home, Isaac. He needs to go home too."

"Hey, little brother. Did you find your hunting good?" He bounced like the energizer bunny over to him and thunked his arm across Dae's shoulders. But Dae could see the irritation trapped behind his glazed eyes—partly for the perpetual state he found himself in from the energy he harvested, but more of it was directed at Dae and what he'd done on the balcony.

"Yes, I got the energy I needed. It won't last long though," Dae said. "My storeground is all sand."

That locked them all, incubus and descendant alike, in a frozen stare.

Isaac managed to break through the manic long enough to ask, "How long has it been?"

Dae shrugged, then turned and started toward the door.

"Damian." Isaac almost managed a growl, and he caught up quickly. "Does Erik know?"

"I have no idea. It's not like anyone has asked me or anything. And you won't be telling anyone anytime soon."

Isaac had suppressed the giggles as long as he could; he put his arms around his middle as they rode the elevator down and took deep breaths to combat them. "Don't..." Breath. "Underestimate..." Breath. "Me." The eyes he pinned Dae with had ice underneath the manic.

Chapter 7

THE STRIDENT SHIP'S HORN blare woke Lexi. It repeated, and she started fumbling on the nightstand for her phone. Even in the haze of sleep, the ringtone for her sister pushed her into action and she answered it without thinking.

"Lexi?" Liz asked. "Were you asleep?"

She mumbled something she hoped was noncommittal and squinted at the clock. *Oh my god, I'm going to be late for work.* She threw the covers back, her sister's voice in her ear.

"What is going on with you out there?" Liz's tone turned sharp. "Dia said she talked to you last week and was concerned."

"Sorry, Liz. I didn't get a lot of restful sleep last night. And now I'm going to be late for work. I've had some pretty intense dreams."

That paused the tirade. "What kind of dreams?"

"Oh, nothing in particular." She blushed as flashes of her dreams marched through her memories. She rummaged one-handed through her closet for work clothes that weren't too wrinkled.

"Alexis, that sounds like a dodge to me." Her sister laughed, and Lexi could almost see her rubbing her hands together as she prepared to start the grill, and her intended main dish was roasted Lexi. "What sort of dreams would have you sleeping through your alarm? You always woke at the drop of a hat."

"Well, I didn't go to bed real early either. I got drawn into a painting..."

"A painting? Now tell me more. You only do portraits. Who's the subject? I suspect that'll give me the info I want."

She groaned, realizing her mistake, and sniffed a shirt to see if it was clean. "I don't *only* do portraits."

"OK, you only get drawn into portraits. Doesn't matter. I'm right, or you wouldn't be dodging the question now, would you?"

"Argh. You make me so mad sometimes."

More laughter echoed down the line. "What's his name?"

She rubbed the sleep out of her eye, the picture of a smooth beach, a mountain glen, a lake shore, and more marched in succession across her vision, and she sighed. "Dae."

"That's an odd name. Send me a picture of the painting. I want to see what he looks like."

"It's short for Damian, and no I will not text that to you."

"That good, huh?"

With a growl Lexi tossed her clothes on the bed. "What did you want, Liz? Shouldn't you be working with Brandon?"

"Ugh, don't remind me. Can't."

Her turn to laugh, she picked at her sister. "What, Brandon too pigheaded to cooperate?"

"That's putting it mildly. I've only barely started the second trimester, and you'd think I was an incapable invalid from the way he treats me."

"He's going to be a new father. From what I've heard that's a pretty typical reaction. Especially after the nausea you had."

"Give me a break. The rest of the family is joining in. So I was hoping to distract everyone by getting you to come over for dinner."

"Ah, well..." She ran a hand through her short hair. "I can't. Not tonight."

"Don't tell me that...*job* has you working late still?" she asked reproachfully.

"No. You see...I've kind of got a date," she finished in a rush.

Her sister whooped. "OK, now I really want a text of that picture."

"Come on, Liz. Don't tell everyone else."

"Are you kidding? I'm running straight up to the big house when we get off the phone."

Lexi groaned.

"I expect a phone call as soon as you're home."

"Liz," she yelped. "I'm not a child with a curfew."

"That doesn't change the fact that anything can happen. How well do you know this guy? He could be a rapist for all you know, or an alien."

She couldn't help it, she burst into laughter. "An alien?"

"And he's going to beam you up to his mother

ship. But seriously, I want a call to know that you're all right."

"Fine. But I don't know how late we'll be."

"I don't care. I'll be on your doorstep at dawn if you don't. Take care of yourself, sis."

"Bye, Liz." She smiled to herself as she hit end on the phone. Rushing into the bathroom, she quickly got ready.

Dressed for work she left her room, but her steps faltered as she passed her work space. Invisible strands pulled, drawing her to her easel. Paintings lay propped on the floor. She avoided the partially done one that kept causing pain, but the new canvas that stared at her from her easel made her breath catch in her lungs.

Dae leaned against the rough bark of an oak tree. His arms were crossed, the hint of a playful smile flirting with the corner of his lips. If she looked carefully enough, she could see the soft strands of his hair move in the breeze. His voice whispered through her mind and she gasped. She couldn't make out the words, but her body responded with a longing that snapped her out of her daydream.

As she sank to her chair, a nervous laugh tried to escape. *Thank god it's only a dream. This obsession is starting to get embarrassing.* Then a more worrisome thought presented itself. *How am I going to hide this? I'm seeing him tonight.*

She stood up in a panic. *I'm never going to make it through work.*

That evening Dae buckled his boots in the entryway.

"Where do you think you're going?"

He stiffened at the tone of Erik's voice behind him. "Out."

"Really?"

With no hint of movement to warn him, Erik pushed his shoulder. He stumbled forward into the wall, then turned a glare over at his center.

Erik crossed his arms, his gaze steady. "You can barely stand on your own. Why should I let you out alone?"

"Damn it, Erik, I need out. I'm just going over to Broadway to hunt for a few hours, OK?"

"Someone has taken you out every day. I don't like this. You're still too weak."

"Then you really don't have to fear me running again, do you?"

Erik snorted and stalked into his space; Dae flattened his back against the wall as Erik's taller frame caged him there. "I'm not worried about you running. You can't defend yourself if any humans try and attack you. You and your pretty face, and the sexual energy you exude. You don't have the strength or the energy to bend the light and disappear. You are a perfect target."

Erik squeezed his eyes shut briefly. "But I can't have you breaking the law either, even instinctively like you have been at night, by hunting in dreams. So I'll let you go, since no one is home to escort you—but you answer your bloody phone, you hear me? And be back in three hours."

"A curfew? Three hours is hardly an appetizer!"

"Take it or leave it. You aren't strong enough for longer. You're still healing from the surgery." Erik rested his forehead against Damian's. "Please, Dae. The next couple of weeks are going to be hard enough without you fighting us too."

Emotion swirled around him, and he felt the stress Erik usually kept leashed. The worry about the consequences Erik would need to face—that they all would need to face—at court when the knowledge came out about their family's situation. The king would not take this well. Damian sagged against the wall and whispered, "OK."

Erik's body relaxed, and he kissed Dae's forehead before pushing away from the wall. "Good. Be back in three hours. I mean it."

Left alone in the entryway, he took a deep breath and rallied his strength. What the hell was he doing? *Not that I seem to have a choice.* After a moment he walked out of the house and huffed getting the carriage house door open. Normally he liked to walk. The Capitol Hill area was exceptionally well suited to travel by foot. But Erik was right; he didn't have the strength—nor the time, now—to cater to that preference.

He wove his car through the stately trees of his neighborhood, then made his way through the traffic leading closer to downtown. He pulled up in front of Alexis's apartment building and realized he'd started to feel her energy wash over him a few blocks back.

He pushed the buzzer for her apartment. "Hello?" her voice asked breathlessly.

"Hi, Alexis." He smiled. "It's me, Dae."

"Give me a sec and I'll be right down."

He descended the steps and put his back to his car to wait. It wasn't long. She pushed the door open and rushed down the steps. At the last moment, she stopped and looked around. He smiled. "Just me. I managed to break free. But only for three hours."

With a laugh she threw herself into his arms. He closed his eyes as he felt her weight settle against him. "Gods I've missed you," he said.

"Me too."

He ran his hand through her short hair, then gently pushed her back as he turned to open the door to his car. She gathered the skirt of her sundress and slid onto the leather seat. After he started the car, he asked, "Do you like seafood?"

"Sure."

"I thought we'd go down to the waterfront if that was OK with you? Since I've only got three hours."

"At least you've managed to ditch the watch dogs."

He blew out a breath and made a right turn. "Yeah. Three hours alone is better than none."

He reached over and took her hand as he stopped at a light. She returned the pressure. Her energy filtered slowly through his sand. Last night at Decadence had been something of a surprise. At home as he lay in bed he went over the evening and realized that only her energy had managed to engage him. It wasn't just that he was more interested in her energy, he hadn't *been able* to absorb the other threads that had wafted around him.

Guilt threatened, but he pushed it aside. He couldn't talk to the others. What he was doing was so far out of legal it wasn't funny. And she would pay the price if they got caught. Because of that, he'd spent the night trying to resist her draw. But in the end he'd been pulled into her dreams again, and he wasn't doing much better in the physical world with staying away.

Only when he was with her, either physically or in dreams, did the need to hunt pull the claws out of his gut. He found a spot on the waterfront to park and helped her out. They walked hand in hand along the sidewalk.

"I wish I could take you to our manor house in France. You'd love it there. Lots of things to paint."

"I've always wanted to travel. Maybe someday after you are better we could."

"I would like that." Wistfully he wished that could ever be possible. "Summer is really the best time anyway. Right now the grapes are in the process of being harvested."

"Grapes?" she whispered.

He cocked his head and saw that her face had paled. "It's a large estate. So there are lots of other crops and animals and things, if you don't like grapes."

"No. No, I like grapes."

Distracted by her response, he stumbled on the curb but caught himself. Keeping a rein on his frustration, he slowed his pace. His leg muscles still quivered with the strain of carrying his weight. *Damn Erik anyway*, he thought, though it was getting harder to be angry at them. His strength was returning, just not fast enough for his comfort. It was harder to get used to the tether that tied him to the others.

He got himself under control and turned his attention back to her, but she seemed like nothing had happened. With a shrug, he walked with her out onto the pier, then opened a big wooden door. The warm salty scents that wafted out made his stomach growl, and she laughed. He got them a table along the big windows that overlooked the waters of the sound and started poring over the menu. His physical hunger still ran higher than before the fade, so food was never far from his mind. Erik had assured him it would return to normal soon.

But until then he still ate like three teenagers at a sleepover. Thankfully with Lexi's energy flowing into him, he could keep it under control. He ordered two appetizers with their drinks and sat back to watch her. She kept absently shoving her hair away as she studied the menu. The tip of her tongue played at the corner of her mouth in her concentration.

"I've never been here before. What would you rec—" She glanced up at him, meeting his stare, and froze.

"You are so beautiful."

She choked, then took a sip of water. "Um…" Her face turned red in the dim light.

He managed a wisp of power and sent it to brush her skin. A shiver flickered through her and she jerked her attention back to the folder in front of her.

He smiled and took a sip of his water.

She cleared her throat. "What would you recommend?"

"The sockeye salmon is pretty good right now."

He reached across the table and tucked a strand of hair behind her ear. Her gaze snapped back to his and he held it until the waiter arrived. He ordered for the both of them, then turned her attention to the view. They chatted and ate appetizers. He couldn't remember the last time he had a real meal with someone who wasn't family or descendants. Not even other Kelusis. They were close to a few of the other Sundered families, but that was it.

"What's it like over there? I've never taken the ferry across." She cocked her head as she studied the mountains and hills on the other side of the sound.

"Really? We should do that. Then I could show you the beach house."

She scooped up some of the spinach crab dip onto a piece of bread. "I would like that."

"We use it occasionally, but mostly the family stays in the house on Capitol Hill when we are in the Seattle area."

"How many places do you guys own?" She laughed. "Seattle, Bainbridge, France."

"I'm going to take the fifth on that."

She shook her head, eyes twinkling, and ate another bite of her appetizer. Through their laughter he felt a power around him shift. His attention sharpened, and he glanced around the restaurant. Not finding anyone else nearby, he let his mind flick out tentatively, and he realized that the shift he felt came from her. Rudimentary shadow-shaping? *That's not possible.* He hurriedly threw a mental blanket around them to douse it.

My power must be reflecting off her somehow. That's the only explanation. But he still looked around swiftly once more. Just humans ignoring them.

Their entrées arrived and they both ate in silence for a bit. The muted clink of china and the soft murmur of voices accompanied them. The sun sank behind the Olympic Mountains across the sound, turning the water into a burning swath before fading to a deep blue black.

Their gazes kept crashing into each other, and after a while they both just laughed, the jokes flowing freely. Power spiked again, and he noticed her shiver and shake her head. He reached out and siphoned it off, gaining a boost for his ground. The sensation dissipated immediately after that.

"That was excellent salmon. Thank you." She patted her lips with her napkin.

He had already finished off his main dish and had scraped the last of the appetizers out of their bowls. "You are most welcome. I love this place. I come here fairly often with my brother Isaac."

"My living expenses take up most of my money, so I don't go out often. You're lucky you can share something like this with your brother. My family don't really share any of my interests and don't understand them. They never understood how alone I was surrounded by close family and the nosy people of a small town."

"We have that in common. It's amazing how

lonely you can be in a crowd." He accepted the check and thanked the waiter before flashing a smile at her. "I still have some time left before my curfew is up. Would you like to take a walk with me along the waterfront?"

She nodded, so he pushed back from the table and held out his hand. She took it and the jolt of energy caught him off guard. He hissed in surprise and she tried to yank back, but he held on and towed her outside to get away from curious eyes. Once in the balmy night air, he breathed a sigh of relief; the tingle of the increased flow of power hummed where their skin touched. The amount of energy he was harvesting from her was remarkable enough, but trying to hide a reaction from observers was more than he needed right now.

At least she covered her response as well. Where is she getting all of this?

He tucked her hand into the crook of his elbow and they paced slowly along the pier, pausing over the water at the corner of a building to watch a couple of seals below twist in and out of the pylons in the moonlight.

He hadn't felt this good in forever. The hunger generated from the need to take in *all* the strands of emotion—those the Chirurgeons cut him off from—forever scratched at him, like phantom pain from a missing limb. But the pain was muted tonight. He turned to her and brushed the soft ends of her hair away from her cheek, then rubbed his thumb along the bone. She clasped her hands together in front of her, and he smiled. This was nothing like who she really was inside, the person who showed herself to him in their dreams. There she felt confident.

He bent his head and let his lips settle on hers. No need to hurry this time.

His tongue slid along her lips, coaxing her to open to him. Her energy rushed forth when she did and he dove in, their tongues dueling. Now her hands slid along the silk of his shirt and branded his chest with their heat. His hand skimmed from her cheek to the back of her head while his other slipped around her waist, then down to cup her bottom, pulling her closer.

She moaned. Abandoning her mouth, he traced a path down the side of her neck. His teeth scraped on her skin, followed by the flat of his tongue; the hard points of her nipples pressed into his chest through the cotton of her dress, and she rose up on her tiptoes to press the juncture of her thighs into him.

He turned them, backing her into the wall, and she shivered at the sudden movement. The sound of the waves lapping below the boards of the dock beneath them mingled with their gasps and groans. Sucking against the skin of her pulse point, he let both hands skim up her sides; his thumbs rubbed circles around her nipples when he reached them. Her hands had inched higher into his hair to pull him more firmly against her neck.

His thoughts arced out, twining with hers, igniting the power he'd doused earlier, and images of places and actions shuffled like a deck of cards between them—acting like lightning to dry tinder. Places they had already been in their dreams and places still left to visit. She shifted her legs apart and he could feel her heat through the thin cotton of her dress and his tight jeans. In response, he rolled her nipples between his thumbs and fingers and rocked the ridge in his jeans upward, the thin cotton hardly any barrier.

She whimpered in his ear. The hot press of her core set his groin on fire and gave it a mind of its own. Her hands gripped his hair as he slid against her again, pressing her harder into the wood of the wall, her feet leaving the ground.

Her sobbing cry echoed off the water and brought him back to reality.

Human.

With a shudder of his own, he let her slide back down to her feet, his tongue soothing the raspberry spot he'd left on her neck. His breath ragged, he forced his hands away from her breasts but let them tangle in her short hair as he rose back to her mouth. The sweet taste of her breath, as rapid as his, panted across his tongue. He tried to untangle his thoughts from hers.

What the fuck am I doing? She's human. This is against the law. I'm going to get her killed at this rate. And why the bloody hell are my dreams moving out of my control?

Still having a hard time pulling away, he groaned and dropped his forehead to the wood above her shoulder. His nose pressed into the crook of her neck, and her scent almost pushed him back into the fray—but her hands skimming unerringly toward his bulge stopped him. He pressed against her body.

It brought his cock into tighter contact but stopped her hands from causing worse trouble.

Laughter echoed from around the corner. She stiffened slightly and he closed his eyes in relief.

"I'm sorry," he mumbled into her neck, and he felt the goosebumps rise on her skin from his breath skating across it. "I just thought we'd kiss. I didn't expect it to go explosive. This is hardly the place for it."

"I…" She trailed off.

Her voice sounded husky and he liked it. He let his tongue have one more slow lick of her skin, then he pulled away. The warm night felt suddenly chill without her body heat pressed into his. Her nipples stood out like beacons to him, but the dazed look in her eyes made him think she didn't notice. He'd enjoy the sight while he could, but his three hours were almost up.

She absently twitched her rumpled skirt from the bunch it had formed between her legs and ran her hands through her hair. He tucked a wayward strand behind her ear, then clasped her hand in his and led her from the docks. "I hope you liked dinner?"

"I…" She cleared her throat. "Yes, thank you."

"I'm sorry I don't have more time." They reached his car and he opened the door for her. Once in his own seat, he glanced at her tightly clasped hands in her lap. "Thank you for joining me tonight."

She smiled, a little unsure, and turned to look out the window. It took about five minutes of silence to reach her apartment steps. She was unbuckled and out the door before he could reach his own belt.

"Thank you," she whispered across the distance of the seats as the door closed. He'd wanted to walk her up, but she bolted, so he waited for her to climb the steps and get the foyer door open. His last glance as he drove away showed her watching out the front window, her hand pressed to the mark on her neck.

Chapter 8

CALLUM SLAMMED THE DOOR to his SUV and ripped his phone out of his pocket. A fierce stab brought up his Favorites menu. With effort he gentled his touch. He'd only just replaced this phone last week. He didn't need to do it again so soon.

"Isaac, home, now. I'll explain when I get there." He hung up on his babbling brother and dialed Cass. "Cassandra, I'm calling everyone home. It's about Dae. No, I'll explain to everyone."

He squeezed his eyes shut for a second, then started his car. He pulled out with a spray of gravel and dialed Erik.

"Yes?"

"I've called everyone home. We have a problem."

Erik's voice turned no-nonsense. "What?"

"It's about Dae, and I only want to explain this once."

"Well hurry up, because he's only going to be out for another half hour. I gave him a three-hour window."

"I'm down at the waterfront. I'll be there in a couple of minutes."

He hung up, then sped up.

When he pulled into the driveway, Cass had left the garage open for him so he went straight in. Isaac's bike was already parked against the wall. He shut his car door and sprinted for the house. The physical surge helped clear a little of the anger energy from his system, allowing him to think more calmly. Inside, the others waited in the formal living room just off the front door.

"I sent the descendants out. I figured better safe than sorry, since I don't know the nature of this." Erik's calm helped center him.

Cass sat perched on the edge of the couch, her dress pooled at her feet, while Isaac hugged his knees and rocked on the floor near Erik's feet, trying not to giggle, and Erik stood by the cold hearth waiting and still.

Anger pounded in Cal's temples and he pressed his fingers to his forehead, pushing it back and down. He started to pace. "I was out hunting but thought I'd grab dinner. Isaac raves about this seafood restaurant down on the waterfront. When I arrived I felt energy threads start to move and found Damian. But he wasn't alone. He was having dinner with a human woman, one I saw him harvesting from for two hours when I took him to the park the other day."

"Are you sure?" Erik asked.

"Yes. It was the same woman."

Isaac started laughing. But the joy link's eyes

turned to Erik. Cal ran his hand through the bristle of his hair and watched Erik crouch in front of the wheezing Isaac, who reached out and gripped their center with a white-knuckled fist.

"Hold on, Isaac," Erik spoke softly and placed a hand against the joy link's chest. Isaac started to hyperventilate but disciplined his breathing quickly. "Better?"

"Yes, thank you. That takes the edge off." The joy link sat up and turned his attention toward him. "What did she look like, Callum?"

He described her, and Isaac's shoulders slumped.

"Damn. I had hoped...I saw him with her last night. I wasn't sure until now, but he met the same woman at the park very briefly the day before Callum took him there." He turned a serious face up to Erik. "He kissed her in Decadence last night. I also found out his storeground is nothing but sand."

Cass gasped, suppressing a sob.

"Four meetings that we know of in as many days? When did he meet her? It had to be before we found out he was fading." Erik scrubbed his face with his hands. "Damn it. I thought the worst was behind us. Sand? Are you sure?"

"That's what he said last night," Isaac said.

"I had wondered why his energy wasn't recovering as fast as I thought it should. It didn't occur to me to look, and it should have. The council and conclave have taken up too much of my time."

"What are we going to do?" Cass whispered. "He's already been on a short leash."

"Well, it's about to get shorter."

Callum heard the growl of Dae's car.

"It's not like we have much choice," Erik continued. "This has to be stopped, before the enforcers find out. Or we have to take care of her. I'd rather not be responsible for destroying an innocent's life."

The front door latch clicked and Damian limped slowly through. Almost like a filter had been removed, Callum could now see how much weight his brother had already lost. He'd done an excellent job of hiding his condition from all of them. Dae paused in the act of shutting the door when he spotted all of them waiting and staring at him. He finished with a click, then faced them as he stood in the foyer.

"Damian, please come here," Erik said in a quiet, pleasant tone, but the command was unmistakable.

"I think I'd rather not. I'm tired."

"It's not open for discussion. We can do this the hard way if you insist, but I'd rather be more comfortable in here."

Dae glanced at Isaac, and Callum saw resignation cross his features before he shuffled into the room. Anger bubbled again, driven by how weak his brother was and the fact that he couldn't do anything to fix it. If he'd only come to them sooner...

Dae came to a stop in front of Erik but looked down at the joy link. "I didn't think you'd manage it."

"Leave Isaac alone," Erik said. "Look at me."

Damian's shoulders squared and he lifted his head. Callum walked over to stand near his sister.

She could have been a statue for how much she moved and breathed. From his new position, he could see everyone's face. Erik had pulled enough energy from Isaac that the joy link could control himself, but the anger Cal could see in Isaac's eyes covered the fear he knew his brother felt. Because it mirrored his.

Dae held their center's gaze unflinchingly. Which took guts, Callum conceded. Erik placed his palm against Damian's heart—then he put his other hand over Dae's third eye. The lust link's legs started to tremble, and with a groan he collapsed to his knees, Erik following him down but not stopping.

"What the hell is wrong with you, man? Why won't you talk to us?" Erik disengaged his hands and sat back on his heels. "You're right, Isaac. He's gone to complete sand. No seed could grow in that."

Callum clenched his fists at his side until he heard his sister's breath hitch, so he laid a hand on her shoulder. She reached up and clutched it.

"I don't know if it can be repaired. We'll just keep doing what we can. And that leads us to the other serious matter we need to discus, Damian." The lust link's head rose up tiredly and met Erik's stare. "What is her name, Dae?"

Shock washed across his brother's features.

"We know you've used the same human donor multiple times and are becoming physical with her. I need to know where to find her."

"No," Damian whispered.

"You know the law. If you've been intimate... Now where is she?"

"Fuck no. Is that clear enough?" He tried to gain his shaky legs. Like a newborn colt, he managed and stared at them defiantly.

"Your leash is now nonexistent. Callum, tomorrow hit the park and see if she comes through. Cass, head over to Decadence tonight and talk to Bob; see what he knows and tell him to keep his eyes open for her. If she comes in, I want her contact info. You"—he pointed his finger at Damian—"will need to hunt every day, but not alone. I'll have to take whatever you manage before it drains away. We *will* find her, Damian."

"Don't you dare touch her," he snarled softly, his head turned to make his point to each of them, then he took a step toward the doors.

"Someone help him to his room," Erik said.

"I can do it myself," he snapped and staggered unhindered across the floor.

"Stubborn fool. What choice have you left us?"

Callum watched Dae put his hand on the doorframe and turn to look at them before he said, "The same as me."

They all watched Damian slowly drag himself up the stairs until the sound of his door firmly closing echoed down.

Alexis sat back in her chair to study the portrait. Her hand strayed to the hickey Dae had marked her with. Like a teenager, she almost felt like giggling from the erotic zap the contact gave her, but reality damped it down. *Why is this so strong?*

All she could think about was him. Being with him. This wasn't like her. His face was constantly there. Every time she shut her eyes.

And that kiss on the docks.

Her body still trembled.

Thank god I got Liz off the phone quick. She thought about the required phone call and how much she had resented giving up her time to it.

Her focus zeroed in on the canvas. She had been avoiding this scene, the started canvas taunting her for the last several days—but the vision was too painful. Now it wouldn't let her go. She stripped her clothes off with little thought, grabbing brushes and squeezing tubes, her movements quick and violent. The scene fleshed out more. His golden body gleamed, every inch of it glistening as it twisted across the rumpled satin of an ancient bed. The curtains hung, partially drawn to the posts. The shadows near the headboard contained the ghosts who'd brought him to this state—their eyes the only thing visible. The cruel pleasure contained in them fell across his torment.

He lay on his back, his arm outstretched toward her, trying to grasp something that disappeared.

Something she felt she knew.

Her pulse thundered, and the slick wet of a tongue slid down her wrist. She gasped, jerked out of the making of her painting. Blinking she looked down at herself, not recognizing what she saw at first. Then the smears and splatters of paint marring her skin penetrated her understanding.

"Damn." She dumped the brush in a jar and grabbed a rag to stop the trail of red paint that had slid down her wrist and was halfway to her elbow. All the colors of the rainbow and anything in between dotted her skin. "At least I put a cloth down when I set up my stuff," she muttered.

The pleasure and pain captured on the canvas drew her back, threatening to lure her in again. Almost like a memory that teased at the edge of the mind. His eyes stared into hers, and she shivered.

The hickey burned.

Backing up a step, she took stock. *Sleep. That's all. I just need some sleep, restful sleep.*

Her body still hummed from the feel of his lips and body pressed against hers; on a sigh, she took herself to the shower. After a quick scrub to remove the paint, she fell naked and damp into her bed. Hugging a pillow to herself, she passed out.

The deep scent of pine writhed through her. Crisp air caressed her face. Her booted feet sank into loam with each step. Soft bird calls floated by, and she turned a corner on the wooded trail. A stone cottage stood in the middle of a huge clearing. Smoke curled out of the chimney, and the setting sun hit the window glass and shot shards of light through the trees.

The path led to the door.

Summer flowers, now fading, rioted around the base of the stones. Red apples still clung among the changing foliage of the orchard trees that she glimpsed behind the English cottage. She stomped her feet on the steps to knock off any clinging dirt, then lifted the antique door latch. Honey, wax, and the musty scent of burning peat greeted her. Inside she stripped off her jacket and hung it on a peg next to the door. Candles already burned in sconces throughout the room, the light from the sun fading from the windows fast.

"I had hoped I could bring you here quickly."

Dae's voice broke the stillness and shivered through her. As her eyes adjusted to the change in light, she found him lounging on a thick sheepskin in front of the glowing hearth. Wooden platters of bread and cheese and things she didn't recognize awaited on the stones. The desire to sink into the plush softness he'd laid out shot through her, but she held off.

"Bring me?"

He smiled. "You set the stage for the previous dreams we've shared. But I had a shock tonight. After I got home from our dinner, the whole family was waiting. Can we say intervention time?"

"Intervention for what?" She bent and unlaced her boots, toeing them off next to the door, then paced across the room to look down at what awaited her. "Where are we?"

"Some place I used to know. I...I needed to see you."

She sank down onto the plush fleece, the softness distracting her for a moment. Then she said, "I don't normally dream like this. But since I met you it seems to be all I'm doing. What's going on? Intervention?"

He sighed and poked at the fire a bit with the poker. "That's what I needed to talk about. I don't understand what's going on. I shouldn't be here. Not like this. Not with you. I haven't dreamed like this in a very long time either. I don't know why I feel this driving need to talk to you. To explain. It's not like you'll remember what I tell you. Humans never do. They can't remember like we do."

"Humans?" She started to laugh, but his eyes turned to her, pinning her with his gaze.

"I've put you in danger. I've betrayed my family. But I can't stop. I. Can't. Stop. Your emotion is the only energy that soaks into my storeground now. I don't know what to do. I just know I need you."

She reached out and brushed her palm along his cheek. "Slow down. I'm not following."

He closed his eyes and leaned into her hand. "I'm Kelusis. What you might know as an incubus. We are a symbiotic species with yours. There's a lot of inaccurate legends and myths surrounding us. Thousands of years ago a group of *Maeuri*—I think the closest translation would be magician? Alchemist maybe?—they discovered us and didn't or wouldn't understand that it's a symbiotic relationship with your species. They viewed us as parasitic. They took it upon themselves to rid humans of our kind. Kelusis are both incubus and succubus; we are able to shift between the two sexes. But a group of humans managed to steal our other half. In my case my succubus, so now I'm stuck as an incubus, which is the male form of my species. When they sundered us, they made it so we could no longer feed properly. Somehow, they knew that would starve us."

She pulled away, but he caught her hand. "Feed?"

"Symbiotic, remember." He held her hand, his fingers brushing her skin. "Yes, we feed off of you. We take in your emotions. Or more accurately the energy your emotions create. By taking it we give your species stability and renewal. We drain the clogging energy humans continuously generate to keep your species from going mad. Since the sundering, we haven't been able to do our job. Look at the last three thousand years or so of your history. You've gone from being a centered, environmentally concerned species to wantonly destroying our planet. Without us filtering the excess you generate, it spirals down into selfish, self-centered, uncaring, self-destructive...in general, mad behavior."

"I'm confused. Why can't you do your job as you put it? You are obviously still here. And you said you are taking my energy. And why am I not freaking out about this?"

"Probably because we are in Shadow, the dream realm. Here anything is possible to your subconscious. So you wouldn't find things you would freak out about in the physical world to be strange." He let go of her hand—the sudden lack of warmth bothered her—and leaned back to look up at the ceiling. "Our doctors were able to come up with a stopgap to allow us some means to feed, but they haven't discovered how to cure us yet. Our court passed laws making concourse with humans punishable with death. The human's death. Which means we cannot perform our other vitally important contribution, renewing your creative bloodlines."

"Our death? That doesn't make sense. We wouldn't have any say if you came along; we don't know about you."

"The sundering happened because of tainted humans. They were sent as a Trojan horse, and when we had sex with one, our other half was ripped out. So the court passed the laws."

"Wait, wait, wait, back up. You crossbred with us?"

"No. Not really. It's complicated, OK? The babies were always human, our involvement just gave them...more? You still have stories and myths of some—Socrates, Merlin, Robin Hood, Benjamin Franklin."

"But those are all people younger than when you say this started."

"True, some were sired illegally, and the Kelusis involved were punished if caught. Some were in the already-established lines of descendants."

"Too many questions." She wrapped her arms around her knees. "Where does that leave us?"

He turned his head to look at her. "I don't know."

"I haven't been able to get you out of my head, Dae. This scares me."

He sat up and turned to face her. "Me too. I don't understand what's happened. I want to stay away. I don't want to put you in danger. But I can't stop."

He lifted his hand and slowly reached for her, giving her time to pull away, until his fingertips brushed her cheek. She licked her lips and his gaze zeroed in.

"Why here? Why didn't you come back to my apartment and tell me this in person?"

"That gets us back to the intervention. They know about you. We are not supposed to feed from the same human more than once, from a distance. Certainly not get to know them or go out on dates. They won't let me out again. This was the only way to see you without letting them know where you are. And they will be looking for you." He closed his eyes. "I'm sorry I wasn't strong enough to stay away."

The lump in her throat threatened to choke her. His fingers, so gentle, stilled. She reached up and brushed the pads of her fingers along his lips. "I need to see you too."

His eyes snapped open. Both held the other with the lightest caress, but the strength locking them together belied that gentleness.

Each leaned in until their lips met. With the first brush of his tongue, the fires he'd started on the dock after dinner reignited. She moaned and he pressed her back onto the fleece. His weight covered her and she shifted her legs restlessly until he slid his thigh between them, pinning her hips. She gasped and threaded her hands into his hair to pull him closer. His hands started to rove, sliding up under her shirt, her skin tingling in anticipation.

The silk of his hair slipped through her fingers, and she fought for control of the kiss. But the moment his thumb brushed against a hard nipple, she lost. He knew just how to touch her to make sure he retained control. She moaned and pressed upward. His teeth nipped her lip, then the flat of his tongue soothed across it. He continued the movement with nipping kisses along her jaw and down her neck. His rock-hard thigh pressed tight to the vee of her pants, holding her hips, preventing her from the movement she craved. She could feel the hard ridge encased in the leather of his pants, pressed against the sensitive juncture of her hip.

He'd managed to ruck up her shirt without her noticing. A hot wet mouth teased at her nipple and she caught her breath. She pulled her hands from his hair and sent them down his sides, wanting to get skin to skin, but he grabbed them both and transferred them to one hand, pressing them into the soft fleece above her head.

She squirmed and he just chuckled against her breast. The vibration made her moan. He continued to toy with her breasts, occasionally sliding his thigh against her. Her breaths came in pants. He finally reached between them and unbuttoned her jeans, maneuvering them over her hips and shoving them down and off before his leather-clad thigh pushed against her again. The buttery soft leather gently abraded her whenever he shifted, and she tried to spread her legs.

His entire body felt incredible against her, but she wanted more. She tugged at her held wrists and tried to push against his thigh. All that got her was a change of position. His. He'd had a soft cord ready because next she knew her hands were still held above her head, but he was now free to use both of his against her. He sat back between her thighs and ran his palms over her skin. Now she could lift her hips but there was no pressure left to help.

"Come to me, Dae. I don't want to wait."

"I know, sweet, but you'll have to. I'm starving, and the more I make you burn the more energy you'll produce."

What started was the most intense experience of her life. Dae played her like a fine instrument. Keeping her writhing and sobbing on edge. He controlled her like she had strings. She was almost afraid at times that her body would have a heart attack with the way her pulse raced.

The torment only got worse when he finally lost his clothes and she had the added stimulation of his slick skin sliding all over her. Begging did little good; true to his word, he fed off of her for what felt like hours. Her only consolation was that his most dangerous weapon against her showed the effects of the torment too.

He made the mistake of bringing it near her face as he concentrated on her chest. She stared at the gleaming purple head, a bead of moisture on the tip. Then he leaned over her and she took her chance. Rearing forward, she engulfed him and he yelled at the sudden intense stimulation. A full body shudder racked him and he pressed forward.

Her pleasure spiraled as she tasted him. A need blossomed and she did everything she could to maintain the control she'd wrested from him. She needed him inside of her, but she needed something else first.

She sucked and his shaft hardened more, then pulsed.

"No." He moaned, and the disbelief in his voice caught her attention, but not for long. She could feel the strangled grip he had on the fleece near her head as he rocked against her. At first she thought she'd won and forced him to come, but what she swallowed was nothing she'd ever experienced before. The burning knot of need it left simmering in her belly made her moan.

He pulled out and stared at her.

"I don't understand. This isn't possible." He looked dazed, but then his body shuddered and he gripped himself. "You are human, I am Sundered. And this is the dream realm. I can't produce *ullaich* here."

The strange word triggered a warm purr deep in her head in a place she didn't recognize.

He covered her and she let the thought slip away, the teasing tormentor gone. He rubbed all over her like a big cat scent-marking before he settled between her thighs and plunged into her overly ready body. She arched bowstring tight as he buried to the hilt and froze.

She could feel the pulsing, the erotic burning, as the *ullaich* bathed her inside before he started the last dance. On a long drawn-out moan, she lifted her hips in time with his thrusts, his control gone.

Sweat slicked them, and she undulated, reaching for the peak that he'd held out of her reach for so long. She wished he'd untied her hands so she could feel him finally. He must have heard her thoughts because somehow the bonds loosened and she ran her hands down the muscles along his spine to grip his backside. His gaze sought hers out and they stared into each other. His arms caged her in as he covered her, the solid strength of him plunging into her. Trembling, she finally caught the edge and started to pull herself over. On a scream, she leapt and he followed.

She could feel the pulsing inside as he made a last couple of thrusts, but the movement didn't feel right. Not bad, exactly, but he should have slid with no resistance—instead he felt stuck. Then, lodged deep inside as far as he could go, he stopped. A deep moan rolled out of him.

Beginning to panic, she realized he really *was* stuck. She felt glued, though the hot spark deep inside still pulsed from him. He tried not to collapse on her, so he fell to the side, pulling her up against his chest, his leg thrown over her, pulling her tighter to him.

Groggy, he kissed her temple and shushed her. "This is normal. We'll be stuck for a while. It's how a Kelusis's body works when..." He trailed off.

"When?" She yawned.

"It's a dream, not truly real. So I don't know what it means. We can talk about it later." He hugged her tighter and rubbed her back—not that she needed any help getting to sleep after the exhausting stimulus he'd put her through.

Erik took a sip of his scotch and looked at his family. They all sat around the big oak table at one end of the kitchen. Maggie puttered as quietly as she could, finishing up dinner. The descendants were all staying in the background, he noticed. *Guess they can tell something's up.* He sighed. The worry caused a knot in his stomach.

"He's still out," Erik continued the conversation.

"How long do we let him sleep for? It's almost twenty-four hours," Isaac said.

He rubbed the bridge of his nose. "I don't know. I drained his storeground before he went upstairs. He probably went to sleep fairly quickly after that, but he was feeding again last night. I couldn't pull his psyche back. That hasn't happened before. Every time he's gone out in his dreams to feed I could yank him out, but not this time. I siphoned the incoming energy off all night. I'm not looking forward to it, but I have to tie his psyche down now. We'll have enough trouble with the enforcers as it is without them finding out he's freely hunting Shadow as well."

Callum snorted. "Oh, he's going to love that."

"He's going to love having me as a hunting partner even more." Erik toyed with his glass.

"But, you don't like to go out," Cass responded.

He shrugged. "I'm the most suitable. I can control him. Isaac would be incapacitated, you wouldn't be strong enough if he loses more of himself and doesn't care if he hurts you, and Callum would likely hurt *him*. Besides, I'll need to siphon him off as he feeds, otherwise he'll lose most of it as it drains through the sand."

They were all silent for a moment.

"Will you be OK?" Isaac finally asked.

He drained his drink. "I'll have to be. There isn't a lot of choice, now is there?" He turned to Callum. "Anything?"

He shook his head. "No luck. I spent a fruitless afternoon sitting in the sun. No sign of her."

"She's a threat. We need to find her. Cass?"

"Bob only knew her first name. Alexis. She hadn't been in before, at least not that any of the descendants working there could remember. Jake worked the gate that night, and he said she seemed especially unsure going in. But Bob was pretty concerned. He told me that Dae hasn't been acting normal or rational. And he confirmed that Dae kissed her. Though what Isaac couldn't tell from the floor was that Dae had everyone's attention. And there were a lot of descendants watching and a few other families as well. So word will spread."

"Clock's ticking." Erik scrubbed his hands across his face, ending with them tented against his lips as he thought. "We have to get this settled before the enforcers arrive. I guess when Dae wakes we'll have to see if we can't get more out of him."

Chapter 9

DAE'S MIND DRIFTED TO wakefulness and he stared at the blank wall of his room when he opened his eyes. His stomach tried to claw its way through his backbone, and his storeground lay parched. None of her energy remained and he wanted to cry at the loss. His mind felt torn again. An echo from centuries ago. He drifted in and out of the here and now. Snippets of memories, physical and dream, floated uncontrolled through his mind. Times from before the sundering, snapshots of the centuries since, and the most vivid—his time with Alexis.

He rolled to his back and groaned unexpectedly. His body needed, and the proof lay like steel between his legs. That brought him to full wakefulness. He was an incubus after all, so he wasn't unused to the drive for sex. But since he was no longer whole, the actual act had come few and far between, and mostly by his hand. All of the links had their challenges. His was the basic need and drive for sex that he wasn't allowed to fulfill. Not since the laws prohibiting congress with humans went into effect. The Kelusis generally didn't want to spend any time with a Sundered, especially of an intimate nature. He'd tried with a few other Sundered early on, but it just made the drive to feed from a human properly harder to control. The memory of physical pleasure, when he'd still been whole, forever haunted him. Add to that the fact that the energy he pulled in was lust energy, which triggered a biological response. He needed to have sex.

But this was worse. *Why did I dream of* ullaich? *I want her more than anyone, but it doesn't make sense.*

An unmistakable burning had started to heat in his groin, and he shook his head in shock. *No. It was a dream. It didn't really happen.*

Still, he couldn't deny the fact that he felt the *ullaich* as it slowly formed in him. He kicked the blankets off his feet and rose shakily. He had too many demands on his body: food, energy, and now this. The physical need would only continue to grow, he knew, until the drive to bond had been completed.

She's human. They would never allow this. Not normally prone to panic, he succumbed to the whirling chaos of his thoughts. *They will kill her if they find out. I can't...*

He doubled over and gripped his grinding stomach. *I've already put everyone at risk.*

Straightening, he hobbled into his closet. He yanked items off of hangers and pulled them on. He plucked his phone out of his dirty jeans and sank into a chair. Resting his elbows on his knees, he stared at the lit screen of his phone. Her number stared at him from the contacts listing. *I'm betraying them. They are my family, they have been for centuries, but this is different. How can I take the chance and try to explain it to them when I know the laws are immediate termination? How could I put Erik in that position with the court? No one would ever believe the impossible. Bonding with a human isn't possible. A human can't be a Kelusis's soul mate.*

His need for her energy pushed him and he started a text stream.

"Lexi, it's me, Dae. I just needed to check on you and see if you're all right. And..." *And what? She's going to think everything that happened last night was a dream and not real. And that's if she remembers. So why would I know what happened to her? But with all the strangeness, why am I assuming she won't remember?* Ullaich *isn't possible either.*

He erased it and rubbed his eyes with a thumb and finger. *It's not safe to assume she isn't affected somehow. If bonding really has started... And she's made references to our dreams together in our physical world encounters.*

He started again. "Lexi, it's me, Dae. Text me when you get this. Please."

He hit send. He waited, but no reply came. *I only just woke up. I need to assume she just hasn't woken yet—not that she wants nothing to do with me. Or worse, that Erik and the others already found her. They've had all night and day to.*

Well, I can't hide in here forever. He rose and

adjusted himself before starting to walk carefully out of his rooms. He could hear the rumble of conversation in the kitchen. So much for just getting some food quietly and going back to his room. He steeled himself and entered. The family congregated around the breakfast table. He ignored them, along with the fact that their silence descended the moment he walked in. Maggie gave him an uncertain smile, but his eyes dropped away from her, and he opened the fridge. She shooed him out of the way and tossed a plate together quicker than he could have. That left him with the uncomfortable situation of no longer having something to do with his hands as an excuse to ignore the others.

"Dae?" Erik called softly.

He stiffened his shoulders and refused to turn.

"Please? You know you can't run from this. From us. You might as well get it over with."

"No, thank you." He closed his eyes and felt Maggie's hand pick up his to wrap it around the plate. He tried to give her a smile but ended up just turning away from the sad look in her eyes.

"Get your arse over here, Dae, or I'll pick it up and bring it over," Callum threw out.

"You've pushed us far enough, Dae," Erik added.

He walked stiffly to the table and dropped his plate with a clatter, his gaze meeting each of theirs in turn. "Get used to it," he snapped.

Erik sighed. "What do you expect? What do you want us to do? You know as well as the rest of us what the law is."

His stomach chose that moment to make itself known to the room at large and he winced and bent slightly before he could control himself. He took several deep breaths through his nose.

"Sit and eat," Erik ordered.

There was no way they were going to let him go, so he pulled out the chair and sat before he started to stuff the food in. He kept his eyes locked on the plate.

"We know her name is Alexis. Where does she live?"

He shook his head and continued to eat.

"Why did you put her in danger if you didn't want her hurt? You know better than to get involved with a donor," Erik said in exasperation.

He stopped chewing for a minute and just met their stares before he spoke, "You don't understand, and there's nothing I can say that will make you understand."

"You can't see her again, Dae. Already what's been revealed will send the enforcers through the roof. You've put me in the position of needing to destroy an innocent life. That doesn't make me happy."

"No one is forcing you to," he said softly.

"Really?"

He clenched his fork. "Those laws were made by scared people who have no care for the consequences of their actions. Be a bigger man and don't follow blindly."

"I don't," he snapped. "But you haven't exactly been forthcoming. We have no reason to think there would be any value in not following the laws."

"I can't take the chance."

Erik barked out a laugh. "So many years. We have been your family. We love you. What happened? Why don't you trust us?"

He spread his arms. "Where am I, Erik? Was I talked to? Given any choice? Listened to? I didn't want the bond conduit opened."

"Don't you dare try and lay that blame on me. No, I didn't give you a choice. I had the whole family to think about. But you made your choice not to trust us before that, Dae. When you lied and ran."

"Erik, you know the fade is affecting his thinking and judgement," Cass said softly.

Dae turned back to his food. "Doesn't matter. I won't help you find her."

"Was it she you hunted last night?"

His gaze snapped up and Erik's trapped his.

"I thought as much. How long have you been dreamwalking with her? You pulled so much energy in last night that I suppose there's a hope that you already took care of the problem."

Horror washed through him and he dropped his fork. *Is that why she didn't answer my text? No, no, when I left her in Shadow she was fine. Don't second guess yourself. You would know if you harmed her.* He rose. "I'm through. I'm going back to my room, if I'm excused?"

"Not yet. We still have a few things to go over, so sit down and finish eating."

He couldn't deny that he was hungry since his middle continued to make noises. He sank back down and ignored everyone's stares by focusing on his plate.

"It'll be you and I out hunting tonight."

That caught his attention and his head snapped up. "You can't."

"Just because it's not easy or pleasant doesn't mean I can't. We leave about nine."

He shook his head. "No. I'm not hunting tonight."

"Boys…" Erik said. His brothers, who sat on either side of him, pinned his arms to the table faster than he could react. Erik rose to walk around the table. "I'm willing to let it go tonight, but we will hunt tomorrow, Dae."

When Erik reached his side, the center reached out and placed his hand over his heart again. He tried to jerk his head away, but the other hand still took control of his third eye.

"We're in enough trouble as it is when the enforcers get here. I can't take the chance of them finding you hunting in Shadow."

No! Alexis. I have to be able to get to her.

He couldn't pull away and Erik made quick work in his head, tethering his psyche so he could no longer travel out. The weight of the mental ropes pressed against him, and his body rebelled. He convulsed. Erik caught him.

"Damn it, Dae. I hate doing this to you." The chair had clattered over as Erik cradled his body. His mind clawed at the imprisonment so he barely noticed when the others surrounded them. "Let's get him back to bed. Hopefully once he's calmed down he can get some actual sleep for a change."

Turned inward, he flexed and pulled, trying to get free, crying out into the gray dreamscape for Alexis.

Gnawing hunger finally pulled Alexis from sleep. She rolled over in her bed, clutching her stomach. The gripping pain eventually faded enough that she could sit up. Rubbing her eyes, she looked at the clock. Half an hour before she needed to be up to get ready for work. Her stomach sounded long and loud in the quiet of the apartment, and she swung her legs over the edge of the mattress. *At least Thursdays are usually straightforward. I won't need to think too much. And it'll give Amber time to grill me.* She grinned and shuffled out to the kitchen.

In the refrigerator she stared at the sparse contents. She settled for tossing some bacon in the microwave and started frying eggs. Her stomach contracting, she ate them as soon as they came off the stove, burning her mouth in the process, and then she cracked more into the pan. It wasn't until she reached for another egg and the carton was empty that she realized that she'd eaten the whole half dozen, along with all of the bacon and almost half a gallon of orange juice.

She cleaned up her mess while her mind wandered and she found herself smiling as she recalled the latest dream. But her smile faded as some of what Dae said penetrated. *An incubus?* She rubbed the mark he had left on her neck. *I don't know.*

She thought about her unexpected and strong attraction to him—and all of the dreams. The obsession. She glanced around at all of the paintings she had done. All excellent. All of Damian.

The last one, of him on the bed, drew her back. She crouched down where she had leaned it against the wall. Her fingers reached out to brush his face and the remembered pain echoed. She jerked her hand away.

Her breathing harsh, she stood and backed away, then headed into the bedroom. She fumbled around, digging under a few piles until she located her phone. The screen lit up with fifteen missed text messages and several missed calls mixed in.

"What the…"

And the date.

Her legs gave out and she plopped to the floor. "Saturday? I slept for two days?"

She stared dumbly at the phone for a few minutes, her brain not processing the truth. *Work. I didn't show up for two days.* Her fingers trembling, she swiped the phone and started reading the messages from Dae. Cryptic, but he sounded worried. *Maybe the voice mail will be more clear.*

The sound of his voice soothed something inside, but the messages weren't any clearer than his texts. Just to text him back as soon as she could, but not to call. Suddenly what he had said in the dream felt a lot more important. She pulled the hair at her temple, trying to remember everything he had said, but the incredible blinding pleasure they had shared dimmed out what she was looking for. Her dreams couldn't be real, but the evidence was making that rational thought harder to believe.

Finally she just set her trembling fingers to typing a message. "I'm here." That was all she could think of.

A return came in immediately. "Thank the stars. Stay home."

"What?"

"Can't talk safely yet. Don't text right now."

Well that was annoying. She huffed out a breath. Now what?

My job, she thought in despair. Two days of no call no show.

She continued listening to the voice mails. The stress in Dae's voice twisted her gut. The worry in Amber's brought guilt to the surface. And the disappointment in her boss's voice when he left a message telling her she was terminated made her want to crawl into a hole.

She wiped the back of her hand across her eyes, then scrolled through her contacts for Amber's number.

"What the hell, Lex? Are you all right? I was worried you were in an accident. Where've you been? I tried to talk to Mathew. He knew this wasn't like you, but it's an automatic termination with two consecutive no shows. Unless you've got a doctor's note?"

"I know, I know. I'm sorry Amber. I wish I did."

"Are you all right?"

"I don't know. I went to sleep Wednesday night."

"What? It's Saturday. Where are you? Did he do something to you?"

"I'm home. No. It's not like that. Dae is wonderful."

"People don't just pass out for a couple of days, Lexi. Have you gone to the doctor?"

"I just woke up."

"You need to go to the doctor now. Get tested for drugs in your system or something. Do you feel all right? Maybe he did something physical."

Oh, he did something physical all right. She smiled at the memory, but then reality intruded as she thought about the story he'd spun. *An incubus?* she wondered again. "I'll make an appointment, OK? But really, he's nice. Nothing like that happened. You know I haven't been sleeping well lately. It probably caught up to me. Though I'm not really pleased to lose my job over it."

"You weren't happy here anyway," Amber said. "I'd prefer if you went into the emergency room."

She sighed. "I feel fine. What would they say? And it's so expensive. I'll get the first appointment the office will give me, OK?"

"If that's the best I can get," she grumbled. "I'll get your desk packed up. We can get together next week so I can give it to you."

"Thanks. I'm really sorry."

"I'm just glad you're OK. I was getting seriously worried. If I hadn't heard from you in the next twenty-four hours, I was going to call the cops."

Lexi rubbed her hand across her eyes. "Thank you, again. You're a great friend."

Amber snorted. "Just make sure that new boyfriend of yours isn't to blame for this."

With a self-conscious chuckle, she bid Amber good-bye. *She hit too close to home,* she thought as she hung up the phone. She rose onto wobbly legs and started to pace the narrow path through her apartment. *Is he really what he says he is? If he'd told me this at dinner, I'd have dumped him into the nutjob category. But either I made it all up myself, and I'm the nut, or he was really there all the times I...*

She felt the blood rush to her face as she remembered how she had acted during some of those dreams. *Oh god.* She took a deep breath to keep from hyperventilating. *He knew. He was there. He remembered the sand from the tropical beach. He mentioned it at our picnic. He came back. Each dream he came back even though I'd... And that last dream...*

She gripped the phone tighter in her hand, willing it to sound an incoming text. *It wasn't me doing the pursuing that time,* she reassured herself.

So if I start looking at the dreams with the assumption that they were as real as now... She flipped through the memories, trying to recall everything Dae had said, especially in the last dream. *He said I would be in danger if his family found out about me. Is that why he called and texted so many times? And why did I sleep for forty-eight hours?*

No answers would be forthcoming until Dae got in touch with her. All she could do was trust him and stay home.

⇜⚜⇝

Dae leaned against the rail and looked down at the floor three stories below. Pacific Place was packed since it was a Saturday night. People jostled one another on the escalators and thronged the restaurants behind him. He and Erik had just finished eating and now he reluctantly sorted through energy threads floating in the air. The relief of having his psyche untied was almost enough to reconcile the guard. Almost.

The family had been in nearly constant attendance. The need to talk to her, to explain, ate holes in his temper. He'd managed a couple of quick texts during the long day to reassure her that he wasn't ignoring her but that he wasn't alone. He could tell she was just as frustrated. He feared she would grow too impatient with his lack of communication and leave her apartment. And with his siblings looking for her...

He stared out over the huge open space; eventually he found a likely thread and pulled. Still nothing. He couldn't absorb any of the power he felt wafting around.

He clenched his fist.

"Do you want to try the theater?" Erik asked.

He looked past Erik's shoulder and across the concourse to the theater's entrance. But the idea of sitting cooped up for a couple of hours, when he couldn't hunt like normal, grated.

"How about them?" Erik pointed to a couple who sat cuddling on a bench. Normally an easy mark, he could push their already focused interest in each other and make them take it farther. If he had wanted, he could have pushed them to full-on sex on the floor. Not that he would do that to someone in a public place like this. But there were parties he'd attended long ago...

"I can't."

"Dae, you aren't trying."

"Fuck off, Erik."

"Are you really going to starve yourself? Cause yourself this kind of pain? Because of a human?"

He turned on his center, grabbing the collar of his shirt, though the threat was pointless because his grip and movements were so obviously weak. "You don't know what you're talking about." He shoved away and limped off. Erik was at his side after a stride.

"Dae, you haven't harvested anything tonight. You have to be in tremendous pain with your storeground so empty."

He laughed and wasn't happy with the hysterical edge he could make out in it. Apparently neither was Erik from the look he cast him.

"We are so done, Erik."

His center shot another worried look at him but didn't respond. He completely sympathized with Erik's worry. The fact that he couldn't harvest any type of energy left him numb in shock and fear. As he looked back over the last few days, he realized that he hadn't actually been taking in any other energy except Alexis's.

He wished Erik would believe him, but he understood why he didn't. What was happening to him had never happened to another Kelusis. It just wasn't possible to have fertile seed form in Shadow, and with a human no less. And only the Chirurgeons could alter his uptake nerves to change what energy he could absorb. So of course Erik would think he was obstinately refusing to feed. He sighed. He needed to go to her. He ducked down the corridor that led to the bathrooms. He paused outside, but Erik just leaned up against the opposite wall. Pushing through the doors alone, he walked past the urinals. A quick glance showed the stalls were empty, so he slipped into one and locked the door, then pulled out his phone.

"Lexi?" he typed and sent.

"Are you alone yet? I've been waiting all day. What's going on?"

"For a second. Not long. They should let me retire to my room soon. Then I'll be able to call."

"Are you OK?"

"I don't know. Promise you won't leave your apartment. The family is looking for you."

"I've told you I won't, but for how long? I don't have a ton of food here."

"Can you call for takeout?"

"Is that safe?"

"Safer than going out, I think."

"What is happening?"

"I don't know."

"So this is all real? Everything you said?"

"What do you mean?"

"The dreams. At the stone cottage. You told me you weren't human."

"How do you remember? You shouldn't. I'm

sorry, Lexi. Yes, it's real. Damn it, I have to go. I'll call you the moment I'm alone for the night."

"I hope it's soon. Bye."

He stuck his phone back in his pocket, kicking the flush valve so it would make noise. After washing his hands, he joined Erik out in the hall.

"Are you sure you won't hunt, Dae?'

"I can't. I've told you that."

Erik sighed and the two of them walked down to the parking garage to retrieve Erik's car.

After he pulled out into traffic, Erik asked, "How long do you think you can go? Hunger striking like this won't help you. Do you really care so little for the rest of us?"

"You just won't listen or believe me, will you? It's not *won't*, Erik, it's *can't*. I can't take in the energy."

"If that's true, then give me the info I need, Dae."

"I won't tell you where to find her."

Erik's hand tightened on the steering wheel. That was the only sign of his frustration. Dae turned to look out the window. The rest of the drive went in silence.

At home Dae slipped his shoes off and put them in the closet. He turned to tell Erik he was going to his room, but his center slapped a hand to his heart and head, invaded at a rush. Dae fell back against the wall as Erik tied his psyche down again.

Grimly Erik took his hands away. "I'm sorry, but you have to stay locked down."

He felt like throwing up as he clawed at his prison on the inside. Outside he turned his hurt gaze on his center. "I need to, Erik," he whispered.

"If you can hunt that way, you should have hunted tonight."

Dae turned away and stumbled up the stairs. Once in his room, he locked the door. Then as a precaution he went into his bathroom and shut that door. He sat down on the toilet and tried to calm his thoughts. They pushed against the restraints to no avail. He took a deep breath and pulled out his phone, dialing her number with shaking hands.

"Hello."

"Alexis." His gravelly voice didn't sound like his own to his ears.

"Dae? Are you all right?"

"No. They're hunting you. I can't get out. I need you."

"I don't think I like your family much."

That surprised a bit of laughter from him. "It's not their fault. I'm sorry this is such a bad introduction to them. They care very deeply for me. That's why they're doing this. They think they are protecting me."

"From what?"

"From breaking the law, from the enforcers, from dangers I wouldn't be strong enough to fight in Shadow. I don't know what's going on between us, but this isn't something that any of us have seen before. That's why they're acting like this."

"I need you too, Dae."

He closed his eyes as her voice washed over him.

"We can be together in our dreams like we have before though, right?"

He swallowed. "No. Erik tied my psyche. That

stops me from being able to dream." He clenched the phone. "I don't know how long I can last, Lexi. I'm so hungry."

"What do we do?"

"I don't know yet. I haven't told them where you are, but they got your name from Bob. So be suspicious of anyone, Lexi. I'd tell you to run, hide. But it wouldn't do any good. I don't think you can be apart from me any more than I can from you. Besides, the reach of the Kelusis is everywhere. It's impossible to hide for long from the enforcers. If something doesn't feel right, get somewhere crowded and stay there. The more people, the harder it'll be for a Kelusis to control them. Above all, control your emotions. They will use them against you. I need to figure out what's happening to us. I'll call you as often as I can."

"OK. I'm scared."

"Lexi, I'm sorry. I wish I could have walked away from you. I didn't want to put you in danger."

"Call me."

"I will, I promise. I need to go. Bye."

"Bye," she whispered, then hung up the phone.

He watched the screen go dark. Finally he got up and checked the bedroom to make sure no one had gotten through his door, then he got undressed and climbed into bed. It was still early, but what did he have to be awake for?

Chapter 10

ALEXIS TOSSED IN HER tangled bedding and gave up the illusion of rest. Wisps of frustrated dreams flittered through her sleep-fogged brain. Dreams of hunting for Dae—and finding him behind a big glass window. She wasn't able to get to him.

Her body needed him just as much as her mind it seemed. She rose and tried splashing water on her face, hoping it would bring her to alertness. All it did was get her wet. With a yawn she checked her phone, glad she hadn't slept through any messages from him.

She popped a couple of slices of pizza from last night into the microwave. Methodically chewing, she assessed the painting she had done yesterday. As good as the others, it thankfully didn't evoke the same phantom memory of pain that the bed scene did. Her gaze slid to the painting in question. Uncomfortable she walked over and flipped it toward the wall, then stacked a few others in front of it for good measure.

Losing herself in the trance of creating was much more preferable to the uncertainty of the unknown she was facing, the unanswered questions, the fear.

She closed her eyes, wishing her phone would ring or a text message would break the silence. But it stayed stubbornly quiet. Looking out again, she picked up a blank canvas and let her mind go, finding the inspiration she needed for the creation. Her eyes stared into a middle ground, between the canvas and her thoughts, and she started to paint.

Later that night Erik sat around the table with the rest of the family. They all looked as tired as he felt. Maggie shook her head sadly when she walked into the room, a full plate of food on a tray that she proceeded to wrap up and put in the fridge.

"All right, we've given him as much time as we can. Something about this just doesn't feel right, and he's damaged enough that he's not thinking clearly. The court has to have gotten word on our situation by now, which means we have enforcers and Chirurgeons in our very near future. I had hoped one of us could get him to open up and give us the information we need to find her and help him. But he's not budging. I really didn't want to betray him this way."

"You're sure he's talking to her?" Callum asked.

"With how obsessed he is, I think he'd be fighting to leave the building more if he wasn't at least communicating somehow. And we need to find out before we are hampered by the authorities."

Callum pushed his chair back with a scrape. "Let's do this thing."

Erik noted the grim look behind the anger link's eyes. They all rose and followed him up the stairs. Erik knocked at Dae's door. No answer, which didn't surprise him much. "Dae, open the door. If you don't, Callum's going to break it."

He listened and could make out slow footfalls on the carpet; he held his hand up to Callum. The latch scraped, but the door didn't move. Erik grasped the knob and pushed it open. Dae trudged slowly back over to the bed where he sat down against the pillows he'd propped up. He clicked the remote for the TV and the box shut off. "So to what do I owe the honor of this visit?"

Erik turned to Cass, who stood just outside the door, behind Isaac. "Call it," he said softly. He didn't want to have to search the entire suite for the phone. He turned back to Dae just in time to see him pale as his phone vibrated. He had it on the bed tucked under the blanket, but the lust link's body language gave it away. Dae grabbed it and hauled back his arm, but Callum sprang across the bed, his big hand engulfing Dae's wrist before the lust link could hurl the phone and shatter it. Which Erik was sure was his intention. He walked over to the bed.

He could hear Cass sobbing against Isaac's shoulder. Dae struggled fruitlessly against the stronger anger link. Erik pulled the undamaged phone from his clutching fingers.

"No, Erik, please," he begged.

Callum kept Dae pinned to the bed, and Erik started to thumb through the phone.

"It's here. And she knows way more than she should." He looked deep into Dae's shattered eyes. "I wish you would have trusted us. Callum, Isaac, stay here with Dae. Cass, you'll come with me."

"No!"

"We'll be back in an hour. Keep him here."

"Cass, don't. Please, no. Don't kill her, Cass."

He walked past Isaac, who gripped him lightly on the shoulder with sympathy, then he pushed the door shut behind them.

Cass looked at him with tears in her eyes. "You want me to use my power on her?"

"If this had been a normal situation, where we had to get rid of a human, then yes. But something's not right here. He's too obsessed. He's sick, Cass. We have to get to the bottom of what's going on. And we can't do that without her. Is she doing this to him? Is it a new Trojan horse? We have to have answers before the court shows up. Not only to protect Dae, but to protect the Kelusis."

The sounds of sobbing reached them through the door, and he turned away, his heart heavy. He and Cass walked quietly down the stairs to his office. The soft leather of his chair embraced him, and he stared at the cellphone he placed on the desk. He blinked, then woke up his computer and started typing. Cass settled into the chair opposite the desk. Erik said, "I have her number now. With a bit of digging I can get her address. I'll lure her out, to the park, I think, by texting and pretending to be Dae. I want you to go to her living space."

"Why flush her out? Why not both of us go to her home?"

"Too dangerous. I doubt she's going to come willingly. Not after the conversation I glimpsed in their text stream. In the park she's just another stranger, less traceable if there's a scene with witnesses. I need you to search her living space and find out all you can. Maybe a clue to the answer we seek is there."

It didn't take long for him to get what he needed out of the computer. He scrawled her address on a bit of paper and handed it over to Cassandra. "I'll let you get a head start before I set her in motion. I'll meet you back here. I doubt I'll be long in securing her, but if you do get back before me don't go near Dae."

She nodded and rose, then with a swirl of her skirts she left. Since he had a few minutes to kill before Cass got in place, he punched the human's name into Google and started to read.

Lexi took a bite of her sandwich and glanced at her phone for the hundredth time. Dae had been texting her steadily all evening. Then it all stopped about an hour ago. She sighed and took a drink. She stood at her kitchen counter because for safety's sake she never ate at her easel. Too easy to get lost in the picture and drink the wrong thing. And she wasn't willing to give up the room in her tiny apartment for a table to eat at. *I suppose I could clear off things from the little end table, but that's too much work. I'd rather scarf then get back to painting.*

Her phone lit up and buzzed on the counter. She dropped her sandwich and picked up the phone before it finished vibrating. A swipe of her thumb brought up the stream.

"Sorry to disappear like that on you. They all came in."

"I thought that was probably the case."

"The good news is they're gone. They all went hunting and left me in the care of our descendant family. I can get past them easily. Can you come meet me at the park?"

She stared at the screen for a moment and chewed on her lip. "But you told me to stay inside…"

"You can't stay inside forever. I just meant not to run around where they could find you, not to stop you from meeting me. I don't know when I'll be able to get free of them again to see you."

"All right. But why don't you come to my apartment? It's more private."

"I can't get my car. I need to walk, and I'm not strong enough to make that distance quickly. The park is halfway between us."

"That makes sense. I'll see you soon."

"Yes."

She raced to her bedroom and tossed on some clothes, covering her paint smears. She didn't want to take the time to wash them off. Slipping her sneakers on, she grabbed her keys and pocketed her phone, then was out the door. The rest of her sandwich lay on the counter forgotten.

She fidgeted in the elevator. It finally opened onto an empty lobby and she rushed through, hitting the door to the outside hard enough to bruise her hand. As she raced across the threshold, a wave of cold shivered down her spine and she froze in midstep to look around her. The porch was empty, the door slowly hissing shut. A reflexive quiver shook her shoulders and she turned away to continue her race to the park.

Cassandra stood in the lobby and watched Alexis look around the porch as the door closed between them. The woman searched but quickly gave up and raced off.

Not many humans can feel us when we are cloaked. She let the light go and texted Erik. "She's on her way and I'm in the building."

"Good."

Cass looked around the lobby and found the bulletin board that listed the residents. After searching for only a second, she picked out Alexis's apartment number and touched the elevator button with her gloved finger to take her to the proper floor. The hall was empty. She paused in front of the woman's door and slipped the lock picks she'd brought out of her pants pocket. A quick probe and twist with the metal and she pushed the door open. She cast a glance over her shoulder and entered.

Frustration roared to the surface as she looked around the cluttered space. She didn't have time for this. *I'll never find anything here.*

Delicately she picked her way through the stuff. At first all she saw was the mess, but then she started to see the pieces. There was actually an order to the chaos, it seemed. That made her feel a bit better. It was more like the woman never took time away from her drives to attend to the small stuff. Why put clothes away if you were just going to wear them again.

Erik had obviously interrupted her dinner. A half-eaten plate of food tilted on the edge of the sink. Not a lot in the fridge or cupboards. She left the small kitchen and slowly prowled the paths through the living room. That was when she noticed the canvases. A lot of canvases.

Dae's face stared out at her from each one.

"Oh no," she whispered.

It looked like the obsession wasn't one sided. She didn't disturb the wet one on the easel, but she gently rummaged through the stacks leaning against one another and the wall.

This girl was good. She had captured him perfectly. Then she found Damian's sundering and froze with a gasp. The scene before her was indelibly printed on her memory. She backed away from the painting, not noticing the other canvases in front clattering over. She only had eyes for the image in front of her. She remembered picking up the pieces with Erik's help, stopping Dae from killing himself that night. So many centuries ago. She pulled her hair back and held it as she stared, then forced herself to turn away and finish searching the small flat. Nothing else of interest turned up.

Needing to get home, she grabbed the painting and headed out of the apartment.

Erik settled onto the bench at Cal Anderson Park and wrapped the light around himself. Even with the lateness of the hour, he could hear people on Broadway a block away. The park held a few homeless that were staking out corners, but otherwise most people wisely stayed out of it after midnight.

It wasn't long before he heard her footsteps running down the sidewalk. She flashed through the circle of light cast by a streetlamp, then into the darkness before hitting the next circle at the base of the stairs to the park entrance. She slowed, panting, and walked up the steps, her eyes wary and searching the expanse of the park. As she paused on the steps right next to his bench, he got a good look at her.

Tight denim and a simple T-shirt encase soft curves, and her hair floated like a nimbus around her face. She flicked her gaze toward his bench, and he watched a shiver travel her spine before she turned to look down the opposite path. He took that moment to let the light go, so when she looked back in his direction she jumped and smothered a shriek.

"I didn't see you."

"I'm sorry, you seemed pretty distracted. Are you OK?"

She looked out over the park before glancing back at him. "Yes."

He made a show of looking around. "The way you came barreling in here, I thought you were running from someone. Maybe you should sit down and catch your breath." He slid over, giving her plenty of room, and patted the bench. The energy currents around her rushed like a flooding river, almost blinding him through the barrier that separated him from the world. He projected calm and reassurance.

"Not from, to." She scanned the park again.

"Excuse me?"

"Running to."

"Oh, I see. Meeting someone then?"

"That was the hope." She sighed and looked at him fully for the first time. "I guess he isn't here yet."

He patted the bench again. She eyed him warily, then took a small step away. The heat of the day had cooled into a pleasant night, but she still shivered. "No, thank you."

"I'm waiting for someone too. Who are you looking for? Maybe I've seen him."

She took another step away before resuming her search of the darkened park. He pulled the light around while she wasn't paying attention and silently rose, his footsteps soundless on the grass at the side of the path.

"I doubt it, thank you though," she said and

turned back to where he had been sitting. Seeing that he wasn't there, she whipped her head around in surprise. "Hello? Where did you go?"

He had drawn close enough to her back that he could feel her body heat, and he whispered, "Dae won't be coming."

She shrieked, and he grabbed her wrist as she tried to run. He let the light go and blocked her free hand as it flailed at him, pulling her back against his chest and holding her.

"Stop, Alexis. Quiet." She struggled, but he easily held her smaller form. "I need to talk to you."

"Who are you?" she sobbed.

"I'm Erik."

She trembled and started to collapse. He scooped her up firmly and headed for his car at the nearby curb.

"Where's Dae? What have you done with him?" She tried to squirm, but he just held on tighter.

"He's at home."

"He said you were going to kill me," she whispered.

"He's not wrong about the law. But at the moment I need to know what is happening more. Dae is sick, and you are the only connection I can find. I won't harm you until I know what is going on."

"But I don't know anything. I didn't even know you existed until a few days ago."

"You might know more than you think." He clutched her with one arm and fished in his pocket with the other hand, then pushed the unlock button on his key fob. He opened his passenger door. After he set her in the seat, he stared into her frightened eyes. "Don't try and get out. You can't run fast enough from me to escape. And now I know you, I'll be able to find you anywhere. If you want a chance to live and see Dae, cooperate."

She shrank back and he buckled her seatbelt. She didn't try anything as he rounded the hood and got in on his side. "What are you going to do with me?"

"For the moment you will be our guest."

"Prisoner, you mean."

"I guess it depends on your perspective." He started the car and pulled out onto the street. "How did you meet him?"

"We ran into each other. Literally. Came around a corner and hit; it broke my grocery sack. He took me to dinner since my food was ruined."

"When?"

She took a deep breath. "Almost two weeks ago."

"I thought it had to be before..." he said under his breath.

"Before what?"

He glanced at her as he drove the neighborhood streets. "It doesn't matter."

She uncurled a bit. "Do you mean before you did whatever you did to him?"

His head jerked to look at her, then back to the road. "What do you know? This will go easiest if you just talk of your own will."

She frowned at him. "We spent several days together where he ignored your calls. Then one day we had plans, but he didn't show. When he finally got ahold of me, we arranged to meet at the park. He was nearly an invalid, but he wouldn't let me help. He said it was dangerous."

"He should have left you alone."

"Maybe I didn't want him to."

He couldn't help throwing another glance at her. She still looked scared, but there was a defiance simmering under her gaze that was growing.

"You have no idea what you've gotten into," he muttered. Pulling into their driveway, he turned off the engine. "Will you cooperate?"

"Why? You've already as good as told me that you will kill me."

"I don't want to. I can't help what our laws state. I'm already breaking them by bringing you here. We need to know what is going on."

"I want to see Dae."

He shook his head sadly. "He wants to see you too, desperately. But I can't allow that yet." He got out, keeping an eye on her as he circled the car, then he helped her out and held her arm as they walked to the front door. Maggie must have been watching because the door opened when they got to it. He brought the human across the threshold, then pointed to the chairs and couch in the living room. "Sit."

He waited until she moved into the room and looked at the descendant. "Anything?"

"Neither Callum or Isaac have been able to leave his room. Even as weak as he is, he's pushing them."

Alexis gasped across the room from the chair she'd chosen and looked toward the ceiling. "Dae," she shouted.

He could see her energy unfurl, and he blinked as

he crossed to her side. "Quiet. Don't make it worse for him. He's distraught enough."

Her eyes glared at him. "He knows I'm here."

"Maggie, get your husband and son in here." The descendant ran off, and a minute later the two men came running in. "Keep her here."

He left without looking back, though he didn't need to; he saw her eyes shrink in fear as the two burly descendants approached with stern faces. He took the stairs two at a time and slammed a fist into Dae's bedroom door. Isaac swung it open. Damian stood in the corner with a chair gripped in front of him, standing Callum off. His eyes swiveled to look at him the moment he stepped in the door.

"If you hurt her..." The whispered threat left Erik cold.

"He's feeding," Isaac said in a hushed voice.

"I can see that. Why do you think I came pounding up here?"

"Alexis," Dae shouted.

"Shut up, Dae."

"I want her, now."

"And your position has changed, how? Sit down and shut up. The two of you aren't getting any closer until we figure out what is going on. You shouldn't be able to reach out to her with your psyche bound. I'll take her out of here in a heartbeat if you don't knock it off. I don't know how you were able to tell she was here in the first place." He didn't take his gaze away from Dae's. "Isaac, she's downstairs. Please get her moved to a guest room as far from here as you can."

Dae's gaze flicked to the joy link, then back.

"Callum, get a couple of padlocks please."

The anger link ran his finger and thumb down his close-cropped mustache and beard, staring first at Dae, then him, before he nodded and left.

"Now listen up, I'm locking you in here because I can't trust you. If you try and go out the window, even though you're three stories up, I'll chain you to that bed. Got it?"

Dae clutched the back of the chair in a white-knuckled grip. "You said you were going to kill her. You took Cass to do it."

"I never said I was going to kill her. You kept saying that. I will kill her if I must, but until we know what is going on, it would be stupid to do that. Now sit, either on the bed or the chair. I don't care."

Dae reluctantly sat in the chair and Erik noticed his movements were already easier. Once the lust link was seated, Erik approached him and watched his brother flinch when he reached his hand out to his chest. He placed his hand over Dae's heart and looked at his storeground. Power seeped into it. He really was pulling energy from the human without even trying. *I can't stop it unless I remove her from the premises. I could take her to the house on Bainbridge Island, but then I split us up and make it more difficult to study what is happening.*

He sighed and pulled away.

Dae fidgeted, then said, "Please untie my psyche."

"No. That's more than I'm willing to do yet. I can't stop you from feeding off of her right now, so just regain some strength." Callum arrived and Erik turned to go. "I'm sending Maggie up with food. I expect you to eat it all. Callum, get the door locked, then install the other on our guest's door." He walked out without waiting for an answer from either.

He went down the stairs and gave Maggie her instructions, then headed to his office. After a moment he heard the front door open, so he wasn't surprised when the sound of Cass's footsteps followed him down the hall. Inside his office, he turned to the sorrow link. She looked pale.

"What's happened?"

She carried a canvas. She blinked her eyes and swallowed, turning the canvas around.

A strangled noise left his throat and he groped for the chair next to him. He remembered that day. That Damian. Every detail of the painting was perfect. From the colors of the fabrics to the textures and carvings of the wood bedposts. The only thing wrong was the perspective.

"She had more than a dozen paintings of him in her apartment. Some seemed familiar, but this one..."

"Yes." He cleared the gravel in his throat. "Yes."

"They couldn't have spent enough time together for him to pose for her. And how could she have gotten this so perfect from just hearing about it? He must have shown it to her in Shadow."

Erik hadn't taken his eyes off of it. He remembered that scene just like it was yesterday. As clearly as his own sundering. If he and Cass hadn't found Damian in time, he would have killed himself. A number of the Kelusis had. But as more Sundered appeared, they banded together and started to help one another. His own father and brother had saved him, which meant they were too late to save their mother. A memory he didn't like to look upon.

"It's wrong. And Dae wouldn't have shown her that."

"How do you know? He hasn't been acting terribly rational lately."

"His behavior has had its own brand of sane, Cass, if you look at it closely. But the perspective, it's wrong. Look at the painting."

She leaned it up against the doorframe and walked over to stand next to his chair. She shook her head. "It looks perfect to me. Like a photograph."

"No. If this was a painting done from Dae's memory, then we would see the room from his eyes."

Her head swiveled back to it, her hand slowly rising to her mouth. "But..."

"Someone else's eyes. It's from someone's memory, all right. But not the Dae we know now."

"Cambion?" she whispered.

"I'm hoping."

He reached up and clasped her groping hand, squeezing as tight as she while they stared at the painting.

Chapter 11

THE SOUND OF THE doorbell ringing a few hours later interrupted Erik's conversation with Callum. Maggie passed by his open office door as she hurried down the hall, then her footsteps pattered across the tiles of the foyer to answer the front door. The anger link turned to look into the hall and Erik sat back waiting.

When the shadow darkened the door, Erik clenched his fist and spoke to Callum. "Go help Isaac."

"Erik…"

"Now, Cal."

The anger link rose and pushed past the incubus in the doorway.

"Good ev'en to you too, Callum," the incubus said sardonically, then turned his stare on Erik, waiting.

"You may as well come in, Karry. You're here and all."

The enforcer walked in and sank gracefully down into the chair that Callum had vacated, his black duster spread out underneath him like a dress. "Three times in the last few weeks. I haven't seen you this many times in decades. How are you faring, Erik?"

"Cut the crap, Karry. We both know why you're here. Though I'm surprised they sent you."

"Really? You truly believe your father wouldn't want to send a friend?"

He glanced away. "Don't."

"Pity. They miss you, of course. As do I. None of us would want this handled by a different enforcer."

"Of course not." He realized he'd started drumming his fingers and forced them still. Karry's eyes looked back up from his hand to his face, and Erik smoothed his expression.

The enforcer sighed. "We need to know that you've taken care of the situation."

"We have it under control."

"Not good enough, Erik. Has the human been eliminated? I assume you sent your sorrow link in?"

"Of course I sent Cass to her apartment."

"And?"

"And we have it under control."

"This is a serious offense. I took care of the first incident at Decadence. But too many eyes saw what happened between him and the human on Friday. He's started to fade, hasn't he?" The silence stretched, so Karry continued. "Your family is ordered to the Chirurgeons before the conclave."

"Not necessary. And yes, we already know. I've opened the bond conduit. Dae hid it from us, he only had a week or two left."

"Erik." Kar's voice suddenly shifted, the emotional tenor filled with sorrow, and Erik turned away for a moment to collect himself. When he turned back, the feminine face that had replaced the masculine stared at him with tears in her eyes. "How long?"

He shrugged. "Who knows? A few months? A few years? If we're lucky, several decades? What difference does it make, Kar? It's not like it's a surprise. We all knew this day would come eventually."

"But not to you."

"Drop it. At least you can bear the news to my father and brother. I appreciate that."

Karry scrubbed her face in her hands, wiping the tears away. When she looked up, the incubus form had returned. "I'm not happy to bear this."

They were silent for a minute, then Karry caught his gaze and Erik knew his childhood friend hadn't forgotten his evasive answer.

"I still need to know, Erik. You know the laws. Dae was seen having physical interactions of a sexual nature with a human. I need to know the details of the resolution."

"And I told you, we have it under control."

"You are not making this easy."

"Was I supposed to?"

"Are you pushing for a summons to court?"

"I have a feeling that I won't be able to avoid that anyway, so what's the difference?"

Karry clenched his fist, then relaxed it and laid his hand flat against the arm of the chair, studying him.

"What are you up to, old friend? What are you hiding?"

"Look, Kar, it's been a particularly hard few weeks for us. This hasn't been an easy transition, and add into that my conclave duties and the upcoming court this winter, so can you just give me a break?"

"You're not giving me a lot of choice."

The look the enforcer cast over him sent a chill up his back. Not from animosity—but Erik knew his old friend could see the secrets he was hiding. And *there* was the true reason they had sent Karry. No one else could have stood up to him. This would be a very brief respite.

The enforcer rose. His coat swirled around his legs. "That's it for now, then. Your family is worried about you."

He shrugged.

Karry placed his hands on the desk and leaned over, his gaze locked on his. "I hope you know what you're doing."

He kept his face blank and finally the Kelusis ground his teeth and stood. "I'll see myself out."

After the footsteps receded down the hall, he said, "Bye, Kar."

Alexis yanked the pillow over her head when she heard the lock click and the hasp swing. Then the door pushed open and light blazed under the protective edge of the pillow. She groaned. "Turn the light off."

Legs encased in dark denim came to a stop at the edge of the bed; she could just see them from under the pillow. She eased the edge back and squinted in the bright light. Erik looked down at her. She glanced at the clock on the bedside table. Four a.m.

"I was asleep."

He cast a glance at the clock, then cocked his head when he looked back. "Sorry. I forget. Waking and sleeping are different for us. Regardless, we don't have a lot of time."

She sat up and rubbed her sleep-gritty eyes. "What do you mean?"

"You painted all of the portraits in your apartment?"

Dropping her hand, she stared at him. "You broke into my apartment?"

"Please answer the question."

"Why don't you answer mine?"

"I don't need to, you obviously already know the answer. Did you paint them?"

She clenched her fist and glared. "Yes."

He ran his hand through his hair, ruffling the short strands, and looked upset. "There was one in particular. Dae was lying on a bed..."

She shivered and looked away. He reached out, gently trapping her chin and forcing her to look him in the eye. She wanted to pull away, but something in there held her, some memory tugged.

"How did you know what to paint?"

Her heart started to gallop in her chest; she didn't want to think about that painting. "Let go."

"Alexis, I need to figure out what is happening,

and we don't have much more time. If you want a chance to live, please cooperate."

She started to tremble and couldn't seem to stop it. "I don't know how. I just can see it. I hate that painting. That's why it was behind all of the others."

He let go of her chin and brushed the hair out of her eyes. "Hold still."

He placed his palm on her chest over her heart. She was about to protest, when the heat of his other hand covered her forehead and the jolt of electricity shot through her. Her body stiffened and froze. It felt like ants crawled under her skin.

When he finally pulled away, she gasped and skittered into the middle of the bed, looking wildly around. The brother that had been with Dae at Decadence now stood in the room with them; she had no idea when he'd entered. He watched Erik, waiting.

"So, is it true?"

Erik stared at her. "I think it is."

"Now what?"

"It's time to talk to Dae, then we need to have a family meeting." He held his hand out to her.

She looked from it to the other man, then back into Erik's face. His eyes held warmth and wariness. The combination pushed her to move and she placed her hand in his warm one.

"Isaac, go get Callum and Cassandra."

He led her from the room and down the corridor, stopping at the other end of the house. Letting go of her hand to fish a key out of his pocket, he unlocked a padlock that probably matched the one on her door. When he pushed the wood open, she saw Dae slowly sit up on his bed. As soon as he saw her, he stumbled toward her. She shoved past Erik and met him halfway across the room. His warm arms wrapped tightly around her, and she gripped his waist, not wanting to ever let go.

"Are you OK?" he whispered into her hair.

She nodded against his chest. She felt him raise his head and look at Erik.

"Why?"

"There's a lot we need to discuss. Karry was here tonight."

His arms tightened around her even more. "And...?"

"We won't have much time. I stalled him, but I know Kar; he'll be back soon. If we could run, I would. But you know as well as I that isn't an option."

She felt him kiss the top of her head. "I won't survive if they kill her, Erik. I don't know why, but I know it's true."

"I won't let that happen. I promise. You have to start trusting me again, Dae."

"You can't promise other people's actions."

Erik sighed, and she watched him nearly collapse in a chair. "True enough, but I can promise my response. If they hurt my family..."

More people rushed into the room and she shivered. Dae led her over to the bed and tugged her onto his lap after he got settled. She happily curled up and let their conversation wash over her. There wasn't anything she could do anyway, and at the moment she was where she wanted to be.

"Cass, go get the painting," Erik said softly.

After a moment footsteps pattered up the stairs. She opened her eye and peeked—the woman held one of her canvases. She figured she knew which one, after Erik's questions. The woman handed it to Erik, who stared at it for a moment, then looked up at Dae.

"This will probably answer a few of your questions." And he turned it around.

Dae froze. She glanced up to his face and saw his eyes wide in shock as he recognized the scene. He set her to the side and slipped off the bed to crouch in front of the portrait. His fingers trembled as he reached out to brush it.

"How?" he whispered, turning to look at her.

"Take a close look at it, Dae. I know it's of a difficult time, but think. What do you see?"

He stood and backed away, then started to pace, his gaze returning over and over to her painting. "I don't know. It matches my memory perfectly..." He slowly stopped and collapsed to the floor. "No. Not my memory. I'm not seeing this scene. My..." He jerked his head to stare at her.

"Your succubus is," Erik finished for him.

Lexi's eyes widened, and she stared at everyone in the room. They all looked at her like she was an alien or something. "What?"

"But she's human, Erik," Dae said.

"I don't have all the answers," he responded in exasperation. "But I *can* tell you she has a budding storeground growing."

"We should hide her, Erik," Callum said.

"Where? How? At the moment Dae needs her to live. We have no clue what is evolving here, or how it's going to affect us all. And the enforcers aren't going to let us keep it quiet and to ourselves. Your displays"—he cast a withering glance at Dae— "made sure too many people knew about her."

Dae groaned and struggled to his feet. "I'm sorry."

"Me too." Erik pressed his thumb and finger to his eyes. "Karry isn't going to give us much time. Pack up. Let's go to the house on Bainbridge. It can gain us some hours to plan at least."

The three people she hadn't been introduced to left in a hurry. Erik cast his gaze over her, then returned it to Dae. He walked up to Damian and pressed his hand to Dae's forehead like he had to her, and Dae gasped, grabbing Erik's arm to stay on his feet. After a moment Erik released him. He studied the lust link, then turned to walk out the door, pulling it shut behind him. She waited. Dae gulped in air as he stared at her painting, then turned to look at her. His face carried a mixture of stunned disbelief and hope. He limped over to her and sat at the edge of the bed.

"Why did you paint that?"

She shrugged. "I don't know. I can just see it."

"Feel it?"

She started to pick at the bedcover. "Maybe."

"Do you know what that picture is of?"

Her eyes darted a look at the portrait without her permission. "No."

"That is a perfect replica, as good as a photograph, of the moment I was sundered. The moment half of my soul was ripped from my body. From my succubus's eyes."

"But that was...how many years ago?"

"I've lost count. Erik would know exactly. But for ease of speaking, let's just say it was close to three thousand years ago."

"How old are you?"

He shrugged.

"How would I know what that looks like?"

He ran his finger down her cheek and along her neck. "Erik believes my succubus is inside you. That she was remembering the pain of our separation."

She didn't know how she felt about that. But she liked the fact that he was touching her again. And this time in real life, not a dream. She leaned into his touch, and he added his other hand as he leaned forward. When their lips met, suddenly everything felt right in the world. Even if she was trapped in an unknown house with strangers who seemed to be creatures from legend.

He pushed her back on the bed and draped across her body, his weight more than welcome. She ran her hands under his T-shirt and felt his skin prickle into goosebumps.

"We don't have time for this," Dae said between kisses. "Erik said get ready to go."

She tipped her head, letting him nibble down her neck. "Why? What's happening?"

He rested his forehead against her collarbone. "Remember how I told you they would kill you?

Erik was supposed to take care of it. But our society has enforcers who are the arms and legs of the crown. They make sure the laws are followed and report back. And if it is deemed that laws were broken...they are authorized to take care of it."

She shivered at the thought.

Dae slid off of her and held out his hand to pull her up. "Let me throw a few things in a bag and we can head downstairs."

Noise erupted somewhere in the house. Dae froze in midstep, then swore. "Looks like we ran out of time." He threw the bolt on the door and took her hand, pulling her to his closet. "Stay in here. I doubt it'll hide you, but it's better than nothing."

She sank to the floor in the back corner of the small dressing closet as Dae shut the door, leaving her in darkness.

⋆⋆⋆

Dae pulled the closet door closed and walked to the bed. He felt better than he had in days because of the energy he was pulling in from Alexis, but he was still weak—and his heart pounded in fear. The noise downstairs could only mean one thing. Karry hadn't waited. Considering how well the enforcer knew Erik, that wasn't too terribly surprising. He didn't figure he would have long to wait. He pulled his dagger out of the drawer next to the bed and slipped it under the pillow he propped up to lean against. Briefly he considered getting his sword out, but realized there would be no point. He was too weak to wield it against anyone, let alone an enforcer. Besides, having it out would tip his hand.

A couple of shouts reached through his door, and he wondered how the enforcers wanted to deal with the human police that were sure to arrive if they insisted on forcing his family to make a scene. Then his blood went cold. The noise and lack of care about it could only mean one thing. They had enough numbers to be able to deal with the minds of as many humans as they needed to.

Feet stomped along the hall, and he tensed. His door rattled. Then a fist pounded. "Damian. Open your door."

He stayed on the bed and the door rattled again.

"Erik, tell him to open it up."

"Go to hell, Karry."

"Fine."

The doorjamb splintered as the enforcer used his foot to kick in the latch. The door swung open.

"Hope you plan to pay for that," Dae said.

Karry glowered and stepped aside so three Chirurgeons could enter. *Damn.*

Behind the doctors, Erik entered with Karry.

"Damian, it has come to our attention that you have recently begun the fade. By order of the court, you and the whole family are to be checked over early," Alden, the elder Chirurgeon, said.

Dae looked at Erik. "They get you already?"

"No."

"Didn't think there'd been enough time." He looked back at the Kelusis. "I'm not really interested."

"We didn't think you would be. No Sundered ever is. Please sit at the edge of the bed."

"And if I refuse?"

"That is why I brought as many people with me as I did, Damian," Karry said.

He sighed and ground his teeth but slid to the edge of the bed. The three moved forward, and he couldn't help the panicked look he threw at Erik. His center stared into his eyes and held his gaze. The two juniors sat next to him and pinned his hands to the bed, while the eldest's form flowed from incubus into succubus and she placed one hand on his heart, the other on his forehead. He tried not to lose sight of Erik, but the shock of the Chirurgeon overrode everything else.

He didn't know how long the elder worked, but when the hand was pulled away, he stared into an incubus's eyes; fear, hope, denial, calculation all warred in them. Erik leaned against the jamb to his closet, partially blocking the door as he watched Karry examine Alexis's painting. Thankfully, while he probably understood what the painting depicted, the enforcer wouldn't have the inside knowledge to grasp the significance of it.

"Enforcer. We must locate this human," the elder said.

Karry sighed and stood to look at Erik. "Well?"

Erik turned away from him, addressing the doctor. "Why?"

"I'm sure you understand the significance of this?"

"Of course. But what do you want? Or more importantly plan to do?"

"This is more valuable than just your family."

"What did you discover?" Erik asked softly.

"Not enough. We must study this. I need to examine this human."

Dae's center met his eyes and he shook his head to the unspoken question; he could tell that Erik agreed. Neither of them trusted the Kelusis who'd invaded their home. Erik turned to Karry. "Get them all out of my house and I will talk to you."

"No," the Chirurgeon said. "We are not leaving without her. We don't know if she's a threat or savior. But she will not be left as a loose cannon."

"Screw that," Damian said. He started to rise, but the two who still sat next to him kept him in his seat. He pulled against them and shot a look at Erik. Erik's eyes bored into Karry's.

"You're sure she's here?" the enforcer asked the elder, though he didn't take his eyes from Erik.

"The link is feeding from her as we speak. She can't be far."

Dae watched Karry scan the room quickly, then take in Erik's location. He took a step toward the center, but Erik didn't budge. Another enforcer, who must have still been waiting in the hallway, entered.

"Please move, Erik."

"You don't have to make this choice, Kar. You are all crossing a line that you will never be able to recross."

"The decision is out of my hands."

"I hope that gives you comfort in the future."

Erik wasn't willing to give up without a fight, but Dae could see that he didn't try very hard either. He didn't blame him. Kar was the best fighter in the royal guard. No point getting hurt when they were so outnumbered. But it looked like Erik was able to vent a little frustration on Kar's body at least. Kar subdued him and handed him off to the second enforcer, who winced as he held Erik back, allowing Karry to open the closet. In a moment Kar came out, leading a resisting Alexis. Dae wanted to tense at the sight of her frightened face, but he resisted.

At Alden's gesture, one of the junior Chirurgeons holding him to the bed left to help Karry with her.

Dae took that opportunity to slide his hand underneath his pillow, the solid hilt of his dagger pressed into his palm. Unlike Erik, he didn't care so much if he got hurt if he could protect Lexi. He tested the hold on his right arm.

"Dae," Alexis shrieked.

Hilt clasped tight, he pulled his hand out, but the elder had seen the threat. Alden slapped hands on his chest and head and dove in faster than Erik ever could. Dae's back arched underneath the old man as the Chirurgeon bound his psyche tighter than ever.

Panting, he writhed on the bed as the Chirurgeon turned from him and approached Lexi.

"No," he managed to gasp out.

She tugged against the restraining hands of both of the incubi. Erik growled out a warning, but it went unheeded.

The elder placed his hands on her and she jerked, then went stiff as a board, a soft whine escaping her lips. Dae could feel her energy scatter like dust motes in the sun. She sagged unconscious in the incubi's arms.

"Karry, please get Damian. Maleath, take her."

"What?" Erik exclaimed, starting to struggle in earnest. "Where are you taking them?"

The Chirurgeon studied Erik but didn't bother to answer. He walked out the door, and the junior followed on his heels, carrying Alexis in his arms. Karry pressed a hand to Erik's struggling shoulder, then came toward the bed.

Dae shifted his limbs but couldn't find the strength or coordination to stop the enforcer from gathering him up. "Erik..." he managed to call to his center.

"I'll get to you, Dae. Remember what I said."

He could hear the other enforcer shifting Erik bodily through the bedroom door and following them down the stairs. Others held the rest of his family from interfering in the living room. They were almost out the door when Erik shouted.

"Kar."

The enforcer turned and Dae could see the rage blazing out of Erik's eyes.

"Understand this. They will be returned to me. Unharmed. If anything happens to either one of them. I will destroy the court. Do I make myself clear?"

Dae felt the tremor that ran through Karry's body.

"You wouldn't," he whispered.

"Yes. Everyone. And you know I can do it."

Karry backed out the door, refusing to take his eyes off of Erik. From the enforcer's arms, he could see the tear-streaked face of his sister, the rage in Callum's body as they held him pinned to the floor, Isaac's unusual stillness as he watched everyone he now considered an enemy. Then the door closed and Karry let out his held breath as he turned to go down the steps.

He addressed the waiting enforcer at the bottom. "As soon as we are gone, release them and return to headquarters."

"Yes, sir. Senior Alden has already left with the human. He said to take Damian to our main house. He will come there after he has examined her more thoroughly, to study him."

Dae could already feel her distance. The energy was almost gone, and what remained in his sand would drain away quickly.

"Understood." Karry started walking again toward a large SUV.

"You've made a big mistake, Kar," Dae managed to get out.

The enforcer tightened his grip. "I know."

Chapter 12

ALEXIS WOKE TO BRIGHT sunshine blinding her through her eyelids. She groaned and rolled away. Her head pounded from whatever that man had done to her, and it felt stuffed with cotton. She struggled into a sitting position and looked around. Fear dried her mouth. Stumbling to her feet, she approached the wall. The view from the window was breathtaking. Two stories below, a street wound along the rocky shore of a beach. A body of water, and she really hoped it was the Puget Sound, ebbed and flowed across from her. Sunlight sparkled off the glittering waves.

She pressed her face against the glass. Some thought must have gone into room placement. The sheer wall held no means of escape through the window. She turned to the rest of the room. Bright, cheery yellow paint—but the room felt sterile. It reminded her of a hospital. A bed, a couple of chairs, and a small dresser, that was all the room contained. She crossed to the door, but unsurprisingly the knob rattled in her hand.

Distraught, she returned to the bed and sat down, her mind playing over everything that had happened in the night. She assumed it was last night, but after her two days of sleep, she wouldn't take it for granted that was the case.

Erik had scared her, but in hindsight she realized that on some level she had trusted him. She didn't have that same sort of reassurance now.

Dae. I need you.

She wrapped her arms around her middle and rocked slightly on the mattress.

Sometime after retreating into herself, she became aware of the doorknob rattling. The older man from last night entered with a tray of food. She inched back into the headboard and watched him warily.

He watched her in return as he set the tray down on the foot of the bed. "Eat."

She hesitated, but her stomach growled and she decided she really didn't have anything to lose. They would do whatever they wanted with her, and she couldn't stop them. So she pulled it closer and took a bite of the fluffy omelet. He pulled up a chair and continued to stare at her. It got so unnerving that she finally dropped her fork with a clatter and said, "What?"

"You should finish eating."

"Well it's a little hard when I feel like a bug under a microscope." She picked up her fork and stabbed at a chunk aggressively. "Where am I? Where's Dae? What am I doing here?"

"You are in our *shalis*. You would understand it as

a clinic or hospital. We don't get sick often, but we do get hurt. Injuries, broken bones, that sort of thing. And we keep track of and help the Sundered. Our research is devoted to the Sundered. The rest I prefer not to answer."

"Of course not." She barked out a short burst of unamused laughter.

"Tell me about your parentage."

"You won't answer my questions, but I'm expected to answer yours?"

"Your view of it would lend a valuable insight to the knowledge, but we don't have to have it. There is a team researching your genealogy as we speak. As well as another investigating your family."

"My family? You leave my family alone."

As she stared at him, his features and body shifted, kind of moved in a disturbingly fluid way, and suddenly an older woman stared back at her. Alexis shrieked and scrambled back on the bed to huddle against the headboard. The dishes shattered on the floor. The woman cocked her head and stared at her quizzically.

"Let me go. Please let me out."

"I had thought this form would appear less threatening to you."

"Yeah, maybe if you hadn't just done it right in front of me," she gasped out and her gaze darted to the door, but it was shut. She didn't think she'd be able to get there and out with *it* sitting there.

"Would you prefer my incubus form?"

Alexis shook her head. "I don't care. Just don't do it in front of me."

"Fine then, close your eyes."

She squeezed them tight.

"You can open them now."

When she did, the man sat in the chair once more.

"I now wonder how much you know of us? What we have been able to piece together without Erik and his family's cooperation has been a little deceptive."

"I want to see Dae. Or Erik." Then she whispered, "Please."

He pursed his lips and shook his head. "Until I can determine whether or not you pose a threat, you will remain here and under observation. I will not expose my people to another Trojan horse if that is what you are."

"I'm just a person." She tried not to cry and managed to keep it to a sniff.

"The most innocent person can still carry a deadly disease that will wipe out an entire town."

She gulped, then asked, "How long?"

He shrugged. "Until we know what you are."

"What I am? I'm human."

"No, that we've been able to determine. You were. What you are? That's not known yet. The hope is Cambion. But we'll see."

"Cambion?"

"When the sundering began, so did the talk of the Cambion. The mythical vessel that was supposed to carry the sundered half of that Kelusis. As far as we have been able to tell, that's all it has been, a myth born of hope for those whose misfortune it has been to become sundered. Both Erik and Damian are beyond certain that is what you are. But until we can determine that for ourselves, I don't put faith into it. We have studied and researched for more years than you can imagine and have never seen a sign that the Cambion could truly exist. I find it hard to believe that one would just suddenly crop up right when Damian had almost reached the point of no return in the fade. I find it much more likely that you are a threat."

His voice held no sign of anger or any emotion really, but that didn't stop her from reacting to the accusation. She started to shake and curled into a tight ball on the bed.

"Since you would prefer not to answer my questions, I will leave now. I have another appointment to attend. Maybe upon my return you will be more forthcoming with your knowledge."

He rose and glanced at the shattered crockery on the floor before walking toward the door. "Someone will be in to clean that up."

Left alone in the sunny room, she curled up tighter and pressed her forehead to her knees, wishing that she could believe this were a dream, or at least escape into one with Dae again.

Dae rattled then pounded on the door another time. He'd kick it for good measure, but he'd been taken out of his house without shoes. He padded across the windowless room, which contained a bed and two chairs, nothing else. Though there were scrapes across the wood that made him think things had been removed. He wrapped his arms around his middle and paced. His brief burst of energy faded, and he crawled back onto the bed. His storeground was bone-dry and his stomach rumbled painfully. Sleep had not come for him in the intervening hours. He twisted his fists in the blankets as he pushed against the ropes the Chirurgeon had bound around his mind, but he couldn't budge them. Trapped within himself, his thoughts cycled through all the bad things that could have happened to Alexis. Only the knowledge that Erik would get to them kept him on this side of the line from panic.

The door unlocked and Karry walked in carrying food. Dae turned his head on the pillow and caught a brief glimpse through the door that let him know it was late afternoon. Then Kar kicked it shut. His eyes tracked the enforcer, but he didn't bother to speak.

The incubus set the food down on the seat of one of the chairs closest to the bed, then pulled the other over to sit on.

"You should eat. Alden will be here soon."

Alden, huh? Until last night, he'd been lucky enough to never actually have to see the elder Chirurgeon. He didn't move.

"Come on, Dae." Kar sighed. "No matter what I had to do, I will see to your health. You need to eat. Erik may want to kill me already, but he'll go about it in a more painful manner if I don't take care of you."

Dae closed his eyes so he wouldn't have to look at the incubus or the room and leaned his head back against the headboard. "Please bring Erik."

"I can't."

"You could. You just don't choose to." He opened his eyes.

"Look, I don't have the freedom that you Sundered have. Living away from the crown…"

"Exile is more like it, Kar."

"It's your choice."

"What is Erik doing?"

"What do you think? Everything in his power. But he's fighting upstream, Dae. He's gone to court."

Dae winced. He knew how hard that would be for his center. He finally couldn't resist asking, "Is Lexi all right?"

Karry pushed the chair closer to the edge of the bed. "Eat if you want me to even consider answering any more questions."

With an exasperated sigh, he sat up and reached over to pick up the plate. He took a couple of bites, then looked at the enforcer.

Karry smiled slightly and leaned back in his chair, crossing his booted feet at the ankles. "So far she's fine. The Chirurgeons are studying her. And they are delving into her background and genealogy. Now I have a question for you. What was important about that painting?"

Dae looked down at the plate and continued to eat.

"I assume she painted it. There were a number of portraits of you in her apartment. But that was the only one that had been removed. Why?"

He shrugged and continued to eat.

"Look, I can't help without information. Give me something."

"Ask Erik."

He crossed his arms. "Like that'll do me any good. Do you really expect Erik to talk to me now? He wouldn't before we took the two of you."

"And how am I any different? I'm one of the ones you took." He scraped the plate clean. "I won't say anything without Erik's OK."

Kar groaned in frustration, leaning forward and squeezing his eyes with his hand. "You all make it so difficult to help you."

"Sorry, not from our perspective."

Karry opened his mouth to say something but stopped when the door unlocked. The elder Chirurgeon and a junior entered.

"Please leave us, enforcer."

"Not a chance, Alden."

The Chirurgeon looked like he wanted to argue but thought better of it at Karry's glare. Dae felt a small measure of relief over not being left alone with them. The Chirurgeons were not the most favored of people to the Sundered.

"How are you feeling, Damian?"

He snorted and handed the plate to Kar. "Why are you even asking me?"

The elder sighed. "This is our job, you know. We are required to look after the health of everyone, but most especially in regards to the Sundered."

"But of course not listen to them or take anything they know into account."

"It is not within your training to make these assessments. It is, however, in ours. Now to start with, we need to do your full exam."

Glaring at all of them, he slid to the edge of the

mattress. He knew there was no getting out of it, so he might as well get it over with. Alden nodded and stepped forward. He tried to brace himself, but a full medical scan from a Chirurgeon was nothing like the intrusion his center caused. Both the Chirurgeons were thorough, leaving him feeling wide open, exposed and flayed from the scrutiny.

When they were done, he fell over. Kar was ready for that and scooped him up, getting him positioned comfortably in the bed. Dae blinked owlishly at them.

Alden pursed his lips and his junior turned to him. "He's starving."

"Yes. I noticed that." Alden continued to stare at him.

But it was the concern in Karry's eyes that surprised him.

"What do you mean he's starving?" he asked.

Alden turned his gaze on the enforcer for a moment as he decided whether or not to tell him. He finally said, "His storeground is a desert. He can't keep any energy in it at all. Even with the braided link with his family, he's fading. I'm not sure how he's still with us actually."

"I need Lexi," he slurred.

"You certainly need to feed. That will be first priority after you wake up. It will take me that long to get it ready."

"I can only feed from her." The Chirurgeon's face swam in and out of view.

"Not possible," he heard faintly before he slid into blackness.

Lexi stood at the window and stared out into the night. The summer storm shot lightning across the expanse of water. She could see the wind bow the trees and hear the thunder crash—and wished with all her might that she could feel it too. Boredom had set in early. She had nothing to do. No books, no TV, no radio, no paper, and especially no paints. She sighed. Her hands itched to paint. At least then she could see Dae. Make him real.

He wasn't in her dreams anymore. She didn't know what that meant, but her fear bubbled to the surface. Except for a couple more meals, she'd been left alone since that creature had come in to see her. She had a hard time thinking of it in any other light. Intellectually she knew that at one time Dae was like it, able to change shape between male and female, but he couldn't now, and anyway she knew Dae.

The lock on her door grated, and she turned. Bright light spilled into her darkened room, and the silhouette hesitated in the doorway. At realizing she wasn't in the bed, the figure stepped in and flicked the light on. Her hand shot to cover her eyes and she growled. She blinked while her eyes adjusted, and her visitor shut the door.

The tall muscular man wore a dark duster over his jeans and black T-shirt; he looked familiar. After a second, she realized why. He was the man who had pulled her from Dae's closet.

She put her back to the wall and watched him. He studied her, then pulled one of her chairs over between the door and the bed and straddled it. His damp coat splayed out behind him.

"Would you be more comfortable with a male? Or female?"

"I...I don't know. Just don't do it when I'm looking."

The corners of his lips twitched. "In that case I'll stay an incubus. Most favor one form over the other. Usually the one they were born in, but not always. It's been particularly hard on the Sundered who got stuck in the opposite form. My name is Karry Yashalla Thuentor. And you are?"

"What? You don't already know everything about me?"

His lips twitched again and he bowed his head in acknowledgement. "Not everything. But I thought polite introductions would be the best foot to start off on."

"'Fraid you lost that chance last night."

He sighed and a sad look flashed across his face. "Very true. So Alexis it is."

"What do you want?"

"I spent several hours with Dae today. And I thought you would want to know. He's holding on, but the Chirurgeons are worried."

She wrapped her arms around herself.

"They are going to try feeding him."

"It won't work," she whispered and turned to look at her reflection on the windowpane.

"Why won't it work?"

She shrugged.

"What was the painting about?"

Her head jerked a look over her shoulder at him. His gaze caught hers and she couldn't look away.

"You had easily a dozen portraits of Dae, yet that was the only one Erik had in his house. Why? What is the significance? I'm assuming it is a portrayal of his sundering?"

"Not a portrayal. A true representation."

"OK, so now I know he dreamwalked with you and showed you his memory. But that doesn't match up with what I'm reading from the situation."

She still couldn't look away. "Not his memory."

His brows furrowed, then a minute later rose in disbelief. "His other half?"

"That's what Erik says."

"Holy fuck," he whispered. "You carry his succubus? No wonder Erik is willing to destroy the court."

She didn't pretend to understand what he meant, so she turned away again. A few minutes later she heard him rise.

"You should get some sleep while you can. Most Kelusis don't follow the same schedule of hours that humans do."

She watched him leave in the reflection of the glass. He'd left the light on, so her view was gone as was her night vision. On a sigh she walked over to the door and turned the light back off, then decided he was right and climbed on top of the covers. Her wrinkled clothes would see another night it looked like.

She found herself sitting underneath a large, shady tree. The smooth wooden chair reclined at a relaxed angle, and she watched the leaves dance in the slight breeze that ruffled them. The fresh scent of the air filled her lungs.

Memory swamped her and she sat up, yelling out for Dae.

Her heart thudding, she turned toward the footsteps she heard coming from behind and she wanted to cry. Not Dae. Erik approached.

"I'm sorry, Alexis. I haven't been able to get him free yet. Alden locked his psyche down to the point that even I can't reach him. But trust me, I'm working on it. I'm doing everything I can to get to both of you. Just hang on."

She curled back up in the wooden chair, forcing the tears back. He sat in another chair that she didn't remember being there a moment ago and watched her. "Are you OK? What has happened? Do you know where they've taken you?"

"I'm locked in a room near the water. There's a road out front and a rocky beach. I've mostly been alone. That thing came in and tried to get me to tell it things. Like about my family and stuff."

"Thing?"

"That old man who took me away."

"Ah, Alden. I take it he switched in front of you?" He smiled.

"Um, yeah. Sorry."

"No need to be sorry. I understand how it must seem. I think I know where they have you, then."

"And the other man, incubus I guess, who was with him came and asked questions."

Erik frowned. "Do you mean Karry?"

"Yes, that was the name he gave."

"What did he want?"

"He wanted to reassure me that Dae was OK for the moment. That he'd been with him all day. And he wanted to know about my painting."

Confusion crossed Erik's face and he mumbled, "He spent the day with him? Why?" Then he looked at her again. "What about the painting? What did you tell him?"

"He wondered why it was important. Since it was the only one you guys took from my apartment. He couldn't figure out the significance, but he knew there was one. I told him. Should I not have?"

Erik scrubbed his face. "No, no it's fine. You didn't do anything wrong. But from here on out, be careful what you say to Alden. I don't know how long it will take me to get to you. It can't be too long though. Dae won't last."

A sob caught in her throat at the reminder.

"I will get to you."

Dae used his mental hands and pushed against the ropes holding his psyche to his body. His fingers skittered along the edges of the binding, looking for a weakness. He flexed against it, but it always returned to its original shape—his mind was trapped. Roaring in frustration, he pounded his fists against it a time or two before he slid into wakefulness. His body lay weak on the bed. The link between him and his family was stretched too taut. He could feel his body consuming itself as it looked for the energy it needed to survive.

He estimated Erik had only a couple of days to get to him before it was too late. His door unlatched, and Alden walked in followed by a man and woman, descendants from the looks of it, since they were human. His eyes tracked their progress across the room, his body too weak to make the effort. Alden pulled a chair across to sit at his head.

The Chirurgeon rested his palm on Dae's forehead. "Damian, I'm going to loosen the binding enough to allow you to feed. Since you are a lust link, I brought you a couple. They are descendants from my household and are willing to be donors. They understand what you'll need to do."

He took a deep breath as the stricture around his mind relaxed. Not enough to branch out and reach Lexi, or the rest of his family, unfortunately. The energy from the pair across the room circled in the air. He could feel it, but it was like trying to catch water with a net. Not possible.

Alden mumbled impatiently next to him.

The couple looked over at him awkwardly, then tried kissing of their own accord. He assumed to try and jump-start the energy. He closed his eyes and sighed.

"Damian, you must feed. You needn't worry about pushing them too far and killing them, I'm here to prevent that."

A snort that sounded too much like a sob escaped him. He looked into Alden's cool eyes. "I can't."

Irritation flashed across the Chirurgeon's face. "Don't be absurd. You haven't even tried."

A coal of anger burned in his gut and he cursed his weakness. He wanted to smash the arrogant doctor in the face. "You are blind then, old man. Because I have tried. Repeatedly. Am now. I. Can't. Absorb. It." He bit off each word.

A huff of disdain left the doctor. "Fine. We'll do it the hard way. Curt, Anne."

The two descendants walked over to him and knelt on the floor before his seated form. Alden reached a hand out and placed one over each of their hearts. The two went rigid and their eyes rolled up. After a moment they gasped and sagged, aware again. They shook their heads and fell back into a sitting position on the floor.

Dae feebly scooted an inch or two away from the hands that now reached out to him. With no mercy on his face, Alden clamped a hand over his forehead while the other branded the skin over his heart. The energy hit his system like a focused blast of water, but when it hit the furnace of the desert sand, it exploded. Screams erupted outside of his room as the power detonated, turning into shrapnel that hit any Kelusis within range.

No sound emerged from Alden's wide open mouth. The chair the Chirurgeon sat in toppled over sideways as the energy shoved him away. The two humans stared dumbfounded at the doctor's flailing form. They still had their hands clamped to the sides of their heads to try and stem the sudden squeal, which was the physical manifestation of the energy feedback. His door was kicked open and Karry staggered in, wiping a trail of blood from his nose. His eyes held murder in them.

"What the hell?" The enforcer's gaze raked the room, then he stormed over to him. Dae would have pulled away if he could have, but Kar's hands were gentle as they checked him over. "Alden, I gave you specific orders. No one is in this room without me. I made that perfectly clear."

The doctor had managed to regain his feet. "I don't answer to you."

Kar's head turned and Dae watched the chief Chirurgeon's face turn even more pale, if that were possible. "If you want to live, you do. I'm the head of the enforcers. Or have you forgotten?"

"But the king…"

"Yes, the king. Trust me, I'm not forgetting the king. And neither should you."

Alden recovered his composure, his face a blank mask once again, and tipped his head ever so slightly to Karry. After a moment more, Kar returned his gaze to Dae. Dae saw the anger in their depths and the concern. "Are you all right, Damian?"

"I need Erik," he rasped out.

Kar's eyes closed briefly. "We're trying. Hold on, OK?"

"I can't much longer, Kar. There's not much left."

Karry cursed, then squeezed his shoulder before rising. "What happened?"

Alden's cold gaze raked him before looking back at the enforcer. "He wouldn't try to eat, so I did a normal energy transfer. Exactly what we would do for any injured or unconscious Kelusis. Routine. But instead of his storeground absorbing it, the energy was repulsed—resulting in a huge packet of energy atomizing at lightspeed and driving like sharp nails into all Kelusis within range. I'm now exceedingly concerned over this human he has had contact with. I'm finding the results to be more than dangerous."

Dae wished he had the energy to get off the bed and throttle the man. "If you hurt her…" The volume of his voice was barely above a whisper. Karry squeezed his shoulder, but he didn't think the doctor even heard him. He certainly didn't give him the respect of an answer if he did.

"Try and rest, Dae. Alden, come with me."

Karry stalked out, not looking back and obviously expecting the Chirurgeon to follow. He wasn't disappointed.

Alone again, Dae battered at the walls that still surrounded his mind.

Chapter 13

KARRY RESISTED THE URGE to put his fist through the wall when he entered the hall. Alden's descendants slipped around him and escaped to the break room. Alden pulled Dae's door shut when he emerged. Some of his enforcers still worked on cleaning themselves up from the energy blast, but everyone seemed to be OK. He turned his head and met Alden's eyes.

"What part of 'do not enter without me' did you not understand?" he asked softly.

Alden put his hands behind his back and straightened to his full height, looking down his nose. "I do not need a chaperone, enforcer."

He spun his body to face the senior Chirurgeon. "Oh yes, you do. If Erik gets wind of what you did, he'll kill you. And there won't be anything I can do to stop it. Not even you could stand against him, sundered or not. I've taken his wrath to protect those under me, but I won't for you if you don't listen."

"All I did was a perfectly simple, perfectly normal, routine action…"

"What part of normal is this situation?" He flung his hand at Dae's door. "Maybe you want to bury your head in the sand over the possibilities? But you certainly aren't forging ahead with any plans that look like they might help one of our own. And if Dae goes down, I remind you, so does Erik and the rest of their bond siblings."

Alden sniffed. "The loss of one, or even the whole of a bond if they are too stubborn to replace a link, is a reasonable price to pay for certainty of safety for the rest of our people. I do not know what this human has done to the Sundered in that room, but she has more effectively cut him off from food than any previous Sundered that has been found. At the moment I feel she is too much of a danger for our race."

Kar just stared at him, then said, "You won't even consider that she could be his Cambion?"

Alden scoffed. "That is just a myth. We Chirurgeons would have found some trace of them in the three thousand years we've been looking for a cure if there were any chance of that. No, she's some new weapon against us."

At a loss, Kar shut his mouth from where it had fallen open. Alden quirked an eyebrow.

Irritation flashed and he snapped, "Regardless of what you believe, you have a duty to investigate all the possibilities. Do not enter Damian's room without me again. And if any harm comes to the human through your hand…you might not have to worry about Erik."

He spun on his heel and stalked off. He had to locate Erik.

A couple of hours later Kar entered the archive building. The air in the old dusty basement underneath downtown Seattle tickled his nose. The archivist succubus shifted smoothly into incubus when she saw him approaching.

"Yes, enforcer? What can I do for you?"

"Erik."

He pursed his lips primly. "Research, milord. I direct research, not turn information on patrons."

Kar smiled. "Good, he's here. Finally." He pushed past the archivist.

"Milord! You can't. Please do not start a fight in here."

He threw a look over his shoulder at the panicked archivist. "Relax, I won't allow damage to come to your precious information."

He strolled through the maze of shelves. Several seekers of knowledge glanced at him. Some, their eyes wide, hastily left, others just shrugged and went back to their tasks. He turned a corner, and at the end of the alcove, spied curly waist-length hair.

His steps slowed. When he got halfway down the long aisle, her back stiffened.

"Hello, Cassandra."

She shoved the book back onto the shelf. "What do you want?" she spat, not turning around.

"I need to speak with Erik."

"Get lost."

"Cass..." Erik's voice rolled out. Kar tipped his head and glanced over his shoulder. His friend stood at the end of the aisle, his arms crossed.

"Fine," she snapped and stormed past him. But when she reached Erik, the slight movement of one hand stopped her in her tracks.

His hand brushed an unruly curl from her face. "Go home. Tell the others what we found. Wait for me there."

"Are you sure?"

"Go, Cass."

Kar saw her clench her fists, then she stomped away. He forced his body to relax. Folding his arms, he leaned a shoulder into the nearest shelf and crossed his ankles. Holding the upper hand against Erik would take all his skill. "So, what *did* you find?"

Erik stared at him, unblinking.

He sighed and cast a glance at the ceiling for patience. "Erik, don't try me. I don't have the time."

"*You* don't have the time?" he said.

Kar pushed away from the shelf and paced. "I've been trying to track you down for a few hours now."

"Sorry to be such an inconvenience."

"Damn it. I just want to help you," he snapped.

Erik smiled, but the gesture didn't reach his eyes. "You really know how to show it, Kar. Storming my house. Kidnapping my family."

He took a deep breath. "You know as well as I there wasn't much choice."

"There's always a choice, and you made yours specifically to hobble me."

"I made the choices that would protect the most

people. You included. If hobbling you protects you, I'll tie you up in knots."

Fear flashed through Erik's eyes, and Kar understood it well. The clock was ticking on Dae.

"I meant what I said the other night, Karry," Erik said softly.

"I know you did." He ran his hand through his hair, then walked slowly closer to his friend. "They sent me because they knew I was the only one with a chance to keep you in line. I agreed because I knew that I was the only choice to keep you safe. The only one willing to help."

"Some help you've been. I'm locked up in red tape. Now, when I actually need to talk to my father, he won't take my phone calls, and neither will Pieter."

"You know how busy they are. And the court in Austria is having issues at the moment. My network says they are going to have their hands full for a time. Which is allowing the court here a free head. Look, I know you're angry with me, for good reason. But I need you to come with me." Erik's slashing look cut him, but he hid the damage.

"Are you taking me into custody, enforcer? Because if you are, you should have brought more hands."

"Damn it, Erik. Get a clue already." He glanced around what he could see of the room. They stood at the end of one of the many long rows, and curious eyes tried not to be obvious in their watching. "Look, we need to get out of the archive."

"Give me one good reason why I should go with you."

"Dae."

Erik's eyes flashed. "What about him?"

"He doesn't have much time."

Alexis picked at the food on the tray, her appetite gone. She had been stuck in this room for days. Though how many, she wasn't quite sure. She hadn't been able to keep track. Fear had left her hollow.

A click at the door let her know visitors had arrived.

The head doctor entered again, followed by two more she assumed were helpers or lower doctors. The reptilian look in Alden's eyes made her shiver, and she covered it by pushing the full tray away.

"When do I get out of here?" she blustered. "My family has to have noticed my absence by now, not to mention my friends. Someone is going to call the cops."

"That is of no concern to me. We can easily attend to any human presence through the psyche. You, however, pose us a problem. Pray you, that I find something of value to study or you're of no use to us."

"No use?" she whispered, then swallowed. The doctor's cold, almost hostile, demeanor toward her had increased dramatically. Had something happened? Her thoughts went to Dae, and her stomach clenched.

"Maleath, you pull first."

One of the younger doctors ducked his head,

trying to catch her gaze. When he succeeded in getting her to look into his eyes, she couldn't look away. The gold-flecked brown filled her vision. Her muscles twitched and she tried to resist, but the pressure of his mind bored into hers. She could see, just on the edge of her mental vision, pictures, waking dreams, that she was sure he thought overwhelmed her mind.

On the verge of panic, she turned inward, away from the invading mind. What she found was something she'd never seen before. Giant trees welcomed her, the vision so real she could touch and taste it. The sturdy roots of the large trees sunk deep into the fertile loam she'd found in herself, while the branches reached, the leaves gathering. The sunlight grew and her leaves soaked in more. Thirsty, she pulled, gathering as much as she could reach. The sounds of shouts echoed through her physical ears, but they didn't disturb her thoughts. More sources of sun came near, and she caught them with her leaves. The beautiful energy bathing her. As one sun burned down to embers, she focused on another until the pulsing lights hovered at the edge of her reach. She waited, her leaves waving in the breeze that circled around her. But they continued to hang back, and watch.

Dae lay on the bed. He couldn't feel the physical hunger any longer, which was a very bad sign, he knew. *I'm sorry, Lexi.*

He tried again to reach outside himself; Alden had loosened the bindings, but that only meant he was no longer immobilized. Now he was just caged within his own mind. More like what Erik had done to him.

Erik, he thought wistfully.

A trickle of energy seeped into him. His eyes jerked up to look at the door. The energy grew and he moaned, the pain akin to a waking limb. After a few minutes, the door opened and Kar stalked through, Erik on his heels.

"Erik," he rasped and felt a tear tickle its way down his cheek, where it soaked into the bed. His center's face turned to stone, but Dae saw the emotion run hot through his eyes when they caught his gaze. Erik knelt next to his bed, his hand trembling slightly when it reached out to burn on the pale skin of his bare chest. His eyes rolled up when Erik shot energy, like a lightning bolt, straight to his core through the braided conduit, and his moan turned to a breathless scream. The pain from the parched nerves was almost more than he could take.

"Breathe, Dae. You can still take energy from me. I need to flood your core and hope that the energy will rehydrate your uptake nerves. They have shriveled almost to uselessness." He tried to do what his center asked, but it came as more of a pant. His arms moved feebly as he tried to bat Erik's hand off of his chest. Erik's free hand brushed them aside, then swept the stringy hair off his forehead. "Shhhh. It'll be over in a minute."

The searing burn, something akin to frostbit fingers getting stuffed into hot water, finally slacked off. Wheezing echoed wetly from his gaping mouth, and he opened his eyes. Both Erik's and Karry's concerned gazes stared at him.

"Did it work?"

"I won't know for a couple of hours. Lexi's energy is the only source he can feed from. The braided conduit still ties us all together. Through that I hope we can sustain him a bit longer, but without his input from hunting, it isn't all of the energy strands—and we'll *all* starve to death soon."

"Then let's get him out of here."

Erik slid his arms underneath Dae and curled him up to his chest. "Blessed stars, Kar, he's lost so much weight. In just a few days."

"He stopped being able to take in food."

"And you didn't come get me then?" His voice cut out. The sound of Erik's heart thudded reassuringly in his ear as his center maneuvered him out of the room and into the hallway.

"I still believed that Alden and the rest of the Chirurgeons would be able to take care of it. But after what happened today…"

"Lexi," Dae moaned, and Erik tightened his hold, hugging him closer.

"We'll get to her next, Dae. I haven't forgotten her."

Kar held the door wide so Erik could carry him out into the humid night air. As they descended the steps to the sidewalk, Karry's phone buzzed.

"What?" he answered. Erik's car waited on the

curb and Kar pulled the door open for them. "Wait, she what? Where?"

Erik laid him gently onto the leather of the backseat and pulled a belt across his body to keep him from rolling to the floor. The sound of Karry's shocked exclamation funneled right through the open door.

"No one else goes in. I will be right there."

"What's happened?" Erik asked quietly.

"I have to leave you. Something has happened with Alexis. No one can get near her without collapsing. They can't tell who's alive or not."

Dae started to struggle to get up, but Erik held him down with a light hand.

"We should come with you."

"No. You need to get him back to the rest of the family. Now. I'll deal with Alden and Alexis."

"Lexi," Dae called again.

"If he's hurt her, Kar…" Erik warned.

"He's already tried, Erik. That's why no one can get near. I'll call you later."

Dae heard footsteps rush off, and Erik squeezed his shoulder before getting out and shutting the door.

He must have dozed on the ride home because the next thing he knew Erik was pulling the seatbelt off of him and slipping him across the leather of the seats. The world spun as he was lifted into the air. Multiple feet thudded down the walk, and he cracked open his eyes to see the expressions on his bond siblings' faces. Tears streaked Cass's pale skin, more anger than normal clouded Cal's eyes, and

Isaac's expression was blank. That was probably the most disturbing of all. The joy link usually exuded an infectious high that was hard to resist.

"What are we looking at, Erik?" Isaac asked.

"I don't know if he's going to make it this time."

Callum barked, "He doesn't have a choice." Then his eyes bored into his. "Do you hear me, Dae?"

It was too much effort to try and answer, so he just closed his eyes as Erik walked. Sooner than he expected Erik laid him on cool sheets, and he opened his eyes to see they had set up a cot on the floor of the formal living room. Somewhere with enough room for everyone to gather around for an extended time. He whimpered when he felt Erik's hand come to rest over his heart again.

"I know, Dae. I'm sorry. We need to get everything we can to your uptake nerves."

The pain consumed him once more, and he bashed against the barrier keeping him trapped in his mind. *Lexi.* He screamed into the aether.

Kar said good-bye to Dante, first chair of the council, and hung up the phone, thankful he'd gotten the injunction he needed. The memory of Damian's pain replayed through Karry's mind as he raced across town to White Thorn, the Kelusis's main *shalis* for the region. He just hoped he wouldn't be too late. For her, or for those trapped.

"What the hell did Alden do this time?" He swore, waiting impatiently at a red light. He only had a couple more blocks to go. The light turned green and he raced the rest of the way. He screeched into a parking space in front of the building and leapt out. Pelting up the stairs, he bolted through the door one of the Chirurgeons held open for him.

The hall surrounding Alexis's door was packed. But no one crossed the threshold. Alden seethed with rage when he spotted him.

"Enforcer. Do your job. That human needs to die. Now. She has several Kelusis trapped, possibly dead."

"What happened?"

"What does that matter? Several of my people are lying on the floor in that room, and we can't get to them without falling too."

"Well something had to have triggered it. I need to know so I can figure out how to get to her and stop this."

"If she's dead, it will stop," Alden reiterated.

Karry stared into the senior Chirurgeon's eyes. "You tried to kill her, didn't you? You tried to drain her."

"No. We tried to sample her energy. But when Maleath started to feed from her, she sucked him in and drained his energy. We tried to get him free and it happened to the next two as well. *Then* I had them try and drain her, and the energy around her changed; now if anyone steps foot across the threshold, they are sucked into the storm. It's up to you as the lead enforcer to kill that human."

"My job is to evaluate a situation and make the judgment and carry it out. Not to execute on your say so. My observations so far lead me to conclude that you are not keen on exploring all this situation has to offer. Now, clear this hall." The rest of the staff jumped to his order and the hall emptied. Except for Alden. He met the elder Chirurgeon's eyes once again. "That includes you."

"This is a mistake."

"I've seen a lot of mistakes happen over the last several days. I don't believe this to be one." He turned his back on the doctor and pulled a chair out of one of the other rooms in the hall. He dragged it as close to the threshold to her door as he could and sat looking into the darkness. He could see bodies lying motionless in the light that spilled across the floor from the hall. When he was sure Alden had left him, he closed his eyes and sent his psyche out. He circled the psychic storm she had encased herself with, checking its perimeter. Finally he lobbed an energy ball at it, knocking, and called her name. He tried it again, and this time the ball passed through. *Alexis. It's Karry. Will you let me in?* He waited, then noticed a spot thinning in the swirling ball. He took a mental deep breath and dove through.

He found himself in a rainforest. He stood for a moment, breathing the humid scents, and tried to place what was familiar about his location. Then the pulse of power had his jaw dropping.

He stood on a storeground. One so fertile that it could grow trees of this immense magnitude. He reached a hand out and placed his palm on the trunk of one of the trees. "Alexis? Can you hear me? Can you answer?"

The branches and vines overhead rustled in response.

"Please try and answer me in words. I need you to wake up."

His best bet, his only bet, was to get her to wake up and become aware, because he now realized that she was too strong for any of them to force. But staying locked up in her storeground would not help her either. And it wouldn't keep her physical body safe from attack. *Damn, I'm glad that hadn't occurred to Alden. They are so used to using their psyche's that a gun didn't cross their minds. At least not yet.*

"Come on, Alexis. I need to talk to you. I have news on Dae."

That got a response. The foliage thundered around as if a gale had suddenly swept through.

"If you want it, then come here and face me," he shouted.

Her voice echoed off the forest, sounding slurred from sleep. "Don't shout at me."

"Then wake up and come here."

She stumbled out of the gloom of the forest, rubbing her eyes. "What do you want? Where am I?" She finally looked around.

"You don't know?" He shook his head and filed that tidbit away. "You've had dreams before, right?"

She nodded. "With Dae, and one with Erik. Why did you bring me here?"

"We don't have time to teach you right now. I need you to wake up. You're hurting a lot of people."

Her brow furrowed. She looked back into the

forest and said slowly, "They were trying to hurt me."

"I know. And I'm taking you out of here. I just got Dae to Erik."

Her head whipped around, her gaze pinning him. "Is he OK?"

"I don't know. But his family is taking care of him now."

"Take me to him."

"We can discuss what happens next in the physical realm. I need you to wake up so we can attend to the injured in your room."

"It's not safe."

"I am sitting right outside your door. I will protect you."

She stared at him for the longest time, then the next thing he knew she had thrown him back into his body.

Soft murmurs rolled down the hall from the milling Kelusis. He shot a glance over his shoulder at the waiting sentry and rose from his chair. He took a deep breath before stepping through the doorway. His hand reached out and flicked the light switch. Eight Kelusis lay sprawled on the floor and across the foot of the bed. Alexis huddled in a tight ball at the head.

He bent down and rested his hand lightly on the first body, which rose and fell slowly with each breath, and he let a coil of tension relax at that knowledge. He rose again and stepped over the downed incubus to stop at the bedside. He wanted to reach out and touch the human but thought better of it.

"Alexis," he called. When she didn't stir, he continued, "Come on. Wake up. I need to get you out of here, but if you suck me in too…"

A soft moan eased out of her, and he felt safe enough to touch her. He brushed his hand across her hair. "Come on. Wake up."

With stiff movements, she uncurled and opened her eyes with a groan. He shivered at the fevered look they held—a sign of the power she had taken in. "So you really were in the dream?" she asked with a raspy voice.

He nodded. "It's not safe for you here. I've got a temporary injunction to move you." He scooped her up in his arms and headed out of the room. Alden blocked the hall when he stepped out.

"What do you think you are doing?"

"I have an injunction from the first chair of the council. You are not acting in the best interests of the Sundered."

Alden reared back like he'd been slapped. "You can't just take something as potentially deadly as that human out of our protected environment."

"Watch me."

"This is insane. We don't know what affect she will have! She's damaged, possibly killed, several Chirurgeons and has stripped Damian from the ability to feed. My professional opinion is that she's a new wave of Trojan horse. We must find out everything we can to prepare our people and try to prevent more losses."

"Be happy, the council agrees with you in that. You will still have access to her and to Damian, but they are now under council supervision."

"Damian!"

"He has already been returned to Erik. When you couldn't feed him, the only way to save his life was to get him back with his bond family. Which you should have arranged." He shoved past the senior Chirurgeon.

"I will be talking to the council. You *will* keep the two separated. And Damian's psyche is to remain in lockdown. Do I make myself clear, enforcer?"

He threw a heated look over his shoulder that Alden met with equal force. "Yes."

He tightened his grip and walked out of the building. Lexi's body shivered in fear. Once he got her buckled into the front seat of his car, she didn't move a muscle as he walked around and got into his own seat. He slammed the car into gear and peeled out, his temper expelling with a mad rush of speed. He took a deep breath and settled down to drive.

"I want to go home," she said softly.

"I'm sorry, Alexis. I can't do that. Your apartment is too close to Erik's house. I will have some clothes brought over for you though. I'm sure you would like a shower. Are you hungry?"

"Was he right? Did I kill someone?"

"I don't know. The one I checked was still alive, if that helps any."

She turned her head to look out the window.

"What am I?"

"That's still being worked out. And hopefully I've bought us the time to do so." He merged onto the freeway, the traffic flowing smoothly at this hour. "I'm taking you home for now. Tomorrow I'll get Erik to come over, and we'll see what we can do."

Chapter 14

Dae woke to a dull pain that had renewed its throbbing. A soft hand brushed through his hair, and he opened his eyes. Cass sat on the floor next to his head, a worried look on her expressive face.

"Erik, he's awake," she called.

He rolled his head to the side and looked out at the large, open room. Erik scrubbed his face as he sat up in the white leather chair he'd slept in. Callum snored on the floor near his center's feet. Erik rose from the chair, stretched, then walked over to crouch next to him. His older brother's gaze captured his.

"How are you feeling this morning?"

He tried to clear the gravel from his throat. "I've felt better."

"I'm sure you have. Hold still." Erik reached out and placed a hand on him and he flinched away, knowing what was coming. His groan woke Callum. When done, Erik sat back and Dae tried to gain control of his breathing. Cass petted his hair in sympathy.

"The good news is he's taking in the energy. The bad news is it doesn't seem to be repairing his uptake nerves. Or if it is, it's incredibly slow."

Isaac walked in carrying a tray. The joy link took Erik's place at the side of his cot and scooped up a spoonful of something. Dae shook his head, but Isaac pressed it between his lips anyway.

He coughed and choked on the mouthful of thick yogurt.

"I'm not hungry," he managed to get out after a moment.

"Eat anyway," Erik ordered and returned to the chair he'd slept in. "Your body is consuming itself too fast. I can't believe how much weight you've lost in the last couple of days. When you are not asleep, you will be eating. And I will be flooding your storeground every hour."

He choked down another mouthful, then said, "I need Lexi. That's the only thing that will fix this, Erik. You have to believe me."

"It's not a matter of believing you. But the execution is the difficulty. The council has—"

A brisk knock at the door interrupted him. Dae watched several emotions flash across Erik's face as Callum stomped over to answer the door. Three council members, flanked by four enforcers, entered. Erik slowly rose to his feet.

The enforcers remained watchful at the edge of the room, but Dante, accompanied by the two other Sundered who sat on the council, continued up to Erik—as if having the Sundered there would somehow give this visit more weight.

"Good morning, Erik," the first chair said.

"Dante," Erik returned the others' nods.

Dante cleared his throat and glanced at his fellow council members. "Ah, well, I'm sure you know why we're here. But before we get to that, the first order we need to discuss is your council standing. Until this matter has been resolved, it is felt that you need to step down."

Erik ran a hand through his hair, the only sign of his agitation. "I have too many commitments with the regional conclave in a few days and the full court coming here in December. You can't just pull me from my duties."

Dante's eyes swiveled to look at him, and Dae held that penetrating gaze though it cost him in strength. "You have too strong a conflict of interests here, Erik. We can't allow feelings, which I'm sure will run high, to color any decisions. Even unrelated ones. I'm sorry. Your tasks are already being assigned to others."

"The vote?"

Dante shook his head. "You know the rules."

"Leaving me with the choice of not trusting anyone since I don't know who sided with whom."

"No one's your enemy here, Erik."

"Right. Then tell me why my lust link is at death's door and was unlawfully removed from my home. Why am I buried in a maze of bureaucratic red tape? Why is our knowledge unheeded and unwanted?"

Dante pinched the bridge of his nose. "I understand how difficult things are for the Sundered…"

"You know nothing," Erik cut him off.

Dae glanced at the two Sundered council members. Both looked away from Erik, but he saw them each nod slightly.

"The Chirurgeons aren't taking the possibility of Alexis being Dae's Cambion seriously. And the time they are wasting is going to cost my lust link his life. Along with the rest of us as a result."

All three council members jerked attentive faces to Erik.

"Explain."

"What? Didn't Kar or Alden give a full report on the situation? Dae found Alexis right when we found out he was in the final stage of the fade. We tied ourselves to him. Then everything blew up. I'm barely managing to keep Dae alive. We need Alexis, Dante."

Dante pursed his lips and shook his head. "I'm sorry, Erik. Really. But the Chirurgeons do have a valid point. We don't know what lasting effect she might have that could harm our people. We need to be cautious."

"Bullshit," Callum exclaimed and took a step toward the council members. The enforcers responded in kind.

"Callum, go sit down," Erik ordered.

"We were all in her presence for hours, Erik, and nothing happened to us," Callum said stomping over to the couch next to Dae, placing a heavy hand on his shoulder.

Erik turned back to the three. "He's right. And while she was here, we learned much. All five of us are on borrowed time and are willing to experiment."

"Erik, you don't know that any effects would be limited to your family. Look what happened at White Thorn. What is she turning Damian into? Does it breed a weakness that can spread to others? I'm really sorry, but the fact that you are all facing the fade is a mark against your judgment. Any hope would be sought for, no matter the cost or consequence. The safety of our whole species has to be taken into consideration. But in light of the information you have given, I feel this needs more discussion." He turned a look on his other two council members. Both gave agreement. "We will be as quick as possible about this, Erik, in deference to the circumstances. The full council will convene tonight. But until then, I must insist that the precautions the Chirurgeons insist upon be observed. Damian's psyche is to remain tied, and no contact between him and the human in question is to occur."

"Even at the cost of Dae's life and what the two of them represent? Are you willing to take that risk, Dante? Did Kar not give you my promise?"

Dante took a step into Erik's space; the two stared at one another. "He told me. Are you really willing to go that far? I'm betting you would have second thoughts."

"Then you would lose."

Silence stretched before Dante whispered, barely loud enough for Dae to catch, "Don't force me to choose, Erik."

"Then you already have."

Dae caught the confused looks the other two council members threw to each other and realized they didn't know about Erik's threat to take out the court. Most had forgotten the strength Erik could wield; even sundered, he was stronger than almost everyone except for the king. Psychically he could wipe out the entire court, killing all of the Kelusis for miles with a thought. And if he hunted through Shadow first...he'd devastate the Kelusis around the world. If the council played politics and it cost the life of one of Erik's bond siblings and their first true hope for the Sundered, then he would have nothing left to lose. Remembered friendship likely wouldn't be enough to counter the pain the loss would cause. And the treatment the majority of Kelusis subjected the Sundered to would seal the fate of the rest.

Finally Dante turned away and headed for the door. "Our orders still stand. No contact. The Chirurgeons will be by to check him. You will hear from us either tonight or tomorrow. Good day."

The enforcers waited until the three had exited before they followed, shutting the door quietly behind them.

Dae struggled to sit up, but three sets of hands stayed his movement.

Isaac shoved another spoonful of yogurt in his mouth. "There's no reason for you to expend energy to get up, and you still need to eat," he said.

He hastily swallowed. "Erik, you can't seriously do this. Let my mind go. Please."

"To what end, Dae?" He ran his hand through his

hair and turned his gaze to meet Dae's. "You know that we'll all be monitored, here and in Shadow. At least at this moment. The enforcers will know as soon as you go out in search of her. For now we need to play by their rules until we can see how to get out of this. Rescuing her will do us no good until we can have a long-term solution in place. Dante's right in one regard, none of us know what's happened and what this connection you have with her truly means."

The spoon shoved between his lips again, and he glared at Isaac, who only raised an eyebrow. Erik sank back into his chair and stretched his legs out.

"We have a touch of breathing space at least. I may be mad at him, but Karry got Alexis out last night. Centuries of trust and belief are hard to fight, especially when I can see his side so clearly and understand where the motives come from. The problem is that none of the Kelusis truly understand the Sundered any longer. We've changed. So getting them to listen to us is like yelling into the wind." Erik paused in thought, then with a blink turned his attention back to them. "As soon as the Chirurgeon has shown here, I'll go to Kar's place to see Alexis for myself, Dae."

Damian swallowed another spoonful, his gaze on Erik's.

"He will keep her safe, Dae. Trust me. Kar will protect her."

"I can't hide up here all day," Alexis muttered. She cracked open the door and looked out into the small hallway. Taking her courage in hand, she stepped out. The small house sat in a quiet neighborhood by Greenlake. She remembered that much from her drive here late last night. Her stomach growled, pushing her to continue her hunt. Footsteps creaked on the stairs and she froze. Adrenaline pulsed through her. A young man crested the stairs before she could make the dash back to her room. He smiled at her.

"Hello." He carried an armload of folded towels that he started to place in a linen cupboard at the top of the stairs. "You missed breakfast, but there's stuff you can make for lunch. Karry's in the kitchen."

"Th-thanks," she managed to get out and skirted past him to scamper down the stairs.

The midday sun beamed in through the open windows as she stepped into the kitchen. A woman sat at the table reading some papers and drinking iced tea. She looked up at her entrance.

"Ah, you finally venture out, Alexis. Please help yourself to anything in the kitchen. I have four descendants that attend to this house, but it's a bit more of a bachelor pad. I don't keep a family; I allow the community of descendants to use it as a sort of dormitory situation for their college-aged children. So their schedules are different. I'm sure you'll end up meeting them all during your stay here. Regardless, at least two of them will be here at all times when I can't be."

She stared at the woman. "I'm sorry?" she asked. "Who are you?"

The woman cocked her head, then looked down at herself before laughing. Her features blurred and blended together, and Alexis had to stifle a shriek, but she couldn't stop her body from slamming backward into the cabinets as she stared at Karry.

"I hadn't realized." He smiled gently. "I just grabbed some clothes this morning and have been busy with paperwork. I favor the incubus form, but sometimes the succubus half just wants out for a bit."

"D-d-don't do th-that." She squeezed her hands together until the bones ached.

"I'm sorry. I'm sure that's a bit unsettling, even if you are a descendant. You haven't grown up in a properly educated family. I'll try and pay more attention." He took a drink of his iced tea. "Go ahead and get some food, then join me. We have much to discuss."

It took all her willpower to turn away from him and search out food. She threw together a quick sandwich and got a glass of water. With dread, she carried them over to the table and sat across from the enforcer. She kept her eyes trained on her plate and started to eat. She was about halfway through when his sigh got her to look up.

"I don't suppose you'd be willing to let me go?" she rushed out after swallowing.

"No."

Her shoulders slumped and she took another bite.

"Erik will be here soon. He was focused on saving Damian last night, so I only managed to relay that I had you in my custody."

"Save Dae? Is he all right? I need to help him."

"Sit back down, please."

She hadn't realized that she'd risen. She settled back into the seat.

"There're too many variables right now, too many fingers in this pie. I'll compare information when Erik gets here and see what moves we have then." He pointed his chin at the wall and she glanced at where he gestured. "I picked up a few of your things, so you can change your clothes finally, and there's some toiletries and whatnot."

A small wheeled bag that she recognized sat against the wall. Relief that she could put fresh clothes on was short-lived as the outrage over her captors pawing through her things hit. He must have seen the signs because he chuckled.

"Would you rather stay in dirty clothes? I've already searched your apartment. Right after we took you into custody." He shrugged. "I could have sent one of my descendants or another enforcer. Be glad I did it."

She still glared at him. He arched an eyebrow and looked pointedly at her half-finished meal. She picked up her sandwich and chomped into it. His eyes crinkled, but that was as far as he showed his amusement at her ire.

A car door slammed outside and the incubus leaned back in his chair to peer out the window. A moment later, Erik strode into the kitchen.

"We don't have long. I broke the laws of physics, and of traffic, to get here before Alden."

She hunched in her seat and dropped her

sandwich at the mention of that person. Erik ran his hand over her head, then sat at the table.

"Don't worry. We won't leave you alone with the Chirurgeon."

"Certainly not after last night," Kar added.

"Is Dae all right?" she got past the dry lump in her throat.

Erik stared at her with the most intent eyes. She looked down at her plate and shifted crumbs around with her finger.

"I won't lie. I'm extremely worried. I managed to get him stabilized last night, but he isn't improving. He's so weak he can't get out of the bed."

"You have to let me see him." She dared to raise her eyes.

He sighed. "I can't. Not yet. I'm fighting the council. It seems that Alden got to them last night." He turned to Karry. "Did you know they were going to relieve me of my duties?"

Kar pursed his lips. "It wasn't mentioned to me, but are you really surprised?"

"Yes, damn it. I still held some kernel inside that who I was mattered. But that seed was crushed."

"Erik…" Concern flooded the incubus's face.

"Don't, Kar. You've all made your choices. Everyone gets to live by them." He turned away from the other incubus. Fishing something out of his pants pocket, he slid it across the table to her. It was her phone. She snatched it up.

"Put that in your pocket and don't let Alden know you have it. There's a no-contact order from the council. Think long and hard over who you call with that. And what sort of danger you would be bringing on any humans."

His gaze held hers as she slipped the phone into her pocket.

More car doors slammed, and Erik leaned back in his chair. It took them longer, but eventually footsteps came into the room. Kar's foot bumped her calf and her gaze shot to his. He smiled in reassurance.

Alden and two others stopped just inside the room.

"How did you get here?" the old man snapped.

A smile stretched Erik's lips, but there was no amusement in his eyes. "I don't drive a minivan."

"You don't need to be here. You can leave."

"No." He sat forward, then stood up to his full height. "There you're wrong. You will come nowhere near her without me present. Not after what you've done to them."

"Girl, come here."

A shiver coursed through her, and she shot a look from Karry to Erik.

"I expect manners in my home, Alden," Karry rebuked.

"I will not do this exam in the kitchen. I want her secluded from all other Kelusis."

Erik burst into laughter, but Karry laid his hand on the incubus's arm.

"Wait, Erik. You didn't see what I did last night. Alden has a valid worry." The enforcer turned his gaze on the doctor. "Though not one I'm willing to indulge."

The doctor's round face turned florid.

"The secluded part. I am willing to take this to a different room, however. But neither Erik nor I are willing to leave her alone with you." He rose and walked around Erik to hold his hand out to her.

She took it, and he squeezed in reassurance before he led her from the room. He towed her along behind him with Erik on her heels. They entered a living room where he stopped her next to the couch. Gently urging her down, he knelt while she stretched out.

Alden stopped beside Karry and stared down at her; she took an uneasy breath.

"The lower Chirurgeons trapped by her last night are still recovering. Most of them were drained dangerously low. Enough of them were able to give me accounts of their experience. Give me yours."

Karry didn't answer right away and Alden turned his unblinking gaze away from her to him. The enforcer relaxed back onto his heels and took his time. The Chirurgeon was obviously getting impatient.

"I arrived to find White Thorn in an uproar. No one could pass her threshold without getting sucked into a drain sink. I ordered the area clear and attempted to touch her mind. As I dreamwalked, I discovered that she was asleep and turned out to be protecting herself. She had hidden away when you attempted to drain her."

Alden made a dismissive noise. "Of course I was attempting to have energy drained from her. Every one of you had made it clear that her energy was the only energy Damian could absorb. We were setting up a standard energy transfer for a transfusion. And that was the result."

"Really? That's all you tried?"

"Del, Maeve," the Chirurgeon said. The two younger incubi stepped up to his side, crowding Karry. Erik stood at the end of the couch. "Stand in the doorway, enforcer. My lord." His nod to Erik was just shy of insolent.

Erik's face looked like stone and Karry shook his head. "Not happening."

Alexis watched all their faces in trepidation. The thwarted look that touched the Chirurgeon's face left her shaking. It was all she could do to hold still as the old man reached for her. His hand settled over her heart, then lay heavy on her forehead. She couldn't suppress the gasp as the thickness of his energy forced its way into her mind. Retreating from the intrusion, she stumbled into the trees of her rainforest, the outside world lost.

Storm winds stirred the canopy, a brewing energy building that she could feel, putting pressure on her skin.

"Alexis!"

She heard Karry's voice, faint.

"Alexis. Stop. Come out to me."

"Dae needs you," Erik's voice added.

The thick energy oozed around the perimeter of the tree trunks. Lurking. She could feel the eyes of the Chirurgeons on her somehow. The breeze grew stronger, and she ran deeper into the comforting darkness of the woods.

Dae fretted on the cot in the living room and stared out into the late afternoon sun, the weight of his phone clutched in his palm. Glancing at it every thirty seconds still didn't result in Lexi responding to him. Erik had swept in a few hours ago, fury riding him though he'd tried to keep it hidden. He'd conferenced with the others but left Dae out of the loop.

As Erik crouched down by his side, the center tried to smile at Dae's irritation over being left out. "Watching Alden with Alexis didn't go as well as we'd hoped. I have to go to the council. I expect it'll be a late night."

"What happened?" His voice faint, he tried to rise, but Erik stayed him with a light touch. *Damn this weakness.*

"You need to rest. Since I don't know how long I'll have to be, I need to transfer energy to you now."

He half-heartedly pushed Erik's hands away when his center locked them onto his skin, but Erik shook his head. "Stop. This will help. You want to be able to answer the phone when she calls, don't you?"

That snagged his attention and reassured him enough to hold still. The expected pain hit, and he hissed through it. Dae thanked all the gods he'd ever believed in that none of them had yet to notice the growing mating urge settling on him. They seemed to believe his obsession to get to her had only to do with his energy needs. He didn't want to even consider the ramifications of that getting out.

Helpless to stop the mate cycle, the restless need plagued him. The *ullaich* grew steadily into a hard knot.

Erik's hand reached out and brushed the bangs out of his eyes, his fingers gentle on his temple. "You will get better. I'll accept nothing less. Isaac, get some more food into him."

He rose and Dae watched him leave. Isaac sat and scooped up a spoonful of rich beef stew. On autopilot, he opened his mouth.

The joy link took his task seriously and spent a long time pushing every spoonful until Dae had consumed the entire serving. Exhausted from the twin exercises, he closed his eyes. But then his phone buzzed an incoming text. He jerked and almost fumbled it onto the floor. Isaac chuckled.

He shot a glare at the joy link and swiped the screen.

"Yes, I'm here. Are you?" she texted.

He stared pointedly at Isaac.

"What?" And his brother fussed around with the dinnerware on the tray.

"Come on, Isaac."

Laughing, the joy link quit screwing around and left him in peace. Not perfect privacy, since he was in the living room, but better than having his brother standing over him. He dialed the phone. She picked it up on the first ring.

They both spoke at the same time, then burst into uneasy laughter.

"Dae, are you all right?"

"I wanted to ask you the same thing. I'm much better now that I hear you. What happened? Why has it been hours? Erik came barreling through here but wouldn't tell me what happened."

There was a pause on the other end, then she said softly, "I don't know what happened. Alden pushed into my mind, and after that everything went black and I woke up in my bed a few minutes ago, with my phone next to me."

"They won't tell me anything. But Erik is with the council. Since he was told this morning to basically stay away, this can't be good."

"What do we do? I have to see you. I don't feel right, Dae."

He kept an eye on the doorways and lowered his voice. "Do you remember what happened the last time we dreamwalked?"

"Of course. It would have been much better in person, I think," she added tartly.

He chuckled. "I don't disagree. What you're feeling is the mating urge. It's going to grow worse the longer we're apart. But whatever you do, don't let them know."

"So the only way to fix this is for us to finally be together? I'm all for that solution."

"Me too, but no one else seems to agree with us. And I can't get out of this stupid bed."

"But you could if I was near, couldn't you?"

He caught his breath. "Yes."

"So, it's up to me. I'll figure out how to get out of here and get to you."

He shifted on the cot; movement in the other room made him pitch his voice even lower. "When you get here, I'll know it. Your energy will start pouring into my storeground. Then I just need to figure out how to get past the family."

"Then what? Where do we go?"

"We won't have long before they know what's happened. And they'll be able to track me through the bond link now. Since running isn't a long-term option, we just need to get somewhere private to complete the mate cycle. Hotels will be too easy for them to get to us." He fell silent. "I think our best bet is to take the boat. We have a yacht moored down on Lake Union. If we can get to that and get through the locks, it'll take them hours to get to us."

"What will happen to us?"

He took a deep breath before he answered. "I don't know, Lexi. This hasn't happened before. But I can't stop it any more than you can, and I don't want to. I want to be with you. All we can do is see it through, I think."

There was a sigh on the other end. "The only way out is through and all that. We don't have a lot of time. I'd better get working on how to get myself over to you. Kar made it clear that I wasn't to leave his house. I wonder why he thought I'd listen."

Damian laughed. "That's a Kelusis for you. And the lead enforcer, no less. He's not used to anyone questioning his orders. Stay safe, Lexi."

"Promise. You start trying to figure out how you're getting out of the house. I'll see you soon." And she hung up.

He swiped his thumb across the phone and stared at it. The others had been near enough to tell when he was done because as soon as he was off, Cal came in with another tray of food. Thankfully the anger link didn't react to the content of his phone call. Reassured that they must have just heard the murmur of his voice, he didn't complain too much about the quantity of food they tried to stuff down his throat.

Their feeding schedule is what's going to be my problem. I'll have to see if I can't get them to agree to an extended sleep period.

Chapter 15

LEXI HUNG UP HER phone and looked around the room she'd been given. Her bag sat lonely in the corner. Thankful she'd gotten a shower last night, she rummaged through what Karry had grabbed for her and found some clean clothes. She also grabbed her hairbrush and wallet and threw them on the bed. *I need to figure out how to get out of here first, but better to be ready. It doesn't sound like we'll be gone long.* She sighed at that reality.

The late afternoon sun bounced off of the lake's surface and filled the house with light. She left her room, exploring the house and trying to formulate a plan. The place was quieter than she expected for a college-house situation. She finally found one of the boys channel surfing in the living room. *Guess they think just sitting where they can see the front door counts as watching me.*

He smiled when she peeked her head in. "Come in."

She stayed on the threshold of the room. "Where

is everyone? I thought Karry was going to be here."

He clicked the mute button and turned his full attention on her. "That was the plan. But he was called away."

Her mind raced. *Could I be so lucky? Is he with Erik at the council?* Getting away from a couple of humans would be so much easier. She put a waver in her voice and asked, "What if that doctor comes back?"

The young man tried to put her at ease. "Don't worry. He's busy too. Do you want to watch something? To take your mind off of it? Jonathan will be home any second to start dinner if you're hungry."

He offered her the remote.

"No. No, I'm fine."

The front door opened and another young man came in with a grocery sack. "Can you believe I lucked out and got a space in front of the house." He paused when he saw her. "Hello, sorry. Kar mentioned we had a houseguest. I'm Jonathan."

"Hi," she said softly, then looked back at the person on the couch. "Do you have any idea when he might be back?"

He shook his head. "Nope. Emergency sessions like this could take all night."

She sighed, but inside she jumped up and down when she saw the second boy hang up his car keys on the rack in the hallway. "I think I'll just grab a snack and go back to my room and go to sleep. The last week has been difficult."

"Do you want us to wake you for dinner?" Jonathan asked.

"No. I'll be fine."

The two shared a look but then let her go. She went upstairs and waited for half an hour before she snuck back down. Loud video game noises came from the living room. Both guys had plates on the coffee table but were totally absorbed in whatever game they were playing. Lucky for her, Karry hadn't seemed to drill into these descendants the severity of the situation. With a smile, she tiptoed down the hall and lifted the keys Jonathan had hung earlier.

She couldn't go past them to get out the front, so she eased open the back door and stepped into the last of the evening sunshine. She glanced at the key fob. *Looking for a Subaru.*

Easy enough to find, it was the only Subaru in front of the house. The key turned easily and she threw her wallet and brush on the passenger seat. With her heart thumping, she started the car and pulled out, her eyes glued on her rearview mirror, hoping no one would come running out after her.

She drove up onto Highway 99 and prayed she could get to Capitol Hill before they reported her missing.

Dae's phone beeped in a text.

"Kar is with Erik. I'm thinking the boys that live there are going to get yelled at for letting me walk out so easily. I took one of their cars. I'm on my way now."

"Got it," he sent back, then deleted the text stream.

Isaac walked in carrying another tray.

He groaned. "Come on. Enough. I can't eat anymore."

"You heard Erik."

"Please, Isaac. Just give me some space. None of you will leave me alone."

The joy link set the tray down and crouched next to him. "We almost lost you. And still could."

"And will, if you don't let me see Lexi. But none of you seem to care about that." He was surprised at the anger that exploded in his chest. The hurt expression on Isaac's face made him feel bad. "Sorry," he said grudgingly.

"Erik's trying."

"And how's that working out, Isaac?"

"Dae, leave him alone," Callum snapped as he entered the room.

"Great, where's Cass? Might as well have everyone in here." Sullen, he glared at the anger link.

Surprise flitted across Cal's eyes, and he turned to Isaac, who said, "Don't worry about it, Cal. He's just scared and feeling smothered."

Dae growled and clenched his fist, wishing he could get up out of the stupid bed. Center of attention in the middle of the living room was not his idea of a great time—especially with Lexi on her way.

"Cass," Callum bellowed, then said to Isaac, "What do you think he needs then?"

Cassandra came running, but the fear on her face

morphed into irritation that she turned on the anger link. "What?"

"Erik's instructions were to feed Dae every hour, but do you think it'll hurt to give him a couple hours of rest?" Isaac asked.

"How about four," he muttered.

Cass walked up to the foot of his cot and tried to catch his gaze. He glared and turned away.

"Come on, Dae. Talk to me."

"Just leave me alone. I'm not hungry. Stop shoving food down my throat."

Cass looked at the other two incubi. "I wish Erik were here. I can't see that giving him uninterrupted rest for two hours will cause any more damage."

"Three," he snapped, hoping to gain them a bit more of a head start.

"Don't push your luck, boyo," Cal growled.

"It's not just food. It's all of you hovering. Will you please just leave me alone?"

"OK, calm down. We can give you some space." Cass turned to their bond mates. "What do you say?"

Callum ground his teeth, but said, "If you guys think it's a good idea."

"I think it's necessary. And it's not like he can get up and go anywhere. Two hours?" Isaac asked. They all nodded.

"Uninterrupted," Dae added. "No staring at me from the doorway or anything."

He breathed a sigh of relief when they left the room. *We'll have less than two hours before they notice. As long as Lexi's absence isn't discovered before I can get out of here, we should be able to make it to the boat. I doubt they'll think about that destination right off the bat.*

The first trickle of energy dribbled into his storeground, and he stifled a groan. A tear squeezed out of the corner of his eye, though. The fresh energy compared to the energy he could take in from the bond conduit was potent. The trickle turned into a stream, then into a raging river. His parched nerves screamed in protest, and he bit his lip to stop the scream that wanted to come out. But for the first time in days, he could sit up and swing his legs out of the bed. Woozy, he went slowly. He rearranged the bedding to try and make it look like he was turned away, sleeping. After a brief pause, he placed his phone on the pillow. Quietly, he stepped out of the room and grabbed his shoes and jacket out of the entryway closet. The sweats that they had dressed him in would have to do.

He worked the front door open silently and stepped out onto the concrete porch, pulling the door closed carefully behind him. Alexis's face peered at him from the driver's side window of a car across the street. Through the pain of her energy pouring into him, he stumbled through the yard and across the road. She got the door open for him, and he fell inside.

"Go, go, go. I don't know how long we'll have before they notice we're both gone." He inched into a more normal position in the seat as she accelerated away. He slipped his shoes on, then buckled his seatbelt. "Give me your phone."

She handed it over. He rolled down the window and tossed it out.

"Hey."

"Sorry. I'll get you a new one as soon as I can. Erik tracked me once already through my phone. I'm not letting him do it again."

She nodded. "Where do I go?"

He leaned back in the seat and closed his eyes. "Work your way down the hill toward the lake. When we get closer, I'll tell you how to get to the marina."

"Are you OK?" she asked.

"Not really. But hopefully I will be soon. What about you?"

"I don't know. I've felt like I'm going to explode. But the pressure is lessening now."

His eyes snapped open. *Oh crap. I think that was a close call. If I have no energy and she has it all...*

It took them about half an hour to weave down the hill because of the evening traffic. But he finally directed her to a parking place. He managed to get himself out of the car, with his strength returning thanks to her energy flooding him. Taking her hand, he led her along the gangways until he came abreast of the *King's Ransom*. He fished his key ring out of his coat pocket and unlocked the cabin door.

"Let me throw the lines off, then we can get ourselves out of here. I'm not going to breathe easy until we're through the Ballard Locks. Go see what we have in stores. It's usually kept fully stocked, but I don't know who had her out last."

She disappeared down the stairway and he took a

deep breath—the energy pouring into his ground still caused pain, but he could move again. Even if it was slowly. He tossed the lines up onto deck and pulled himself on as well. He cranked the engine in the wheelhouse, and it turned over right away. With care he maneuvered the boat out of the marina and made his way toward the locks.

Erik scrubbed his face with his hands as he listened to the council debate ceaselessly. The incident this afternoon with Alexis had lit a fire under Alden, which pushed the council into an emergency meeting.

Now he sat in the first row of gallery chairs across the open space from the council's table, with Kar's support next to him, as they pondered whether this human deserved to live. *As if they have the right to decide such things,* he thought with venom and tried to keep a leash on his temper. So far they'd done very little listening to him.

Every once in a while, Kar's knee would rest against his or his shoulder would bump him, the contact enough to bring him back and remind him he wasn't alone. As angry as Karry's part in the situation made him, their long history and his actions to help made it difficult to stay mad.

"This human is dangerous. She has an unknown power, and it's growing. We can't take the chance that she could be the final piece that will destroy us. It is just too coincidental that she shows up now. Right when Damian is about to die. If the Cambion were true, we would have seen them centuries ago. No. They are a myth. I'm sorry to take that hope away from the Sundered, but there is no such thing as the Cambion." Alden sat down after his latest reiteration to the council on his opinion.

It grated on his nerves that the Chirurgeon was allowed to speak freely while they silenced him every time he tried to speak up in his family's defense. Unable to help himself, he ground out, "Alden is not doing his job. He is willfully ignoring evidence and instead supporting baseless fear and propaganda."

"Erik," Dante snapped.

"No," he shouted, finally losing his temper. "You are debating life or death sentences for my family. Possibly for all of the Sundered. I have a right to be heard."

Dante's face filled with compassion. "The human is not a member of your family, Erik."

"I disagree. But none of you will listen. Now I know why Dae made the decisions he did. She does carry Damian's succubus half. I don't know how to prove it to you, but I know."

"Please sit back down. We know your feelings on the subject and we promise to ask you questions, but for now you need to let us work through this."

Kar's grip on his sleeve pulled him back down. He hadn't realized he'd risen.

"Erik," he whispered, "they will eject you from the room."

He looked at his friend. "No, they won't. They don't want me out of their sights."

His phone rang and he pulled it out. Callum's caller ID. "Yes?"

"Erik, we need you home, now."

"What's wrong?"

"Dae's gone."

He froze. "How?"

"We don't know."

"I'm on the way." He hung up and found Kar's gaze locked on his.

"I need to go. Let me know what happens."

Karry's hand kept him in his seat. "What's going on?"

He shook his head and tried to pull his arm free.

"Is Dae all right?"

"Let me go. I need to get home."

"What happened?" He'd raised his voice so a few of the council members looked over at them.

"Hush." He lowered his voice. "Dae's gone."

"What? He can't even sit up. How...hold on..." He pulled his phone out and made a call. "Jonathan, what is Alexis doing?" There was silence for a minute, then Kar continued, "Go check on her. Now. I don't care if you wake her up."

After a longer silence, Kar swore. "All right. We'll discuss your lapse in judgment later." Kar turned to look at him. "Well, we know how he left now."

"I have to get out there and track him." Erik started to rise and a throat cleared pointedly. He looked at the council table.

"Where are you going?" Dante asked softly.

"I'm needed at home."

"We've heard enough of your conversation to

know we need to know more."

He shook his head, but Kar turned to the council. "Both Damian and Alexis are missing."

"What?" Alden screeched.

Dante turned a glare on the Chirurgeon, then looked back at them. "When did this happen?"

"We don't know. We've been here the whole time."

The head councilman turned his attention to the rest of the council and they all nodded. "Fine. Whatever resources you need, Karry, find those two. And when they are located, you are to bring them both here. They will now be under council hands."

Grinding his teeth, Erik turned and stalked out of the room, Karry on his heels. Out in the corridor, he snapped over his shoulder, "You could have made some sort of excuse."

"No. Maybe you would, but I have duties to uphold."

He spun on his childhood friend, and a lesser Kelusis would have shrank away from his rage. "If you want my help to locate them, then I suggest you find a way to convince me to trust you."

"I don't need to, Erik," he said sadly. "I know you're the only one who can locate Dae. Through your link. You will lead me there because you won't leave him out there alone. You can't leave him out there without letting the rest of the family die. All of you need his energy to live, and you haven't had a full feeding in too long as it is because of this situation. Letting him go is your only choice to keep me out of it. Because as of now, you are in my custody."

Disbelief followed by fear blanked his mind briefly. Kar reached out to him, but he flinched away, turning to stalk out of the building.

"Daphne," he heard Kar say behind him. "Grab Rastin and put together two teams, then meet me at Erik's house."

He didn't make it to his car before the lead enforcer caught up. "Take your own damn car," Erik snapped.

"No. I was serious. You are in my custody. I'm happy to ride in your car if you wish, but we will be together."

Erik slammed his door. He revved the engine as Kar leapt into the passenger seat. He peeled out of the parking lot. The drive home was completed in silence. The car squealed as he slammed the breaks and threw it into his driveway, then he pelted up the walkway and into the house. He found them all gathered in the living room. The bedclothes on the cot had been yanked clear. Cushions from the couch lay end to end in the center of the cot. He stumbled to a stop next to it and looked down at Damian's phone, placed square in the middle of the pillow where his head should be.

A pointed message.

"Damn."

"We would have already tried going after him if he'd taken it," Cass said quietly.

"What about Alexis's phone?" Kar said behind him.

He looked over his shoulder. "Cal."

His anger link looked pleased and moved in on Kar. But the enforcer held up his hand. "I wouldn't if I were you, Erik. You know two full teams are on their way here now. If you want to have any help with this, then your best bet is to work with me."

"Why? So you can take them both from me again? That's what the council ordered. That's what you'll do. If we aren't here when your teams arrive, then we don't have to worry about that."

"You can't outrun me or the court. Do you really want to go rogue? No support system, hunted down?"

"If it means life for my family, then yes, I'll embrace that."

"But we aren't there yet, Erik."

"We've been one step shy of it for days."

"But still on the right side of it."

Isaac squeezed his shoulder. He looked Cass in the face, then met Cal's eyes. "Well?"

"Why don't we find him first and see what we have to deal with?" Isaac said.

"I don't know, Erik. How'd he even get out?" Cass asked, bewildered.

"We're wasting time; we need to find him," Callum growled.

"This might be our only opportunity, Isaac, and as for how he got out, Alexis escaped first. As soon as she got close enough, Dae would have had the strength to leave."

"Please, Erik. Don't make a choice you'll regret. I don't want to be your enemy in truth."

He stared into Karry's eyes. But then the sound of

car doors slamming made the point moot.

Cal pulled the drape to the side. "Eight enforcers," he said.

"In my office." Erik started to leave the room. "Kar, you can greet your friends."

He shut his office door after the three links were inside. "I don't know how long we can keep him out. He's taken me into custody, he claims. Mostly he's making sure I understand that he's not letting me out of his sight."

Cal looked out the window in this room. "He's serious, all right. Three of the enforcers have been left outside. I expect to make sure you don't try to go out the window, Erik."

He sank down into his desk chair.

"How are we going to find him this time?" Cass asked.

"I can track him through the bond. It won't be easy, and the quicker we get on the trail the better. But I don't know what to do when we find him. The council has ordered they be remanded to their custody. After what happened with Alden, I'm not comfortable with that."

"Maybe we should let them go?" Isaac whispered.

"I can't. I need to take care of all of you too. And without Dae, we all die. Now, any thoughts on where they would go?"

"More importantly why?" Isaac looked at all of them. "They can't be thinking clearly. Why did they do this? What do they hope to gain? Damian knows that you can track him down, so what's the point in running? This doesn't make sense."

A knock at the door stopped the conversation. Erik looked at each of them. "Do we trust him?"

"He's been trying to help," Isaac said.

Cass frowned but nodded. And Callum added, "I don't like it, but I don't see much choice."

"Then let him in."

Kar's gaze swept the room, but he stayed at the door and leaned casually against the doorjamb. "Looks like she told the kids she was tired and didn't want to come down for dinner. As soon as they were engrossed in a video game, she snuck out with Jonathan's car keys and came straight over here. I should have been more clear to them about her situation. I didn't think she'd have the initiative to do anything yet. I had my team track her phone. They found it on the side of the road a couple of blocks away. They are searching for the stolen car now. What have you decided?"

"I don't trust you." If he hadn't been looking so closely, he'd have missed the flash of pain Kar suppressed.

"I didn't think you would."

No, but you want me to. Damn it, I want me to. "I need to start tracking him immediately. The farther away he gets, the harder it's going to be."

"What do you need?"

"Cal, get the SUV ready. Cassandra, grab my laptop. Isaac, get our jackets. We can continue the discussion of why in the car."

The rest filed past Kar, but he placed his hand on Erik's arm to stop him. "I should split you up, but I won't. However, I will ride with you."

"Fine."

They walked down the hall, where Erik grabbed his coat from Isaac. He gave Maggie a reassuring nod and walked out the door.

Callum had the big SUV running in the driveway. He climbed in the passenger side and let the other's sort themselves out. He closed his eyes and concentrated on the conduit he had to Dae. West. He felt the car start to pull out and he opened his eyes; the blaze of the setting sun shot out over the peaks of the Olympics and turned the Puget Sound into fire.

"West."

"Is his psyche still locked down?" Kar asked.

He looked over his shoulder at the enforcer, who sat behind Callum.

"Yes. Regardless of what you believe, I've tried to follow the rules."

"I know, Erik."

"So, back to why?" Isaac said behind him.

He sighed. "I have no idea. What are they doing? Or...what are we missing?"

"You think he hid more from us?" Callum asked.

"He must have. He knows he can't outrun us for more than a few hours, just like Isaac said. So why?"

"We won't find out until we locate them." Isaac sighed.

Chapter 16

THE BURNING SUN SET behind the Olympic Mountains as Dae navigated the boat out of the mouth of the canal and into the open water of Puget Sound. The passage through the locks went smoothly, though their fear of being stopped ate at them. Alexis leaned into his side. He adjusted the wheel and set a course across the shipping lanes for Port Madison. There he figured they could drop anchor in the middle of the deep water of the bay. A little harder for Erik to get at them, but not impossible. As soon as Erik realized they were on the water, they wouldn't have much time.

"How long do you think we have?" she asked.

He sighed. "I don't know. I'm hoping we got the full two hours' head start. Which means they probably know by now that we're gone. My hope is that they think we're still in the car and that they don't think of the boat. I'm heading for an open water area. We'll be able to see them coming. Unless we aren't looking." He smiled down at her.

She laughed like he'd hoped she would. It didn't take long for twilight to settle and the stars to twinkle on as the darkness deepened. For the time being, they were content to hold each other in the quiet as they crossed the sound. Finally he asked, "Are you hungry? You can go make something before we drop anchor."

"I'm not hungry for food."

He squeezed her to his side. "Me either," he said with a roughness in his voice.

"So, can you tell me what's happening?" she asked timidly.

He rubbed his hand up and down her side, brushing the swell of her breast in the process. She pressed closer. "I really don't know. And it's not fair to you to have gotten dragged into this. Not that I meant to. I haven't had any more say than you. I can tell you what I'm feeling. I need you. But not just because I'm starving and want your energy. It's more than that. I want to be with you. I enjoy your company. I love the way you look, the way you smell." He bent his head to her hair and breathed deep. "I can't stop thinking about you. The only time this ever happens to a Kelusis is when they've met their mate. But I'm Sundered and you're human, so I don't understand. We have two types of reproduction in my species. There is the form that creates the descendants, but that isn't true reproduction. In that situation, we have sex as a succubus with a human male, then we change into our incubus side, and using the sperm we harvested from the human, we have sex with a human female, impregnating her. The resultant offspring is a first generation descendant. They are more than human. Something happens to the sperm as it passes through our bodies that give the babies gifts.

"But true reproduction, the kind that results in creating another Kelusis, is different. They have to find a compatible mate; once that happens, their chemistry pulls them together. The true test comes when they have sex for the first time. The response in the succubus half of the pairing is more subtle, but the incubus half knows right away since the *ullaich*, fertile sperm, starts to form. And the mate cycle begins.

"It takes about a week for the sperm to mature. During that time the more uncomfortable they both become. Staying close and having sex helps alleviate it. What I can't figure out is how it's happened. We mated in Shadow. I've never heard in any of our histories of that happening. I never would have believed it possible."

"So what do you think will happen?"

He shrugged. "I'm hoping it means we'll bond like true Kelusis. But I don't know how that's possible. I'm only an incubus, and you're not even truly a succubus. Though I'm surer than ever that my succubus half is in you. Maybe you're becoming a succubus? With my psyche still locked down, I can't get inside you to see what's going on. I do need to warn you, though, I meant it when I said *fertile* sperm."

He felt her freeze against his side. "Do you mean...?"

He pulled her tighter. "Yes. You will likely get pregnant tonight. If we were full Kelusis, I know you would. You won't hate me for that, will you?"

She was silent so long he worried she would, but she finally whispered, "No. I want to have babies. I just hadn't thought about it being soon."

"If I had any choice, I would wait…"

"It's OK. Neither of us planned any of this. That's something I can put off worrying about until later. Right now I'm more concerned about when they find us."

"Me too. I figure we have a couple of hours, tops. Enough time for us to do what we need to." Deciding they'd reached about the middle of the open water in Port Madison, he cut the engines and dropped anchor. After making sure all the alarms and controls were set, he picked up Alexis's hand. "You ready?"

She looked nervous and shy. He didn't blame her. Even though his sexual experience was off the charts, this was new for him too. He led her out of the pilot cabin and down below to the living quarters. They ignored the galley and went straight to the main cabin. It had the largest bed. He smiled.

Ushering her inside, he closed the door. He'd turned the heat on as soon as they set sail, so the room would be cozy, and he lowered the brightness of most of the lamps so the starlight could shine through the windows.

He brushed the hair away from her face with both his palms. "I can't believe I'm really standing here with you. I keep feeling like I'm going to wake up in that cot, unable to move again, any second." The pain from her energy flooding his storeground settled into the back of his mind as he became focused on touching her.

"I know what you mean. Every time I would wake, I would reach for you and all I found was an empty bed." Her hands skimmed lightly up the muscles of his stomach underneath his shirt.

He bent his head and touched his lips to hers. Their softness fluttered the lightest bit under his lips and her tongue caressed the seam of his mouth. That was all it took. His hands firmed on the sides of her head and tipped it back, his tongue sweeping across her lips in a long flat stroke that made her gasp and gave him entrance. He dove in. His tongue tangled with hers, their breaths mingling.

Her hands clutched at his muscles, then skated around to his back, pulling him closer to her. The gentle rock of the boat pushed them together.

He walked her back one slow step at a time, their tongues sparring, until her legs hit the side of the bunk. He pushed again and followed her down to press her into the mattress. Spreading her legs with his knee, he settled into the juncture of her jean-clad core. She twisted her head to the side and moaned when he rocked against her.

He dropped his head to the crook of her neck and nuzzled the soft skin, his tongue licking and teeth scraping. As he continued to slide his rigid length along her, she arched up, her hips searching for firmer contact. He sucked at her neck and drew a mark to the surface that made her shudder.

Her hands started to tug at his shirt, and he let her try, but he continued the slow seductive teasing through her clothes. He swayed back and forth across her chest, enough to make her nipples poke through the cotton of her T-shirt. She groaned.

"Come on, Dae. I want these clothes off."

He chuckled and let her get the shirt over his head. Her hands skimmed up his chest, then swept out over his nipples, and he shuddered, pulling her shirt off too. Then after a second thought, he ripped the bra off as well. She sighed when he pressed his chest back down to hers, skin to skin.

Still not satisfied, she started trying to work his waistband down. He ground into her core and she went limp and moaned as he circled his hips. He captured her lips again, and she devoured him. He gasped, throbbing from the stimulation, but turned his attention to her accessible breasts. He rubbed the palm of a hand lightly over the tip until she arched up, trying to get a stronger touch. Then he pinched. The effect was electric. The jolt that shot through her jerked every muscle underneath him.

Warm heat ran the length of his cock. No longer able to move comfortably against her, he opted to remove her damp jeans. He slid down her body, her hands brushing and gripping.

He dipped his head between her legs, her warm spicy smell wafting through her clothes. He undid the snap and slid the zipper down slowly, then let his fingers tickle the skin under the tight waist band, her hips lifting, wanting the barrier away.

"Hurry, Dae."

"We only have a short time, Lexi. But I'm not willing to rush it unless they are pounding on the door."

"No," she whimpered. And he was sure she was remembering him tormenting her during their dreamwalk.

He chuckled, which made her shiver. He continued to tease her skin as he exposed it slowly and peeled the jeans from her legs. His fingers brushed along her panties, and he soaked in her sound of need.

Having enough, she shoved the scrap of cloth off herself, then grabbed at his waistband. He shackled her wrists in one hand and pressed them to the bed above her head. "Too bad I can't conjure a rope in the real world like I can when we dreamwalk."

She twisted, panting. "I'm naked. I want you to be. It's only fair."

"Don't worry. I'll get there eventually."

"No, no, no, now," she chanted, then cried out when he sucked in a nipple and sunk his fingers fully in her channel with no warning. Her hips bucked and hot liquid bathed his fingers. He froze as he imagined what that would feel like around other body parts. It had been so long since he'd had physical intercourse of his own. His own breath panting, he wasn't sure he could make it last as long as he wanted.

He pulled his fingers from her and brought them to his mouth. He closed his eyes at his first real taste of her. His body trembled. When he opened his eyes, he caught her staring at him.

He felt his mind trying to reach for her, but the ropes binding it were too strong for him to break. He beat at them uselessly.

"Dae..." she said softly. "Will you let me try something?"

He cocked his head.

"I need my hands." She gave them a tug.

He let go and she brushed one across the skin of his chest like she was looking for something. She finally settled over his heart, then her other hand reached for his face. Surprised at the action and what it would normally mean, he forced himself to hold still until her palm rested over his dream eye. Then with a bolt of lightning, she was inside of him. He gasped and would have jerked away, but his muscles were locked.

Before he could really grasp what she'd done, his psyche was free and he sobbed in relief. When he opened his eyes, he met hers, and she brushed her palm from his forehead and across his brow down to his cheek, catching the tears that had escaped.

"Now I think we can carry on."

"Thank you," he whispered and dropped his forehead to hers.

Her soothing hands rubbed up and down his back, reigniting the flames that had died temporarily. This time when she tugged at his waistband, he let her pull the sweats off. He kicked them to the floor. Her hands brushed him as she made a grab, but he pinned them over her head again. "If you touch me, we won't be here long."

"That was kind of the point," she said with a

touch of frustration. "I'm all for a quickie tonight."

"This is a quickie for me." He laughed at her glare. "Trust me. On a normal night, I'll pin you down and torture you for hours. Not letting you come, or making you come more than you can believe possible. Both are in your future."

Her eyes clouded as the uncertainty of what would happen intruded.

He brushed his lips across hers. "Trust me. I will do that to you. There will be a future. We will be together. We have to believe that."

She nodded, and he let his hands drift again until she was squirming. The *ullaich* was burning; he couldn't last much longer. He gasped when she succeeded in rubbing her thigh the length of his rigid cock.

"Are you sure you're ready?"

"Quit talking."

She managed to rub against him again and drew a moan out of him. He shifted and lined up, brushing the broad head against the hot softness of her and drew a matching moan from her. With a flex of his hips, he teased the both of them, sinking just the tip in and withdrawing. Her muscles clenched, trying to pull him deeper. Not able to wait any longer, he slid home. The silky wet grip squeezed his length, drawing a shudder, then he pistoned out.

After a couple of thrusts, he slid his hand between them so his thumb brushed across her clit. She screamed and convulsed around him as she came. He managed to get a few more satisfying thrusts in before the *ullaich* stiffened and forced him into climax. He collapsed as his body convulsed through the first physical release he'd had in centuries inside a living being.

All barriers down, his mind thrown wide open from the joining, he felt her mind respond in kind as their psyche's crashed together. He screamed as a pain he'd experienced once but had never forgotten drove a spike through his heart. Her answering scream echoed through the ship cabin.

Then blackness engulfed him.

Warm breath tickled his neck and he opened his eyes. He tried to shift, but he was still firmly stuck. Her eyes fluttered open at the jostling.

Confused, she tried to shift, then moaned at the aftershock her movement caused. "What happened?" she rasped.

"I don't know." But he took stock and froze in surprise. For the first time in some three thousand odd years, he felt whole.

But not the same.

More than he could take in, he turned away from that thought for the moment and looked at his storeground. Tears burned his eyes and he felt them fall. He met her gaze. "My storeground. It's no longer sand. It's loam, with seeds sprouting."

He buried his face in her hair and let the tears fall, her hands gentle on his back and her whispered words soothing in his ears. Eventually he took a breath and pulled his head back. Her gaze traveled his face and he winced. She smiled and smoothed her thumb over his tear-stained cheek.

"Well, we're both still alive."

He bent forward and kissed her, her lips clinging to his. "So far," he whispered against them. "But I doubt the enforcers will be far behind. Erik won't have a choice about leading them to us."

"Why? Why are they doing this?"

"My family? Because they are worried about us and they need the energy only I can bring in for them to survive. The enforcers, because what I've done has broken some pretty strict laws. It was through humans like you, they think, that brought about the sundering. Nothing like what's happened to you and I has happened before, so they don't see us as we are, they see the past danger."

Her eyes looked sad, and she nodded. Then she laid her head to rest against his shoulder for the last of the time they were together.

A few minutes later he was able to pull out, and they gathered up their clothes and crowded into the tiny bathroom. He handed her a wash cloth. "I'm sorry. I wish there was time to shower, but I don't think there is."

They scrubbed up and got dressed. Back in the bedroom, she looked at him. "So now what? Where should we wait? Up top to see them coming? Down here?"

"Which would you rather?"

"I'd rather you hold me."

"I like that. Make them come and take us." He climbed onto the bed and patted the rumpled covers. She crawled up and spooned against him. He pulled her tight and pressed his nose into her hair, memorizing the scent.

Chapter 17

"DAMN HIM," ERIK CURSED again under his breath, and Kar gripped the wheel tighter. The boat bounced on the waves.

"He's not stupid, center. He knew just what to do to give them the most time," Isaac consoled. "Look at how long he kept his fade from us."

"Don't remind me," Erik growled.

Kar watched Erik stand, staring out the window next to him. The confines of the pilot cabin allowed the center to take a step or two to the side in his restlessness, but that was it. Kar could tell by Erik's movements that they were still going in the right direction.

They'd lost precious time earlier. Erik had followed the pull to the west, all the way to Magnolia Bluff in Discovery Park. But when they ended up on the beach, and the pull didn't stop, Erik stared out over the water and swore a blue streak.

"Fuck. He has to be on a boat. I don't think he

could have gotten all the way south and around the Tacoma Narrows as fast as we started tracking him. Not with traffic at that time of day. I would have felt him to the south. Not west and north."

"Ferry?" Cass had asked. "Maybe they headed to the beach house."

"Maybe..." His shoulders had stiffened, then he turned and Kar winced at what he saw in Erik's eyes. "How stupid..." He swept back to the SUV. "Kar, send your people to Chinook Moorage. See if your missing vehicle is there."

"Shit." Callum jumped into the driver's seat and revved the engine.

Sure enough the *King's Ransom* was not in its slip when his people found Jonathan's car. He ordered them to get the *Relentless* ready. With some careful phone tag, they met up with the vessel already underway in the ship canal. So they managed to get through the last locking of the night at the Ballard Locks. Now Kar followed Erik's body language as they tracked Damian to ground.

Isaac's questions still circled through his head. *What were they doing?*

The number of bodies on the *Relentless* was a tight fit. The Sundered were too agitated to pose a serious threat at the moment, he'd decided, so he let them stay up top with each other and only kept one of his junior enforcers with him. The rest were below decks waiting for the end of the hunt.

Isaac moved out to check on Cassandra, but Callum made Kar's shoulder blades itch with his focused stare. The anger link sat, still and silent in the corner of the bench, keeping an eye on his center—and on him.

They'd left the mouth of the ship canal and had started out slowly into the shipping lanes using Erik as the lodestone. Steadily their speed increased.

Erik groaned and Kar threw a worried glance his way, then suddenly Erik screamed and collapsed to the floor. The other three links had similar reactions, though not as severe. Callum crawled to his center, whose back arched in pain before relaxing.

"Dae? Is he?" The anger link moaned and pulled Erik onto his lap.

A sob burst out of Erik that he quickly quelled. "I don't know, Cal. Gods, I haven't felt that since…" He gripped his anger link and hauled himself into a sitting position. "Go check the others."

"Are you all right? What happened?" Kar snapped.

Erik refused to look at him and pulled his body to a standing position with the console. "No. I'm not all right. Pick up the speed. We need to get there. It's too late to stop whatever he was up to. All we can do now is pick up the pieces."

He opened the throttle and followed Erik into the dark waters.

Another tense twenty minutes passed before Erik told him to slow.

"He's near here."

He turned on the floodlights and illuminated the dark glassy water around them. Ahead, a boat bobbed in the open water. Mostly dark.

"That's it," Isaac called.

He tacked up to it until they got close enough to grab it with the hook. Isaac and Callum tied on, then jumped over. He and Erik followed. He didn't wait to see who else came over, staying on Erik's heels.

They descended into the cabin, and Erik continued straight through like a line pulled him in. He hesitated at the bedroom door but then turned the knob and pushed it open. He froze after he walked through. Kar followed him and looked in the doorway to see Damian's eyes glitter at him where he lay on the bed curled around Alexis. Her hand clenched tight on his forearm, holding him to her.

Without a word Erik spun on his heel and pushed past him, back into the main cabin where he sank to his knees in the middle of the floor. Stunned by his response, Kar stared at him for a second, then entered the bedchamber. The scent punched him in the gut.

"*Ullaich*," he whispered. He stared around at the rumpled bedding, the two forms lying still yet watching their every move. He backed out of the chamber and pulled the door shut. An iron fist grabbed his arm and yanked him around. He stared into Callum's face, always so full of anger, but fear dominated it now. He waved at Erik, but Kar shook his head, clearing his throat. "*Ullaich*."

"What?"

"Stay out of that room until I've talked to Erik." He walked away and called for Daphne. She ran down the steps, then stopped and stared at Erik on the floor, her face pale. He quickly assured her, "It's not what you think. Leave two on the *Relentless* to pilot her home. Get the *King's* engines going and let's get moving."

He knelt by Erik's side. "Eirikr?" he said softly, using the old-world pronunciation they grew up with.

His friend looked up. Hope, fear, and emptiness shown in his eyes. "They will kill them."

"No. I won't let that happen."

Erik snorted. "Right. You do everything they tell you."

"If that were true, we wouldn't be here now. I let you give her the phone when we both knew there was a no-contact order. If they couldn't have communicated, they couldn't have arranged this. So don't tell me I don't break rules."

"This is a bit different. Alden is going to scream bloody murder. We have no idea what we're dealing with in there. And to have to acknowledge that Alden was right about the Cambion..."

"How is he right? We don't know, and won't know until we face them, what they are."

"A mate bond? Setting aside the utter impossibility, it shows that we will never be whole again." He turned his head away.

Karry grabbed Erik's chin and forced him around. "Maybe not. Whole, but different. Could you ever be the same as you once were? You've lived life too long as Sundered. Would it be possible for the pieces to ever fit together again? Break a bottle and toss it in the ocean. Will the pieces fit back together after meeting the sand?"

Erik's shoulders slumped.

"You need to keep fighting. If what happened in there is what we think, just imagine. How many of us ever find our mates?"

"Erik?" Cass asked softly.

"What's going on?" Isaac crouched in front of his center.

Erik looked over his shoulder at Callum, who still stood by the door watching. He scrubbed his face with his hands and rose to his feet. Kar saw only the slightest tremor, which he tried to hide. "It looks like Dae and Lexi mated."

"What?" they both said in unison.

He smiled mirthlessly at them. "The scent of *ullaich* was unmistakable when I stepped foot in the room."

"But…"

He squeezed Isaac's shoulder. "You guys stay here. We probably shouldn't crowd them right now. I'll go see what's going on."

"We will," he added, and Erik turned a glare on him. "You need a witness. But before we go, you have to understand that when we dock…"

"What did I say? It's not like it's a surprise," Erik said, but he couldn't hide the betrayed look in his eyes.

"I told you I won't let them be killed. That doesn't mean they don't go back. This is too important. For the Kelusis, and the Sundered." He turned with Erik and they both walked back to the door. Callum stared at him but moved so they could enter. The three Sundered spoke in hushed voices as he pushed the door closed. Erik paused in the middle of the room again before continuing to the foot of the bed.

The two stared at them.

Erik cleared his throat. "Dae?"

Lexi pressed closer and the lust link tightened his arm around her. "What's going to happen?"

"I don't know." He threw a glare over his shoulder and Dae followed it.

"I see."

Erik sank down on the edge of the bed. "I need to know everything I can, and we don't have much time. Once they dock in downtown, they'll take you from us."

"I figured that. I'm sorry. Really. We didn't have a choice."

"Why didn't you tell me?"

"The same reason you didn't tell me, Erik," Kar put in.

"How did it happen? I didn't think you'd managed to go that far together."

Dae sighed. "We didn't. It happened when we dreamwalked. I didn't believe it at first because the reaction was slower and not as strong as I was taught it would be, but it grew."

"No wonder the two of you were going nuts. I don't know how you managed to hide it." He paused, then said, "I felt the pain."

Dae blanched and looked over his center's head at Kar. "I want him out."

Kar shook his head and crossed his arms.

"I do too," Erik growled. "But we're stuck with him."

Damian kissed the top of Alexis's head. "I'm

sorry you felt that. Was it because of the conduit?"

"Probably. I had it wide open tracking you."

"As much trouble as this has been and will be, you're going to be glad it happened. We would both be dead, probably within a day, maybe two, if we hadn't completed this."

"An uncompleted mate cycle is uncomfortable to incredibly painful, but not deadly," Kar said.

"That may be true for a full Kelusis, but I assure you it wasn't the case for us." Damian looked back at Erik. "You guys knew my uptake nerves no longer worked and I was close to dying. I couldn't take in any other energy but Lexi's. Well, no one thought of the other side of the coin. By not allowing her to give me the energy, it had built up to explosive levels."

Kar's arms fell to his side in shock and Erik's head whipped around to look at him. He could see the understanding in Erik's eyes of how close they had been when Alden had pushed her that morning. It was that incident that had precipitated the emergency council session.

"Let me see you, Dae," Erik ordered.

The lust link ran his hand down Alexis's hair and kissed the top of her head, then whispered, "It's time."

She nodded and they both sat up. She sat cross-legged in the middle of the bed, and Damian swung his legs over the side. Erik rose and went to stand in front of his lust link. He placed his hands on Dae's heart and dream eye. A moment later, Erik crashed to his knees, cupping Damian's face in his hands as tears started to flow. A matching tear ran down Damian's cheek.

"It's no longer sand," he said brokenly. "You're fertile again."

Sand? He couldn't have been. Kar stared at them.

"It happened when we bonded. I'm completely healed."

"Lexi?" Erik asked. "Come here."

She slid over to the side and Erik checked her out. He withdrew, then looked at Damian. "You did tell her what happens, didn't you?"

"Yes. Though I wasn't sure it would since this is something new."

"Well, it did."

"She's pregnant?" Kar snapped.

Erik threw another disgruntled look at him. "Well that is usually the end result of a mate cycle."

"Center," Dae got a worried look on his face. "Have I killed all of you now?"

Erik grabbed Damian by the back of the neck and pulled him to his shoulder in an embrace. "No," he said tightly. "I think I can take from both of you now."

Damian sagged against his center, and Kar looked away as the sobs reached his ears. The pain they released told a lot about how much stress and fear the lust link had been under—was still under.

And he had to add to it.

"We don't have much longer, Dae." Erik ran his hand down Damian's hair, then nudged him up. "Are you up to seeing the others? They'll want to make sure you're all right."

Dae dug the heels of his hands into his eyes and nodded. Erik cast Kar a pointed look, so he went to the door and motioned the rest of their family in.

They clustered around the bed. Their love for one another was a painful reminder of the loneliness that most of the full Kelusis lived with. He listened to their conversation with half an ear, then heard what he'd hoped he wouldn't.

"Stop."

Erik's gaze turned cold on him.

"I can't allow you to feed from him, Erik. I'm probably going to get a lecture that I let you near them in the first place, let alone allowed you to check his storeground. But I can't allow this. We don't know enough about what happened."

"You would starve us?"

"Damn it, you know that's not where I'm going with this. But you do need to wait."

"And if we don't want to? You only outnumber us by two."

"Not anymore. We're docking. I have many people waiting." They stared each other down. "Please. Don't turn us into enemies, Eirikr," he whispered.

His old friend turned away and the family closed ranks, blocking him out as they tried to say good-bye. He gestured to Daphne, still waiting in the main cabin. She stepped over and he instructed her to get as many of their men below decks as she could. She paled and glanced at the closed circle, then raced off. The boat jolted against the bumpers as it docked. A number of enforcers had gathered in the cabin, so he cleared his throat.

"It's time, Erik. Let's go. I want each of you to exit the room one at a time."

"You can't be serious."

"Oh, I am. I know how dangerous you can be. I'm not about to let you do something stupid. Your father and brother would kill me. So you first. Come on."

Frustrated anger burned in Erik's eyes when he turned away. He cupped Alexis's cheek and kissed her forehead, then ran his hand over Damian's hair again. Kar couldn't hear what he murmured to them. Erik rose and stalked out of the room; three enforcers met him, and Kar watched them escort him up the stairs. One by one the others said their good-byes. He knew he would soon have his hands full when they realized they were all being kept separate for a bit. None of them would be happy with him. But if it kept them alive as he navigated the political perils...

Now he was left with just Damian and Alexis. She watched him with fear, Dae with power. *And this is why we need to be careful. We have no idea what has been created.* He held out his hand. "Do you want to go first, Dae? Or Alexis?"

"We're bonded. It's against the law to separate bonded pairs."

"The law doesn't apply to you. And you know it or you wouldn't have hidden your state."

"Kar, please. She doesn't understand."

"I know. I'll try and stay with her, but I can't guarantee anything."

"This could be really bad." Dae got up and pulled Alexis with him, wrapping his arms around her.

They clung to each other for a moment.

"We need to go."

Dae kissed her forehead, then touched her lips. He stalked past, and Kar couldn't believe the difference in Dae's condition. He'd helped Erik pull him out the other night, weak and helpless. Now...

He shivered and turned back to Alexis. She stiffened her spine, but he could see she'd wiped away some tears. He held his hand out. When she came forward, he escorted her off the *King's Ransom*. She craned her neck, but Damian had already been loaded into one of the waiting SUVs. Most of the family had been also. Only Erik and his escort remained on the dock. And he looked even more pissed, if that were possible.

Karry sighed and looked at the handful of enforcers around his friend. "He's supposed to be loaded already."

"What the hell are you doing?"

"What I have to, Erik. Now just cooperate for once in your life."

"And leave my family's fate in your hands?"

"For now."

"Why should I trust you?"

"Because you once did. And you don't have a choice."

He took Alexis's arm and walked her to one of the waiting vehicles, then climbed in after her.

Erik paced the holding cell, rage burning in his

stomach. The threat to his family kept him from acting. His mind yearned to lash out and leave, gather his people and go. But his power was too great a weapon. One best suited for catastrophic events. Instead he turned on his heel and kept it leashed. He'd been waiting for at least an hour. Tentative brushes across his mind assured him they took his rage seriously. The door clicked, then pushed open. Dante stepped in, pulled out a chair, and sat at the little table.

"This is against the law."

Dante shrugged. "A gray zone."

"Bullshit. Where are they?"

"Your family is unharmed. But until we've resolved this, I think it's best to keep you all separated, to keep you safe."

Erik burst into ridiculing laughter. "Safe from whom? The only people that want to hurt us are those holding us."

Dante flinched from his scathing glance. "The council is working on this, Erik."

"I've already told you what will happen if any of my family is hurt. What has my father said?"

Dante looked away, clearing his throat. "We haven't been able to get in touch with him. I'm starting to become concerned."

"Pieter?"

"Same. I need information, Erik. What is going on? From all accounts, Damian was on his death bed, yet when they dragged him in…"

"Dragged him in? Where's Alexis? You separated them? They are newly bonded."

"Impossible. He's Sundered and she's human. Karry mentioned something insane like that, but I don't have time to deal with manipulations of that nature in an attempt to keep them together."

"Get your head out of your ass, Dante. We were here earlier because something unexplainable was happening between those two, and now you just want to pretend it's business as usual. This whole problem is because people like Alden refuse to see something new. What have you done with Damian and Alexis? They are bonded. Think about the danger you're courting if you've separated them. And she has no knowledge."

"Then I have no choice about turning them over to the Chirurgeons."

Erik slammed his hands down on the table and leaned into Dante's face. "If you let those butchers anywhere near a member of my family—and I include Alexis in that—without me present, I will destroy you." He let enough of his power free to back his promise.

Dante stilled. "Do you have any idea what you are setting in motion?"

"None of you are giving us any choice. It didn't have to be this way."

"You could work with us."

"Work with you?" He laughed. "What have we been doing? You've forced everything from the get go, and we've been railroaded into it. The impression I'm getting is that it would be much more acceptable if I were to slit the throats of every member of my family, then fall on my sword. Then we could go out in a nice convenient manner that won't disrupt the status quo of the Kelusis, and we can become just a footnote in the history books."

"That's a bit melodramatic."

"Is it?"

They stared at one another for a few minutes.

"Well, I'm not going along with it anymore, Dante. I don't know what Alden is up to, but he doesn't have the Sundered's best interests at heart. And the council is too hidebound to see. The longevity of the Kelusis works against change or moving quickly enough, as we found out tonight. My family would have died if Alexis and Dae hadn't escaped."

"What are you talking about?"

"Alexis and Damian had started the mate cycle. Damian could no longer feed from any other source. But no one bothered to take what was happening seriously enough. Alexis was producing all the energy, but no longer had Dae siphoning it off. She was a ticking time bomb."

Dante blanched. "Alden is a highly respected Chirurgeon..."

"I don't care. He's proved to *me* at least that he doesn't want this to be reality. He's already tried to harm Alexis."

"What do you want us to do, Erik? We have laws. And as they stand, they've been broken."

"Damn it. That's the hidebound talking. Let us go."

"I can't just let you go." He sighed. "But I will

take you with me. For now, the rest of your family can stay our guests, however."

"Do you really think that would stop me?"

"Stop you? No. Just slow you down." He pushed away from the table and rose. "Shall we?"

Chapter 18

DAE WANTED TO TEAR his hair out. He needed to get back to Alexis. Newly bonded couples had to stay together. Their energy was chaotic for a while and needed proximity to balance each other out. Alexis would have no idea how to control her energy yet. He hadn't felt the stirrings of his full range in so long that he didn't think he could control his, so how could she?

Normal hunger gnawed at his belly, and he gave a quick thanks that the insane, obsessive hunger was now gone. This was just a normal response because of how much weight he'd lost. He leaned against the headboard, his forearms on his drawn-up knees. His psyche reached out and brushed against Lexi's. At least they had that much contact.

The lock on the door clicked, then it pushed open. Alden walked in. An enforcer outside pulled the door shut, and he heard the lock reengage.

He stared at the head Chirurgeon and his power unfurled. A defensive cloak automatically wisped around him. Alden's eyes narrowed as he stepped closer, and Dae felt the other incubus's power reach out and test his.

"Your psyche is no longer leashed."

"Stay away from me."

"Erik should never have freed your power. I must examine you and see what you have done."

"No. Where's Alexis? I demand to see her."

"Move to the edge of the bed."

"I said no. Where is Erik? I need to see Alexis."

Alden continued toward him, and he slid off the other side of the bed, keeping it between them. The Chirurgeon's eyes widened at his ease of movement. Dae's power surged around him; he tried to control it, but he saw the Chirurgeon's gaze grow focused. He felt the other's energy. It pushed into him even over the distance. Normally they used physical contact, but apparently they didn't need it.

He fought back as Alden gratingly forced his way in. Alexis surged into his mind. Together they held the Chirurgeon off until the door opened and Dante and Erik walked through.

"Erik," Dante snapped, and the chief councilman's arm slammed across Erik's chest as his center tried to rush past. "Alden, back down."

The Chirurgeon released his hold, and Dae sagged, his hands pressed into the mattress.

"Erik, you know they need to be examined. Alden, you should have known better than to come here yet."

"We don't have time to waste. We must know what sort of threat they pose. The fact that you insist on bringing them here, into the heart of one of our busiest structures, full of our people, I will never understand."

"And that is why you are not on the council." Dante grabbed Erik and pulled him to the side, then shut the door, not letting him go. "You"—he shook him—"get yourself under control. And tell Damian to cooperate so we can get through this."

Erik shook him off, then turned a scathing glance on Alden before meeting Dae's gaze. "You heard him, Dae." He folded his arms and leaned against the wall.

Dae could tell his center was less than pleased, but having Erik here was a relief. Unhappily he stood straight and turned to let Alden approach. The Chirurgeon caught his gaze, then placed his hands. He gasped at the attempted intrusion, and his psyche acted without his thought to keep the Chirurgeon out. Alden used a heavier hand to force him open, then changed tactics and dove into his link with the rest of his family, managing to go through a back door none of them were aware of being a weakness.

His mind fought, but he didn't have coherent control of any of it yet. It had been so long since he could access it. Next thing he knew, Alden roped his psyche and tethered it. He screamed and convulsed back into the wall. He heard Alexis echo the scream, but hers was one of rage.

Erik tried to come to him, but Dante held him back while Alden picked him up and placed him on the bed.

"You knew he was going to tie his psyche. It's not a surprise," Dante murmured to Erik.

"They are bonded," Erik insisted tightly.

"That still needs to be determined."

No longer able to fight the internal battle, Dae watched in horror as the Chirurgeon rummaged around. The incubus traced his pathways. He tried to close down those that led to Alexis like he would the bonds they put in place with his family. But when the Chirurgeon turned to look at his storeground, Damian felt him freeze in shock. The sand was now replaced with a grove of young saplings.

That momentary lapse in concentration was all Alexis needed to rush in and sever one of the ties and allow him to free his psyche.

He threw Alden out of his head.

When he opened his eyes, he found the Chirurgeon staring up at him from the floor, fear in his eyes. Dante looked concerned and Erik smiled grimly at him.

Alden rose and turned to Dante. "I need to see her. Now. This is dangerous."

The councilman asked, "Are they mated?"

"What?" Alden looked shocked. "That's not possible."

"Well, what did you see then? Karry insisted that when he picked them up there was *ullaich*."

Alden shook his head. "He has to have been mistaken. This incubus is sundered. That is simply not possible."

Damian felt hysterical laughter burble forth that

he couldn't stop. "Not possible. What the hell do you know? You didn't feel it grow in you."

"There was *ullaich*, Alden. I was there as well. Those two bonded," Erik said.

"I don't argue that somehow that human managed to take control of this Sundered's power, but mated? No, I don't think so."

"Then how did Dae throw you out? You bound his psyche. He broke free, didn't he?" Erik taunted.

The Chirurgeon got a mulish look on his face.

Dante sighed. "Enough. We won't get answers this way. We need more information."

Dae scooted up into a sitting position. Erik threw him a frustrated look as he left with the others to examine his mate. When the door shut and locked, Dae slammed the back of his head against the headboard.

Alexis looked up into Kar's eyes from where she lay on the bed.

"Are you all right? What happened?" he asked.

She shook her head, trying to clear it. Someone had done something to Dae. He'd needed her. "I don't know. Something was wrong with Dae."

"And you did…what?"

She rolled to her side, then inched her way into a sitting position. "I don't know. There was disorienting pain. And a feeling that I could help. I reached out to him, but it was like a window between us. I smashed at it until I could reach him."

"Crap. Someone must have tried to bind his psyche."

She shrugged. "I can reach him now. But it isn't enough. The restlessness is too much. I need him here."

"I know." He rubbed a reassuring hand over her knee. "If they were in with Dae, it won't be much longer before they come here."

The sound of the door lock disengaged, and he snorted, catching her eye as if to say "See?"

She rubbed her palms down her jeans as the door opened. A tall, dark Incubus walked through, followed by Erik. She could have sobbed seeing him. But she held her tongue when that doctor and two of his people followed him in. She shrank back on the bed.

"What is he doing here, Dante?" Alden demanded.

The dark one raised an eyebrow at Kar. Karry shrugged and relaxed back in his chair beside her bed. "I'm an enforcer. I'm enforcing a lack of stupidity."

"Kar," Dante warned.

"It's obviously needed since you've already tried to tie Damian's psyche. And failed from the sounds of it."

"What?" Alden snapped. "How would you know?"

He waved at her. She lifted her chin but clenched her fists. Dae brushed through her mind and helped calm her.

"What the hell do you think is going to happen to

a newly bonded pair, Alden?" Kar said.

"This is ridiculous. That is simply not possible. We must determine what she *has* done, however. She has completely taken over that sundered incubus." He stalked toward her, his two helpers flanking him. "I want everyone else out of this room. She has proven extremely dangerous. I don't need you three high-ranking officials as collateral damage when she attacks."

Her eyes grew huge, and she shot a look at Erik, leaning closer to Kar. Kar put his hand over hers, where it rested on her knee, and squeezed. Erik glared daggers into Alden's back. The dark one, Dante, looked from one to the other in the room, a curious expression on his face.

"We told you before, Alden, that you wouldn't be permitted to examine her alone, and that hasn't changed. Both times now I've had to go in and rescue anyone dumb enough to enter her at your behest. And now? When she'll have Dae's expertise to draw on?" Kar said.

"She is dangerous and must be dealt with. You won't do your job, enforcer. The law has been broken and she needs to die."

"That would kill Damian," Erik snapped.

"He was thoughtless enough to continue on with his foolish contact. Besides, he was already dead. He's just gained a few extra weeks."

"Enough." Dante stared at them all. He pointed at Erik. "You, stay near the door. If he's right and she's that dangerous, you need to be protected. You" — he turned his finger on Alden — "examine her, but without the prejudice. Kar, do whatever it is you need to."

"Erik." Her voice wavered when the doctors approached again.

"Try and relax, Lexi," Erik growled. "It'll go faster then."

"I'm right here," Kar said softly beside her. "Focus on me. I've found you before in your ground. I'll keep you safe. Trust me."

She felt like hyperventilating as all three of the doctors reached out to touch her. The shock of their invasion swept her out of her consciousness. She ran for her trees but before she could get there this time, a disorienting pain struck and she struggled against thick ropes that held her away from her safety. Starting to panic, she could hear voices shouting outside.

Another power swept into her. This one she welcomed because it felt like Dae. He pulled at the ropes.

Damian, no! Just hold her. Don't.

She couldn't tell where those words came from or from whom. She pulled and pushed but couldn't get out of the net. Then Dae's energy settled over her, net and all, and she shivered in her own mind.

She wasn't sure how long she huddled there, but finally Dae's energy lifted off of her and he somehow pulled her back to the outside world. She opened her eyes and found herself huddled against Kar's chest.

"Dae," she gasped.

"Hush." He rocked her and she noticed everyone

else in a knot at the door. "Let them go. Just rest now."

Erik seethed. Kar had protected Alexis as much as he could from the Chirurgeon's invasion while he watched helplessly. He hoped Dae was all right alone, because he was stuck with Dante. They left Alexis's room. The Chirurgeons seemed shocked and frightened as they huddled in the hall. Dante looked grim.

"Now will you believe me?" He turned on Dante.

"I never doubted something different was going on, Erik. But what it is still needs to be determined."

"We know that it is dangerous for all concerned, and that's all we need to know," Alden snapped.

"Damn it. You saw what nearly happened in there as much as I, Dante. If Kar hadn't managed to get Dae to help hold her instead of free her psyche like he intended, then her power would have consumed all of us."

"I warned you she would attack."

"Defending oneself from an attack isn't the same thing."

"Enough," Dante barked. "The rest of the council should be assembled by now. They need to be apprised of the situation. We will work through the details already established."

Dante grabbed Erik by the elbow and pulled him alongside, but he threw a glare over his shoulder as the councilman dragged him. Alden, flanked by his two subordinates, followed in their wake. Down a flight of stairs and through the large marble halls of the building, they passed several Kelusis who backed away to let them forge by. Erik yanked his arm out of Dante's grip and matched his pace. The council head threw open the chamber doors and pointed him to a seat in the front row of chairs as they walked down the aisle. Grumbling, he flopped down into it instead of taking his own seat at the council table.

Dante joined the other nine members. The full Kelusis constantly flowed between their halves, a sure sign of their agitation. The two remaining Sundered on the council cast worried glances his way.

Dante pulled his seat up to the table. "They have been brought back."

"And?" Cyrus drawled.

"And there's been some complications."

"More?" Arete asked.

"How can this get even more complicated?" Paris, one of the Sundered, asked.

Dante swept his gaze across all seated at the table. "That's what we need to determine. Alden?"

The Chirurgeon approached the table, his two underlings with him. "I am still firmly of the opinion that the laws are in place for a reason; that human needs to die. She has completely taken over the Sundered that she latched onto. He no longer survives on his own."

"So are you saying that if we eliminate this human, we will lose a Sundered?" Hector interrupted.

"Unfortunately it has now been allowed to progress to that state, yes. From what my colleagues and I can ascertain, he can no longer survive on his own."

"She's his Cambion." Erik couldn't hold himself in check any longer. "And now they are bonded. It is cruel and dangerous to keep them separated."

The council all turned to look at him, but Alden made a scoffing sound. "She certainly has set her hooks in him, but Damian didn't take back his succubus. He is still sundered. So this assertion that she is his Cambion is spurious. I think she's another danger sent to finish off what was started. We can't allow this to spread or we could lose even more than what we lost before."

"You didn't even bother to look. You call yourself a Chirurgeon, yet you won't see. Dae is just as strongly entrenched in her, so it's not one-sided by any means. And you refuse to acknowledge the *ullaich*."

The whole council froze and Alden rose.

"I still say you were mistaken. There is no way a Sundered and a human could bond. He is no longer physically capable of creating fertile seed."

"Well it was there. Send people over to the *King's Ransom* before it is too late. It may already have dissipated by now. But both Karry and I know what we speak to be true. They bonded. And even now the result of the *ullaich* is growing in her storeground."

"If that human is pregnant, then it is from before the incubus broke the law and lay with her."

"Any excuse," Erik said heatedly.

"You are sure, Erik, that there was *ullaich*?" Selene, the other Sundered on the council asked.

"That is not something that can be mistaken, and you know it."

"But we only have your word," Cyrus replied.

"No, Kar witnessed it too."

"Where is the enforcer?"

Dante answered, "He's remained with the human in question."

"Why?"

"When threatened, she has posed a danger. But she seems to trust him enough that he has been able to diffuse the situation each time."

"So she is as much of a danger as the Chirurgeons believe?"

"I am too," Erik said softly. "Are you going to kill me for it?"

"All right. That's enough." Dante took control. "Birch, please get Karry."

A younger Kelusis who sat in a chair against the wall rose and headed toward the door behind the council table.

Alexis pulled away from Karry and brushed the hair from her face with a trembling hand. She scooted back against the headboard of the bed. "So now what?"

Kar settled deeper into the chair, watching her. "I guess we wait."

She pushed against the binding on her mind. Strange how easy it was to miss something she hadn't ever even known about before. Kar caught her attention by squeezing her foot.

"Try and ignore it. I know how uncomfortable it is to have your psyche bound, but it's necessary right now."

"This is what they did to Dae, isn't it?"

"Yes."

"Why?"

"It keeps you in your own body, and stops you from having access to your psychic side. You don't know enough to control it yet. After what you've done—and almost just did—it's safer."

"Safer for who? Not me I'm sure, since I can no longer effectively defend myself."

"I will stay with you."

"Right. If this council decides to kill me, you'll do it since that's your job. Otherwise you wouldn't have brought me here."

Whatever reply he was about to make was cut off when the door opened. A young man, though she didn't know how to tell if he was Kelusis or a descendant, walked in carrying a tray. Kar cocked his head when she looked at him. The man set the tray down on the foot of her bed and took the lid off, revealing a bowl of white chowder.

"Who sent you?"

The man fumbled the silverware as his head shot up to look at Kar.

"E-Erik convinced Dante, sir. I was told to bring her food."

The smell of the chowder wafted through the room, and her stomach growled. Kar sighed and waved at him to continue. She accepted the warm bowl and sniffed deeply. She took a big bite, then cringed as her mouth burned. Kar chuckled and the guy left the room with the tray. She took a smaller bite with caution. The clam chowder was saltier than she normally liked—but after burning her mouth, it wasn't as much of an issue, she mused.

"So," she said with her mouth full, "how long until we hear anything, do you think?"

"Honestly, I don't know. It could take hours, or even days."

"This is so unfair. I didn't have any knowledge or choice here."

"I'm sorry you've fallen down this rabbit hole, Alexis. I'm trying to help all of you. Even if Erik doesn't believe me."

She scooped up more of the stew. "Well you certainly haven't seemed to give him a reason to believe you, from what I've seen. I take it you've known each other a long time?"

"Since we were children."

"And when was that?" She scraped the last of the soup out of the bowl, then ran her tongue across her teeth, noticing the bitter aftertaste for the first time.

"It's hard to keep track of the years, so to know for certain, I would have to go and consult the chronicler, but it's probably safe to say it's been over thirty-five hundred."

Her heart thudded, heavy in her chest. "Three thousand years?"

"More than."

She fumbled the bowl when she tried to set it on the nightstand; her heart squeezed in her chest as it pumped slow and hard.

"Hey, I didn't think you would react so strongly or I wouldn't have told you. You've been doing great with all the other knowledge bombs dropped on you."

She swayed, finding it hard to catch her breath, and Karry caught her shoulders. She shook her head. "Can I have a drink?"

"Look at me."

She felt so tired and still couldn't catch her breath. Her muscles relaxed, and she would have slumped down on the bed if Karry hadn't gripped her shoulders tighter. She whimpered from the pain.

"Look at me."

She tried to lift her head, but it was too much work. He laid her down, then squeezed her chin in his hand as he turned her head. Her vision tunneled, but it finally settled on his eyes when he leaned in and peered at her.

"Shit. This isn't good. Your eyes are wrong."

"What's wrong?" she managed to get out in a whisper.

"I don't know. But I'm guessing something was in the food."

She pushed against the ropes holding her mind and cried for Dae. He must have heard her because she felt him settle over her mind again.

"Alexis," Kar snapped. "Open your eyes. Look at me."

She tried to do what he said, but she was so tired and each breath came so slowly.

"Can you tell me what else you're feeling? Is Damian there? Is he with you? Dae, if you can hear me, she's been poisoned."

Her mate let out a roar in her head, and she felt the ropes holding her psyche tear free. She would have sobbed in relief if she'd had the strength. Dae wrapped his energy around her and squeezed. She tried to struggle away, but he wouldn't let her go. With each rhythmic press, she felt her breath escape.

Chapter 19

ERIK WATCHED AS BIRCH reached the door, but another Kelusis burst in before he could pass through.

"The sundered incubus has gone mad. He's broken free," the succubus panted.

Erik started forward, but Dante lunged around the table and grabbed him before he could latch onto the messenger.

"What happened?" the head councilman demanded.

She shook her head. "I don't know. He started screaming, then turned his psyche on everyone when they went in to calm him. He dropped anyone who tried to stop him."

"He's gone to her. You know that, Dante."

"I told you she needed to die," Alden snapped.

"Shut up, elder," Dante snarled, yanking Erik toward the door. "Erik, you'll be the only one who can get through to him."

They broke into a jog. The sound of multiple feet

followed behind. Several enforcers hovered in the open doorway of Alexis's room when they arrived. Karry stood blocking.

"Kar?" Dante asked.

"Someone poisoned her," the enforcer said and glared over Erik's shoulder. Erik glanced behind at Alden.

"Don't look at me," the Chirurgeon said. "I've been with you the whole time. But obviously I'm not the only one who feels the law should be followed."

"I've sent for Sasha," Karry continued.

Alden sneered behind him, and he wanted to plant his fist in the Chirurgeon's face, but instead he pushed past Dante until he stood before Kar. His childhood friend continued to block the door.

"Move."

"I don't know if it's safe for you to go in there," he said.

"They're my family now, not my father or brother. I'm no longer needed or wanted by the court, Kar. These recent developments have proven that beyond a doubt."

"You're wrong," Karry said with force but still stepped to the side.

Erik walked past with Dante on his heels. Damian held Alexis in his arms, her too-still body stretched between his legs. The lust link had his eyes closed, and through the link they shared, Erik felt the power he used to hold her, to make her stay with him. He was keeping her breathing.

Erik gestured Dante to a stop and continued alone to the side of the bed. He reached out a hand to Dae.

The incubus's eyes snapped open, and Erik couldn't see recognition in them at first. Power coiled and Erik pushed through their link. Dae blinked at him.

"Center, I can't stop it," he said brokenly.

Before he could reply, there was a commotion at the door. Sasha rushed in with a male descendant.

"Move, Erik," she snapped.

He stepped to the wall, staying near Dae's head. Sasha and her descendant started checking Alexis out.

"Pupils constricted, pulse slow. What happened, Kar?"

"Someone brought her some clam chowder."

"Is there any left?"

"No, she ate it all, but the bowl is still here."

"David? What do you think?"

"Heroin. They could have masked that in clam chowder." He reached into his bag and pulled out a package, stripping the syringe out of the plastic. He snapped all the pieces together, and Sasha pushed Alexis's head back. David shoved the thing up her nose and shot half of whatever it was in, then used the other half in the other side of her nose. "If it is heroin, we'll know in a couple of minutes."

The room grew silent except for the soft sounds of Alexis's shallow breathing and the movements of the Chirurgeon and her descendant. A few minutes later, Dae looked up and Erik saw the tears in his eyes as a look of hope filled them. Then he noticed her sudden deeper breath. Her hands twitched and she shifted. Opening dazed eyes, she blinked slowly.

"Somebody slipped her a bowl laced with heroin

or some other opiate-based drug," David confirmed. "Sasha, we'll need to stick around in case the Narcan wears off and there's still too much heroin in her system. Everyone else, please get out."

Erik bristled at the command and Kar put a hand on his arm.

"The descendant is right. There's too many people here."

That's when Erik looked up and realized the whole council stood in the room.

"I want Callum here, Kar. No excuses."

Kar squeezed his arm but didn't answer. Dante held out his hand and indicated he should lead them out. Erik looked down into Dae's eyes once more, then strode through the crowd and out into the hall.

"It didn't work."

"How was I supposed to know that his psyche was tied close enough to her to be able to keep her alive? Or that that radical Chirurgeon and her pet could come in and save her? Now what? I sent my descendant home so no one could question him."

"And you're sure no one can trace his family back to you?"

"I'm sure."

He paced across the small office and felt his body shift into his succubus. "The council will reconvene in fifteen minutes. Erik's family is now on alert, so we won't get another try from that direction. At the moment our best hope lies in getting the council to vote in favor of upholding the law and ordering her destroyed. I'll see who I can sway. You report back to the others and let them know what's happened. And find out how much longer they'll keep the king occupied. He's going to be breathing down our necks as soon as he's free. Once he's heard what's happened to Erik, our tasks will become much more difficult."

"Yes, milord."

"We must hope we can stop this here with the council, but we have to plan just in case. Bring Jakob into the city. We might need to set one of our hounds loose."

"What about the others? You haven't checked with them about bringing him in."

"I'm in this position for a reason. Now don't question me. I have to return to the council chamber before I'm missed."

"Yes, milord."

⧫

"Sit down, Erik, and eat." Dante sighed with exasperation.

Erik glared at the council head. The last several hours had been a nightmare. Only the update that Kar had thoughtfully sent to him during the interminable session had kept him from unleashing his psyche on the obstinate gets. Sasha and her descendant had Alexis stabilized, and she was recovering quickly. The thought of how close he'd come to losing Dae…both of them…

He could feel the anxiety through all the bonds he shared with the family. He wasn't sure whether to be grateful that they had no idea what had almost occurred, or to be annoyed that they were scared and alone.

"Erik, you need to eat. And when's the last time you shared power?"

"None of your concern."

Dante made another exasperated sound. "Look, I know you don't like it, but there's not a lot of choice. The council is divided. They must be brought in and a projective dreamwalk done."

"She's not strong enough." He pulled out the other chair at the small table and dropped into it.

"I don't think that's the case."

"She doesn't understand." He eyed the food on the plate, not sure he wanted to trust it, but Dante had already eaten most of his and didn't show any ill effects. "You don't understand. Asking them to relive that..." He looked up into Dante's eyes. "Asking us to live it..." He swallowed. "You don't know what you're asking."

"I'm not asking."

He clenched his teeth together and turned back to the food.

"Look, Erik, it's the only way I can see to prove beyond a shadow of a doubt that she's his Cambion. Unless you have any other ideas?"

"Well, since trusting us is out of the question, I guess not." He took a bite.

Dante sighed. "Look, we will all be there. If what you believe is true, then Alden will not be able to brush off the truth we all see. And if he's right...it's better to know about it now."

He forced the food down. He wasn't hungry, but he knew it was going to be a long night. "How long are you willing to give them?"

"This should be settled, Erik," he said. "As soon as the recess is over."

He pushed the food around on his plate, then looked up at Dante again. "At least let me go talk to them. Tell them what's coming."

The council head leaned back in his chair and watched him for a few moments. "OK. But not alone."

He snorted, then said, "What could I possibly accomplish?"

"You? A great deal. Finish that and I'll go with you."

Exhaling sharply, he took another bite.

Lexi walked beside Dae through the marble halls. The building had the feel of one of the old buildings in downtown Seattle. Erik and another Kelusis who exuded power walked before them, and Karry and the nice doctors followed behind them. Nervous, she rubbed her palms down the denim of her jeans. She felt mostly back to normal after her close call. She still found it hard to believe that she had almost died. *I know they've said by their laws they will kill me, but to have someone almost succeed?* It really brought home the reality.

Then what Erik told me the Chirurgeons are going to do to us... I don't like the picture I painted, but to live through the scene... She shivered. *I don't want to do this.*

A whisper of Dae's power circled around her and he reached for her hand. She squeezed and clung to the reassurance.

A big, dark oak door stood open, waiting for them. An enforcer, from the looks of him, pulled the slab shut after they all passed through. Even more nervous, she followed Erik down an aisle that bisected a gallery full of spectators, leading toward an immense wooden table at the other end of the room full of unsmiling people. A heavy hand stopped her in front of a chair, which was placed in the open area between the council table and the audience chairs. Dae was pushed to sit in a matching seat several feet over.

Alden stood with his arms crossed, glaring at her from the farthest end of the council table. Dante's chair scraped back, and she looked around anxiously. Erik sat at the edge of his seat in the front row behind her, and Kar beside him. She swallowed and turned back to the silent room. Everyone stared at her. She felt her power unfurl inside.

"Lexi," Dae said softly.

Heeding the warning, she tried not to let the power control her and put a restraining hand on it.

Dante cleared his throat. "It has been a number of centuries since we've needed to witness a public dreamwalk. But too many questions have been raised in this situation. The main being the truth of the existence of a Cambion. Does this human woman carry the sundered half of this Kelusis? Or is she the next stage in the plot that was unleashed against us to kill our people? After much deliberation, it seems that the only evidence deemed acceptable will be to see what these two contain for memories."

Fear shortened her breath when Alden stepped forward. She wanted to jump up, but the hands clamped down on her shoulders again, and Dae caught her gaze. He stared into her eyes, and she felt his energy smooth around her, soothing. Erik's words echoed in her mind of what he said was to come. How both her and Dae's memories would be projected onto the big, blank, screen-like wall to the side of the conference table for all to see.

Alden purposely placed himself so that he blocked her visual connection with Dae, and with a hard smile, he reached his hands out. She didn't even feel him touch her before he forced his way inside her mind. Instinctively she dove for her trees, but he'd been ready for that move and netted her psyche once again. She was sure she heard a scream in the room but was too busy clawing at the ropes to think about it. She could sense Dae's energy just outside of the net, pulsing with violent emotion that seemed to be held back with sheer willpower.

As soon as the Chirurgeon had trapped her, he left. Panting, she opened her eyes and saw him move in on her mate. Dae stared daggers at the elder. Damian convulsed in his seat as soon as Alden touched him and his guarding enforcer kept him upright.

The Chirurgeon stepped back, and she felt him in her head again like a strangling piece of vine twining about her. She flinched away, but he held tight. She could do nothing but watch as he sank claws into her deepest recesses, places she didn't actually remember—but when he touched, she could recall the feelings.

Deeper he burrowed. After an eternity of a few minutes, flickers of movement appeared on the open wall. The movement solidified into two matching movies, side by side. Torchlight flickered on stone, and the sound of footsteps echoed. Soft whispers reached her ears; she couldn't understand the language, but after a glance around, she realized others could. Dae's eyes stared at the scene, and the pain in them hurt her. Two of the men on the council looked upon him with a mixture of sympathy and a pain of their own.

Laughter drew her gaze back to the unfolding drama. A beautiful face swung into view in the flickering light. Male hands reached forward and swept her hair back from her cheeks. She said something, and Alexis heard Erik growl behind her. Dae hunched in his chair like he'd been punched in the gut.

The woman laughed again and tugged a hand. Alexis gasped. They'd passed a reflective surface, and she recognized Dae's face. She knew it was him, but seeing him dressed in ancient clothes made it more real.

Conversation from the gallery behind her caught her attention.

"The two memories match perfectly," a female voice said.

"It could be he shared with her in a dreamwalk. I've heard they dreamwalked several times before caught," a low voice added.

"I don't think so. I'd think if it was shared, then her own perceptions would have colored the memory of it. So then they wouldn't match perfectly."

The projected couple on the wall paused beside a wooden door and embraced, then they opened the door. Alexis felt her heart clench. The room looked exactly like she had painted. The large curtained bed stood sentinel in the far corner. More words, then Dae tumbled the woman onto the bed. Alexis had to look away, embarrassment warring with jealousy.

Plus the anticipation of the pain she vaguely remembered to come.

As the coupling grew heated, more murmurs started up. No longer watching, she realized she could tell which people in the room were Sundered by their reactions. A greater number than she had thought were present.

Then she noticed the Chirurgeon. His agitation, while he tried to hide it, was obvious to her because she could still feel him sitting on her psyche like a bloated spider.

He did something and the images cut off. Silence fell throughout the large room.

"Alden?" the head councilman questioned.

"We've seen enough. We don't need to put the Sundered in the room through the pain of watching or the rest from seeing what our brethren went through. Damian obviously shared his memory with the human so completely that it took all of him in."

Dante leaned back and folded his hands on the table. "Really? I don't remember you taking my position, or any position on the council actually. It isn't your place to decide what we see." He glanced around the table, and all nodded at him. "I'm sorry for the sorrow we will cause, but the rest must be seen."

The thwarted look Alden turned on her scared her. After a mental jab that she figured was unnecessary, the images started up again. She didn't enjoy watching the man she'd come to love rolling around the bed with another woman, even if it was centuries ago. The Chirurgeon sped up the playback, so to speak. It didn't sound like a high-speed tape, but the memory movie did move into fast-forward. Then he brought it back to real time right before the moment of climax.

She shot a look at Dae. He stared, his hands gripping the sides of his chair, white-knuckled. Erik had gone to him. The other incubus knelt behind Dae with his hands on his shoulders, whispering into Dae's ear.

Then the pain ripped through her. Their matching screams tore through the quiet chamber, quadrupled because of the echo of the psychic playback. She would have fallen out of her chair if Kar hadn't caught her. Erik held Damian. Tears coursed down her cheeks as she looked at the wall.

Now the two images no longer matched. The

right-hand picture was an exact replica of her painting—Dae sprawled across the ancient bed, pain etched through his twisted body as he reached toward the watcher.

The other image shocked her.

She knew immediately that what she was seeing was from Dae's eyes. But it was the visceral remembrance that she could *feel* that left her cold. The frozen picture depicted the human woman Damian had been having sex with, her long hair wrapped in the fist of a burley, uniformed man as he dragged her across the floor. Her body contorted with the struggle to reach Damian again. Yellow torchlight gilded the scene and the acrid smoke still filled her nose.

The woman's sobs echoed in her ears as her ancient memories pushed to the surface—the pain in her scalp as she was dragged away, tossed, cold and naked into a small stone room. Confusion as the soul of the succubus burrowed into the woman and neither understood what happened. Fear, as strangers came and took her away.

A lifetime of memories skated by in the blink of an eye. Then multiple lifetimes as the succubus passed from descendant to descendant. More time than Alexis could grasp.

Kar's grip on her shoulders tightened painfully and pulled her back to now. She cried out and tried to wrench away, but the stronger enforcer held on. He pulled her sideways out of her chair and wrapped her in his arms. His voice in her ear finally penetrated her wheezing sobs.

Quiet murmuring filled the room, an awed tone prevalent. In the matching chair several feet over, Erik helped Dae. She pulled, trying to go to him, but Kar held her back.

"You can't. Not yet," the enforcer whispered in her ear.

The memory echo still ached and she took a deep breath. She realized that reliving it wasn't as bad as living it. And the bond she held with Dae was absorbing it.

"So she truly is his Cambion," one of the council said into the silence of the room.

Alden looked ready to spit nails, but he held the dream images. His voice hard, he called out, "Is she? It looks like maybe something in her might have been, but what is she now? If she carries his succubus, does that really matter or change anything? He didn't take back his other half when they bonded."

"So now you acknowledge the bond?" Erik challenged.

He looked down his nose at their center. "For lack of a better term, it changes nothing. He didn't reclaim his succubus. How do we know she's not the rest of the plot to destroy us? What did they do to *her*?" He pointed at the woman frozen on the wall. "We can't take the chance of letting this go any further, endangering our entire race. We can't forget that one of the first casualties was our crown prince." He stared at Erik. "And I find it hard to believe and a bit too coincidental that this new development is so close to our former heir now."

The look Erik cast should have killed the Chirurgeon, and Alexis relaxed, dumbfounded, into Kar's hold. "Is...is he?"

"I'm afraid so," the enforcer whispered grimly.

"And that is exactly one of the reasons why I feel we shouldn't be hasty about doing anything irrevocable. If we kill her before the king knows what is happening, heads will roll," Dante countered.

The head of the council met the gaze of each member at the table. "He has acknowledged they do have a bond and I feel sufficient proof has been offered"—he waved a hand at the pictures still displayed on the wall—"to show that she carries his succubus, or some remnant of it. Are we agreed?"

After a minimum of comments, seven of the council agreed but three still felt that Alden held the right of it. Outnumbered, the dissenters grew quiet.

Dante smiled finally and looked at Erik. "You may take your family home, Erik. All your family. However, this is still an unknown. You aren't under house arrest, but none of you are to leave the region. And I want you under Chirurgeon care."

"Not him," Erik snapped, jerking his head at Alden.

"No. I understand. Will Sasha be acceptable?"

Dae whispered in his ear, then Erik looked back at Dante. "Yes. We'll tolerate her and her descendants."

"Thank you," Dante said. "I'm sorry this isn't completely over, but you can relax for now. I will call on you tomorrow so we may discuss the next steps in more detail."

With a hiss, Alden cut the images, and Alexis

groaned when he yanked himself out, leaving her psyche tied behind him. She glared at his back.

Erik stood and helped Dae to his feet. Karry lifted her to hers. With an uncomfortable look, she glanced out over the audience, pausing at the hope etched in numerous faces. A gentle shove to her shoulder got her moving, and she fell into Dae's arms. He buried his face in her hair.

Kar's voice spoke softly behind her. "Take them down to the garage, Erik. I'll get the others and meet you."

"OK."

Quiet conversations filled the room. Erik gave them a moment, then cleared his throat. "Let's get out of here."

Dae lifted his head and his arms loosened. As he looked into her eyes, she could feel her psyche reach for him but couldn't get past the tie.

"Sasha can take them off for us. Erik probably could too, but Alden did a thorough job." His hand slid down her arm, and he linked his fingers with hers. She followed as Erik led them out through a smaller door behind the council table. So many eyes bored into her back she let out a sigh of relief when the door closed behind her.

Their center led them to an elevator, and after a quiet ride, they got out in an underground garage. Erik held out a key ring and pushed a button. One of the fleet of black SUVs flashed its lights and beeped. They headed over and Dae helped her into the front seat.

Erik started up the car with a roar. "I don't feel

like waiting any longer here. Kar will bring everyone home."

She twined her fingers with Dae's, where they rested over her shoulder from the backseat, and finally let her body relax.

Curled up on Dae's lap on the leather couch, she listened to the conversation float around her. Some part of her knew these people. She couldn't remember them. Didn't know them. But a feeling of childlike happiness and trust that she realized was directed at them filled her.

Their happiness and welcome was unfeigned.

Kar's voice held a note of concern. "I still don't like it, Erik. Someone tried to kill her. We have no idea who. And they could try again. No matter what the council has decided. Obviously more is going on than we'd realized and all of you need to be protected. Alden was right about one thing, I too find it too coincidental that you were one of the first to be targeted when you were sundered, and now? But it also brings up another question: How many thousands of years has it been? And there's a cohesive plot that has survived the time span."

Erik sighed. "What do you want?"

"For now, they don't go anywhere alone." He pointed at her and Dae. "And I want you to be sure of where your food comes from."

"Been a long time since the days of food testers," Callum added.

"And I wouldn't have thought it'd be needed again either."

The doorbell rang and feet pattered to the door. Quiet voices murmured, then Sasha and her descendant partner walked into the room. She smiled. "I'm glad to see all of you here. I want to do a full workup on all of you."

Groans filled the room.

"Come on," Cal snapped.

She smiled at him. "Cope, anger link. I need to see how this new bond is affecting all of you since you still require your lust link to feed you. Do you really want to trust Alden's assessment?"

"OK, good point," he groused.

"The council wants a full report by tomorrow morning. I'll start with the love birds, then you next." She winked at Callum.

Lexi couldn't help the snort that came out from the look on his face. Dae lifted her off his lap, and she sat beside him on the couch so they both faced the doctors. When Sasha reached for her, she only flinched slightly, then relaxed when the Chirurgeon's soft hand pressed against her forehead. The invasion was nothing like Alden's, and in seconds, Sasha had freed the ties binding her psyche, and she sighed in relief. After that she wasn't sure how long the succubus rummaged around in her head, but a light squeeze of her hand from Dae had her opening her eyes.

Sasha smiled at her. "I was too busy saving your life earlier to check you out. You have the most fertile storeground I have ever seen. And it's a true bond you have with Damian." She glanced around at the people in the room before she took a deep breath. "Now comes the hard part for you. You no longer register as human."

Alexis gasped. "What? I'm me. I don't feel that much different...I don't think..." She trailed off.

"When I look at you, read you, you appear exactly like one of the Sundered. I know this is going to be hard for you to come to terms with. It probably won't become real to you for a few decades...when friends and family age and start to notice that you aren't."

"But...my family..."

"Eventually you will have to leave them. Unless they are descendants?"

She shook her head and Dae broke in.

"They are, but not aware of the fact."

"I'm sorry," she sympathized. "You don't have to worry about it right now. You have years yet before your lack of aging will be noticed. But of more immediate concern is that you will need to learn how to hunt and feed because your body now requires emotional energy just like all of us. The two of you are currently running through a stockpile she has, but it'll end eventually."

"What about the pregnancy?" Erik asked.

"No way to know at the moment. Will it run like a Kelusis? Or a human? I think I'll be spending a lot of time here." She smiled.

"Lovely," Callum muttered, which made Dae chuckle.

Sasha quickly untied Dae's psyche and ran a quick check, pronouncing him well.

"You are sure he had gone to complete sand?" she queried Erik.

"Positive. I saw it for myself. He could hold nothing in his storeground. The only thing keeping him with us was the open conduit I made. Though I think she had something to do with it as well. Even though they couldn't share any energy and Dae couldn't dreamwalk, he was so far gone... He shouldn't have been able to stay with us."

Sasha shook her head. "I just don't get Alden. This is such an opportunity. I wish I could have seen you before you bonded. But the best I'm going to get is some dreamwalking."

"Well, before you move on any further, Sasha, I've some business the family needs to discuss." Erik turned to look at them and addressed Dae. "Since your honeymoon is housebound, I can't send you to Port Townsend now."

He groaned. "I forgot. Sorry, Erik."

"Don't worry about it. But I need one of you"—he looked at the rest of the family—"to take Dae's place in the negotiations. Jeremy's main branch of descendants want that house for their business, and Jeremy thinks it'll be a perfect new location for their family. With the crisis the last couple of weeks, I've let business slide and now there's competition for that property. The owner is seriously balking at our offer now."

Callum cocked his head. "It can't be the money? No one could reasonably top any offer we make."

"True. Mr. Davies isn't saying, but I get the

distinct impression that whoever has countered us has caught his fancy."

Isaac laughed. "He's in his late eighties, Erik."

The center smiled back. "And that makes a difference?"

"I'll go," Callum declared.

Erik turned to the anger link and studied him for a moment. "Are you sure?"

He shrugged. "If you drain my ground thoroughly, I'll be fine for a few days as long as I don't feed. And we can go for at least five days before the need becomes problematic for the family. We've shown that before. I can pick up the *King's Ransom* from where Kar left her docked and take her up to Port Townsend. Then we don't have to worry about me mixing with too many humans by staying in a hotel. And how long should this take, really? Two days should be plenty."

"All right. But stay in close contact. If anything goes south, I need to be ready to get up there."

"Then I'll leave in the morning." He stood and looked at the Chirurgeon. "I assume you want to look at me before I go?"

She rolled her eyes and followed him out of the room.

"And I think that's our cue for the party to end," Dae said and rose to his feet. He pulled Lexi up beside him.

A smile flirted with Erik's lips. "Staying close to home isn't just meant in the physical; for now it'd be best if you two didn't venture out in the Shadow realm. She will have a lot to learn, and there will be plenty of years to take her places. Until we know more about this threat, I don't want you out in Shadow, especially in any of the public meets."

"I understand. I can't guarantee that we won't walk, because she drew me out unknowingly. But I'll take the lead and bring us home if I find us out."

"As long as you stay safe. It's good to have you home and back to normal, Dae. And welcome, Alexis."

Erik rose from his chair and gave them both hugs. The rest of the family followed suit. Dae took her hand and she followed him up the stairs. The damaged door to his room swung on loose hinges and Dae sighed. They pushed it shut and stuck a shoe in front of it to hold it closed, as best they could. She looked around the room, the memories flipping by. Dae must have realized, because he took her in his arms.

They rocked together for a moment as their bodies relaxed, and they came to terms with being alone after everything that had occurred.

He cupped her face, his gaze roaming over her, then his hands slid up into her hair and his head lowered, his lips brushing hers. She shivered and let the tip of her tongue slip out to brush across his lips. The kiss deepened until their breathing grew heavy, then he pulled away. A smile lighted his face.

"I can't believe you are here." He ran his fingers through her short strands. "I know, since you carry my succubus, that we are compatible, but it's more than that. You aren't me, even though some ancient part of me is in you. You are your own person, and who you are, I love. I love you."

"I love you too," she whispered, her heart swelling, and her power flowed around them.

Author's Note

Thank you so much for reading. If you enjoyed the story please consider leaving a review on Amazon and Goodreads. And if you follow the link to my website you will find my mailing list sign up button to get updates on new releases.

http://www.sianawineland.com

Coming Soon…

HEART OF FURY

by Siana Wineland

MELODY CARLISLE STARED GROGGILY up at the ornate ceiling panels of her hotel room as she tried to get her mind in gear. The alarm had blared its second snooze and she knew if she hit it for a third she wouldn't get up. The clang from the ancient radiator finally got her moving. She yawned and slipped her feet into fuzzy slippers. At least the thing worked to heat the room in the morning. Summer in the Pacific Northwest was usually a short lived affair. The hottest time of the year was generally August. The month just past. At the start of September one could hope for summer like days but usually only after cool misty mornings.

This was especially true when you were out near the water. The wind came barreling through from the Strait of Juan de Fuca and up over and around the little seaside community of Port Townsend. Thankfully today she could see the sun burning off the fog already, so it promised to be a nice warm day. She let the drapes fall back across the glass.

"Well, Mom." She spoke to the empty room. "I'm this close to the dream." She pulled two clean cotton skirts in graduated shades of blue and pink out of her suitcase. "I'm hoping today Mr. Davies will decide that he likes me well enough to let me have the house."

She slipped the skirts on over each other, their complimenting colors overlapping, then tucked in a lilac blouse. "He can't really want his beloved house to go to some city developer from Seattle. People with that kind of money don't care about the property. Just what they can get out of it to make more. I bet they'll just tear the old Victorian down and build a condo."

She found her sandals under the wingback chair then started the daunting task of getting the brush through her thick hair. "And why would they care? Probably live in glass condo's that look out over downtown Seattle, they would never understand the lure of quiet and no hustle and bustle. Mr. Davies will see that. I'm sure he will, Mom."

She got the knots out of her hair and let the heavy mass fall back to her waist. She put a couple of clips in the side to help keep it out of her face then picked up her wool sweater. The sun may be out but so would the wind. She hooked the clasps closed and grabbed her string wallet and walked out the door. She'd found a wonderful little coffee shop across the street that served the best chai and bonus of bonuses was full of organic and vegetarian options. That was one thing she'd come to love about this little piece of the Peninsula, plenty of choices for good food.

⋙⋘

Callum stared into the early morning sun across the water and let the anchor drop. Once he was secure he wandered around the King's Ransom making sure everything was battened down. The soft lilt of the flute that flowed out of the speakers throughout the boat followed him from task to task. He was going to savor his freedom for as long as he could. A vacation from the damning anger he'd lived with for thousands of years was a welcome reprieve after the stress of the last few weeks.

He could hardly believe everything that had happened. The emotional ups and downs were enough to make a human commit suicide, so his need for a little space was totally understood. He'd almost lost his brother. He couldn't contemplate that yet. But the alternative was almost more unbelievable.

He was more than happy for Dae and Alexis, but a small portion of him was jealous. His brother had his succubus back. No, it wasn't in the form any of them had ever expected, and the revelation that they would never truly be whole again was another piece that would take time to come to terms with.

But after so many centuries he wasn't sure he cared how he was healed, so long as he found his other half again. *I've been an Incubus for so long I don't know if I could adjust to my female half inside again anyway.*

Not that he expected it to be an issue any time soon, he chuckled. He shut the music off and locked the cabin door. Once on deck he stretched in the sun. No humans close enough to push their energy at him so he could relax. Erik had drained his storeground so thoroughly that he felt light hearted and carefree. He couldn't remember the last time he'd been free of all anger. As the anger link for his family his power had been altered after his sundering to only be able to draw in dark violent emotions, anger being the strongest and purest of the band he could access.

They had all been tuned to bring in one spectrum of the rainbow of emotional energy that humans produced, then their center used his power to pull it out of them. Erik was able to mix all the colors together and feed it back to them. It managed to keep them all alive when their sundering had crippled them and made it so they couldn't feed.

That had been the purpose behind the attack so many years ago. An attempt by a small group of scared humans who misunderstood that the Kelusis were actually a symbiotic species, not parasitic.

But all of that was hard to remember when he looked out over the deep blue of the water as the sun dazzled the tips of the gentle waves. He looked at his watch. He still had over an hour before he was to meet with Mr. Davies. He dropped the dingy then climbed over the rail into it. The little motor putt putted him across the short distance of water to the slice of public beach that fronted the shops of Water Street in Port Townsend. He pulled the craft up past the high tide mark then clomped his way up to the sidewalk knocking the sand out of his boots.

The smell of coffee wafted out of a door and it pulled him like a rein on a horse. He mounted the steps up to the cheery opening. He steeled himself at the chatter of the humans and tightened his mental hold on his power. His empty storeground begged, but he wasn't even close to being ready to feed it yet. He still had three to four days of freedom before he had to start filling his 'ground to take food home to his family and he wasn't going to waste any of it.

Inside the coffee house was perfect. Hand lettered chalkboards, coffee was brewed by the cup to your specification. But not automated like an espresso machine. A row of drip baskets open to the air greeted his eyes. The scent was heavenly. He frowned a bit at the food choices as his stomach growled. He finally found something more filling then rabbit food and got three of the ham and cheese quiche slices.

Energy threads wafted past him. Most he could ignore, though there were some darker ones that pressed for his attention. But one spiraled around him trying to force its way in. He pushed back and firmed his thoughts.

His coffee finished dripping and he took a huge sniff and sighed. The man behind the counter grinned at him and handed him the plate of warm food. He turned away from the counter and looked out over the crowded room. Tables big and small, comfortable couches and seating areas filled the space with the huge panes of picture glass looking out over the water. Everything seemed full.

Then a hesitant hand caught his eye. A woman sat alone at a bistro table in the corner of the big windows. Prime real estate for the view. He froze as he took in her mahogany curls, the energy swirled around him again and he pushed it aside absentmindedly. Drawn toward her he smiled when he neared. "Everywhere else seems to be taken. May I sit?"

Melody couldn't believe her luck. The huge man actually had a trace of a burr in his voice. If there was one weakness she had it was a Scottish accent. She'd watched him pilot the little boat to the beach from the ship anchored out in the water. The whole way across she couldn't take her eyes off of him. His bristly red hair competed with the sun that glint off the water, the green plaid flannel's sleeves had been rolled up to his elbows and his jeans had hugged his butt appreciatively when he'd pulled his boat up the sand.

"Feel free. It is the only space available."

"Thank you. I've never been here but the coffee smells wonderful so I hope the food is as good."

He got a tick mark off on his food and beverage choices but that wasn't a total surprise to her, looking at his muscular frame. Not a dainty vegetarian. She wasn't strictly vegetarian herself but she leaned that way. She raised her chai to her lips and took a sip. "I've been coming here every morning of my visit and haven't been disappointed yet."

"That's good to hear." He took a sip of his coffee and closed his eyes. After a second he looked at her again, a wicked glint of humor touched his eyes. "Test one, passed. I suspect they'll pass the rest with flying colors."

He dug into his food and barely paused between

bites to take a sip. After a few moments only crumbs remained and he sat back with a contented smile. "So you're visiting?"

"For now. I'm hoping to move here soon though."

"From where?"

"Nowhere in particular. I haven't had a real home in a long time. But now I have the chance to settle finally so I'm looking forward to it. What about you?" She wanted more of that delightful hint of brogue.

He shrugged. "I'm visiting for a few days. My family needed me to look at a business thing so I get a mini vacation out of the deal."

"Fun."

"Yeah," he smiled. "Life's been stressful lately. Almost lost my brother, so I'm looking forward to some down time."

Her heart contracted and she caught herself before she reached out and touched him. "I'm sorry. Is he ok? I lost my Mom recently. So I sympathize."

He looked out over the water before he answered. "He almost wasn't, but yeah he's going to be fine. Scared us all though. I'm sorry about your mother."

"I'm Melody." She held out her hand. He engulfed it with his. The skin was warm and calloused. He obviously did a lot of physical labor from the feel of his hand. "Thank you. I'm sad she's gone but glad too. She'd had cancer for a while."

He squeezed her hand before he let her go. "My name's Callum. I hope her passing was swift." He took a drink and stared into her eyes.

He had the most extraordinary eyes. Blue, but as

she stared closer they had a yellow starburst that turned them into a soft sea foam green when his mood changed. She cleared her throat and looked away, fiddling with her cup. "At the end it was."

They sat in silence for a bit then he glanced at his watch and drained the last of his coffee. "Will you be in town another day or so? Maybe we could meet here again?"

"I'm definitely here until tomorrow and maybe for another day after that. I've come here every morning." She smiled.

His grin showed even white teeth and he bowed his head. "Then I look forward to seeing you tomorrow morning Melody."

He rose and she watched his tight ass saunter through the crowed tables with a sigh.

SIANA WINELAND lives in the beautiful, but soggy, Olympic Peninsula of Washington State. When she is not writing urban fantasy or paranormal romance she is spending her time shepherding her young children, or the goats and sheep she raises on their little farm. For updates on her writing, please visit her website at sianawineland.com or follow her on Twitter: @SianaWineland.